Star Frontier
Star Frontier: Beyond the Veil
Star Frontier: Dangerous Games
Star Frontier: Descent
Star Frontier: Intrepid

The Sentinel
Fringe City Nightfall

The Sun Always Sets

The Martian Archaeologist

The Veya Child

hamishspiers.com

STAR FRONTIER

Hamish Spiers

STAR FRONTIER
Copyright © 2012 Hamish Spiers

This book is a work of fiction. Names, characters, businesses, organizations, places, events and incidents either are the product of the author's imagination or are used fictitiously. Any resemblance to actual persons, living or dead, events, or locales is entirely coincidental. For information, visit hamishspiers.com

The cover art for this book features the following images used under standard license from shutterstock.com:, 1335835925 (Ana Aguirre Perez), 1358905778 (sdecoret)

ISBN: 978-0-9923706-9-5

First published: 2012
This edition published: 2020

6 5 4 3 2 1

This book is dedicated to my wife Erin, my son Jason and finally to my brother Rob for all his feedback and advice on this story and others.

1. The *Lady Hawk*, the Resistance and the Federation

"WELL, HERE WE ARE," ASTEN KORR announced, checking the chronometer on the instrument panel. "The Impaati system. And since we're five hours early—" He was cut off as two fighters shot past on the viewscreen.

"Carla, where did *they* come from?"

"I don't know," his navigator replied from behind him, checking her scopes. "We must've just cut across their flight path when we came out of lightspeed."

"What, space isn't big enough for them?" Asten muttered. He then saw bright flashes in the distance on the viewscreen and the fighters were heading right for them. "Looks like a party over there."

His co-pilot stirred. He was a Harskan, humanoid and with somewhat human features but hairless with lightly pebbled golden bronze skin suggesting a slight reptilian quality. His size and physique suggested a lot of raw strength but his intelligent gaze was not the look of hired muscle. "Asten, are we still going in?"

"I'm thinking," Asten said, watching the distant skirmish. Maybe it *was* a pirate raid but for pirates to be attacking ships so close to a planet with the defenses this one had…

"Hey, Asten," Carla called out. "We've got more fighters coming in on our six."

Asten sighed. "All right. Drackson, slow down and divert some power to the rear shields."

His Harskan co-pilot raised a hairless eyebrow. "You don't want to try to outrun them?"

"Let's see what they're up to first."

A brief sequence of flashes lit the viewscreen and the second group of fighters shot past while, up ahead, several Federation frigates came to engage them.

"Well," Asten said, "I think we can safely say this isn't a pirate raid." He powered up the main drive again, ready to hightail it out of there. "Notice anything?"

"The fighters are ignoring all the civilian ships," Carla said. "They're going after the frigates."

"Exactly. Maybe these guys are resistance fighters or something." He shook his head. "All right. Change of plans. Carla, set a course back to Halea and I'll contact our client once we're clear. If he can hold off his delivery for a couple of days, we'll escort his freighter then. If not, he'll just have to pay whatever the Shipping Guild's charging."

"This doesn't go with the job?" Carla asked, but only in jest.

"Well, the Federation's navy boys are out there and if they're around, the average freighter should be pretty safe. Whereas people offering affordable alternatives to the Shipping Guild's escort services..."

Carla chuckled. "You don't like those guys very much, do you?"

Asten grimaced. "I don't like *anything* Corinthe's brought in. All right. We're out of here."

With the yank of a lever, the *Lady Hawk* accelerated to the speed of light and entered a suspended field, allowing it to act as a massless particle and bypass most of the distance between Impaati and Halea.

Asten leaned back as the automatic systems came online and let out a breath. "Home and dry."

"Asten," Drackson asked, "did you get a look at those fighters?"

"Not really. Why?"

"They were Harskan Corteks."

"Huh." Harskan Corteks were a close match to the best fighters for speed, while packing almost as much punch as a decent sized gunboat.

"Friends of yours, Drackson?" Carla asked.

"I doubt it," the Harskan replied, frowning. "I'd say those ships were stolen. Renegade Harskans sometimes make off with naval ships then come here and turn pirate. Or they sell their wares."

"So it *was* just a pirate raid then," Carla said, sounding a little disappointed. "Nothing to do with the resistance movement."

"Probably not," Asten told her. "We're a long way from the Frontier."

For millions of years, the Therah asteroid belt had been ignored by the outside galaxy. Now, in the midst of the field, there was a decent sized base in one hollowed-out rock. And it was bustling with activity.

General Draedon, a weathered looking man in his late fifties, wove his way down a corridor past technicians and general staff with a younger man keeping pace beside him. "And where did Captain Fera say this was?"

"The Usile system," the man replied.

"Nicely out of the way." The general stopped. "They didn't see Captain Fera snooping around the place, did they?"

"I don't think so. He was pretty sure no one saw him."

"Good. We don't want the Federation moving the operation on our account. Still, I can't say I like the idea of them building these warships off the books. They've got enough heavy cruisers as it is."

"The Resistance is still growing at a good rate though," the other man pointed out. "And more systems are signing up."

Draedon sighed. That was true but with every Frontier nation that joined the movement, the Federation seemed to annex two.

At first, it had been legitimate enough. Corinthe, the new Federation security minister, had approached a number of Frontier systems and offered them the opportunity to merge with the Federation. With the ending of the Levarc War just over twenty years ago and still very much in everyone's collective memory, these systems had initially been quite receptive to the idea of being under Federation protection. However, several systems Corinthe approached later had not been as open to the suggestion. And things had turned nasty.

"That's true," Draedon agreed. "But we have to bring all the stronger systems in. Get the Hie'shi on board. The Phalamkians and the others. And I think these new warships call for another attempt at contacting the Harskans."

It erred on the side of wishful thinking, he knew. But if being turned down was the worst that could happen, there was no harm in trying.

"Shall we get Lieutenant Janson again?" his aide asked.

"Do it."

The planet Corsida, the heart of the Federation, was the most heavily defended world in all its territories and one of the most densely populated.

In one of its largest cities, two men met in a small office. One was middle-aged, evidenced by the lines in his face and his receding gray hair. He was also clearly military with a spotless white uniform and the insignia of an admiral.

The other wore a gray uniform but neither the decorative shoulder trimming nor the badge sewn onto it signified his position. He looked a good ten years younger or more than the first man as well... and rather smug.

The older man eyed him with thinly veiled disdain as he sat across from him. "Commodore Hallyd."

"Admiral Roth," the man replied, making a concerted effort to put some gravity into his voice to match his elder. "I thank you for coming."

"I trust this is important?" Roth asked. He never found the commodore's tendency to feign politeness towards him endearing.

"It is," the commodore replied, clasping his hands. "I wish to discuss the recent incident in the Impaati system."

"There's not much to discuss, Commodore," Roth said. "I've filed a report with Corinthe if you want to read it."

"Yes," Hallyd said, glancing at a pad on the desk. "I've seen your report. I have some questions about it though."

Roth raised his eyebrows. "*You* have some questions?"

"*We* have some questions," Hallyd replied, attempting to hide his irritation. "Corinthe has some questions. Your deduction that this attack on Federation ships was carried out by renegade Harskans, for instance. How do you know they weren't acting under orders from the Harskan command?"

"The Harskans have never been concerned with affairs outside their territory, Commodore, unless those affairs directly affect them."

"Well, they helped your father when he contacted them," Hallyd pointed out. "After they'd beaten back the Levarc."

"They offered him advice," Roth said. "That's all. I'd also remind you that their advice benefited the Federation. But as for your question, why would the Harskans attack the Impaati system? It's not even close to the Harskan sector. And there are numerous systems that would make better strategic targets. What would they have to gain from it?"

"I see your point," Hallyd conceded. "However, the fact remains that Harskan Corteks were used in the attack."

"I wonder if you missed a paragraph in the report," Roth told him, feeling his patience stretch a little. "Renegade Harskans are known to operate outside their home sector, primarily because they know the Harskan authorities will not pursue them beyond their borders. The theft of military hardware by such individuals has been an ongoing concern to both the Harskan leaders and the Department of Security for some time, as Corinthe can no doubt tell you."

Hallyd nodded but Roth knew he wasn't listening. He and Corinthe were playing this for some other end of their own.

"It seems to me though," Hallyd said, "that renegade Harskans wouldn't want to go around bringing attention to themselves. They may well raid major trading routes and engage in other acts of piracy but we're talking about an attack against Federation frigates and cruisers here."

"An attack for which they would have been well-paid," Roth pointed out. "Possibly by one of the resistance movements that's been formed against Corinthe's expansionist activities."

"Activities which you quite openly disapprove of," the commodore told him. "Perhaps you're subconsciously trying to form a link between this attack and our operations in order to give more weight to your objections to them."

"I wasn't looking for a link, either consciously or unconsciously," the admiral said. "But the link is obvious."

"There may be some link," the commodore told him, "but that can wait. For the time being, our first priority is to deal with the Harskans."

"And what have you and Corinthe decided you are going to do about them? Set them up as secondary scapegoats along with your mysterious Minstrahn insurgents? To help justify your activities along the Frontier in case people start questioning the present story?"

Hallyd smiled. "Admiral, we've been over this before. The official intelligence reports don't lie. The Minstrahn are not the peaceful people we have thought them to be. Agents *are* mobilizing to attack this region of space."

"And I've told you before that I believe those official reports have been doctored. However, since I know neither you nor Corinthe are interested in any genuine discussion regarding the matter, let's put that aside for now. You were going to tell me about the Harskans, yes?"

Commodore Hallyd looked aggrieved and took a moment to compose himself. Roth used this chance to glance through the window at Corsida's three brilliant moons. They were all in the same area of the sky that evening, offering a pleasant distraction from the discussion at hand.

"We have no ulterior motives here, Admiral," Hallyd told him. "We are simply taking precautionary measures to ensure the safety of Federation citizens."

"And what are these precautionary measures you have in mind?"

"Corinthe and I have decided to issue a small warning to the Harskan leaders, to tell them that Harskan vessels breaching our territory boundaries and attacking Federation ships are acts of war and that if they should happen in future, the Federation will be obliged to respond."

"Yes, that ought to go down well. And will you be delivering this message or will Corinthe take the responsibility?"

"Corinthe has instructed me to contact them on his behalf," Hallyd said. "He has also requested that you provide me with passage aboard your ship to our outlying systems so we can establish a clear communication channel."

"I see," Roth replied. This was getting better and better. "I'll send a shuttle to bring you to the *Sentinel* at your convenience."

2. The Job

PALANAMI HAD EVERYTHING. SHALLOW, lifeless seas. Scattered islands like this one that were just rocks with a bit of complimentary sand. Lieutenant Janson put down his glass and smiled. Okay, maybe 'everything' was an exaggeration but he still kind of liked the place. Here on the long balcony of the one and only establishment in walking distance of the spaceport, with a pleasant breeze, it was pretty agreeable. Plus, he could see the ocean—and the shallow canyon below him, just ten meters deep, was a natural spectacle in miniature. Sadly however, he would soon have to leave this little corner of the Federation.

It had been several weeks since the request had come through from the Therah system to locate and hire a suitable emissary he could send to the Harskan sector. Several weeks with nothing to show for his efforts. And now he was being pulled off the job altogether.

A reconnaissance team had gone missing on Bestira and as he was the closest operative, resistance command had asked him to check it out. It was a shame he had to abandon his original job and it was a shame he had to leave Palanami just as he was getting comfortable. However, what trail was left to the missing team wouldn't be getting any hotter and that was assuming there was one to begin with.

Sighing, he got up to leave then stopped. Ten meters down the balcony, he saw a human man, a human woman and a Harskan man at a table. He hesitated. It was rare to find Harskans beyond the borders of their home sector and the ones you did were mostly dangerous renegades. However, Janson didn't get that vibe from this one. Of course, he couldn't neglect his orders to head to Bestira but he couldn't ignore this opportunity either.

His mind resolved, he approached the trio while thinking of an excuse to sit with them that wouldn't attract too much attention. Glancing over his shoulder, he saw just one other occupied table outside. A lone dark-haired woman in a sequined dress sat there stirring the remains of her drink. And an idea came to mind.

Still glancing back at her, he slid in at the trio's table next to the Harskan. "Mind if I sit with you guys for a moment?"

The young man across from him frowned but shrugged the interruption off. "Sure. No problem."

The fetching red-haired woman beside him, younger still, gave Janson a slight smile then looked away.

"Avoiding someone?" the man asked.

Janson gave quiet thanks that the subtleties of his performance hadn't gone unnoticed.

"Ah, no one," he said. "Just that woman over there. We had a bit of a falling out. She thinks I'm a lay-about and she's probably right."

The Harskan chuckled while the man smiled. "Well, we won't tell her you're here. You local?"

"I work all over the place," Janson replied. "Which is part of the problem. Actually, I'm off to the Frontier today. Have you been out there recently?"

"We get the odd job there now and again," the Harskan said.

Again, Janson felt the assurance that he wasn't one of the dangerous ones that people had to be wary of. Also, his clear enunciation sounded like that of a high-born Harskan, which was most strange. He'd never come across one of them this far from their home sector before.

"It's crazy out there at the moment, isn't it?" he said, keeping the thought to himself. "I was delivering a shipment of hydrelium to Nyev'ji the other week when I got caught in the middle of one of the Federation's attacks. With the planetary bombardment and everything else, I'm lucky I'm still alive." He shook his head. "And all our own worlds are being turned into military supply depots to keep this crazy thing going."

"Yeah, it's a joke," the human man agreed, "especially with that flimsy explanation about the Minstrahn threat that Corinthe expects us all to swallow."

"A lot of people are buying it though," the woman pointed out. "They couldn't get away with it if they weren't."

"I don't know," the man said. "Who'd stop them? One of those lame little resistance movements? Or a lonely independent Frontier world?"

Janson bit his tongue at the man's casual dismissal of the resistance movements. He was glad these people didn't like Corinthe's war mongering but if they didn't think any of the resistance movements were worthwhile then it might be hard to convince them to help out.

Then a terrible thought occurred to him and he almost kicked himself. It seemed quite unlikely now that they were Federation spies or off-duty naval officers but those types usually had a few tricks up their sleeves. He couldn't assume they were clear just yet. Not without something a little more convincing.

He glanced over his shoulder and saw that the lady in green was gone, totally unaware of what a great job she was doing. Professional backup couldn't have timed it better.

"Ah, that woman's left," he said. "How about a drink? Something heavy? Something light?"

The man shrugged. "I don't know. Maybe later."

"Yeah, I'm fine for now," the woman said, while the Harskan just shook his head.

Now, Janson could relax a little. He'd thrown them one of the lines Federation field operatives sometimes used and they hadn't taken the bait. Which was just as well. 'Give me something that the light sparkles off' was a pretty pretentious recognition code.

"Fair enough," he said. "Actually, since I've got you here, I might have a proposition for you. Are you in the shipping business?"

"We're more on the escort side of things," the man replied. "Although our schedule's pretty full for the next little while." He gave an apologetic smile.

"Well, if you've got prior commitments, I don't want to press you," Janson told him. "But it would pay well."

"What's the job?"

Janson took another glance around the balcony but there was no one nearby. "Well, I'd better introduce myself first. My name's Masec Janson and... I'm a lieutenant in the resistance movement. I should also add for the record that I don't know that woman I saw earlier. I just needed an excuse to join you. But what about yourselves? Who do I have the pleasure of drinking with?"

The young man across the table extended his hand first. "Asten Korr. Captain of the *Lady Hawk*."

The woman beside him went next. "Carla Casdan."

"Very nice to meet you both," Janson said.

And last but not least, the Harskan took Janson's hand in a firm grip. "And you can call me Drackson." He gave him a curious look. "Incidentally, which of the resistance movements are you in?"

"Well, that's a tricky question," Janson admitted. "Officially, we don't have any other name to distinguish us from the other groups out there. We just call ourselves the Resistance. Although we'd like to think we're the largest of the various organizations... Although we're still nowhere near as big as we need to be to halt the Federation's expansion efforts. Which is what I wanted to talk to you about. We need more allies. More resources."

Asten's expression was blank. "And how can *we* help?"

Janson turned to Drackson before he replied. "I thought you might be able to contact the Harskans on our behalf and ask them for aid. Anything they could give us. I know it might not be much but every bit helps."

Drackson nodded. "I see. You haven't contacted them before, have you?"

"Not yet, no."

"It's just that we think we saw a resistance unit in the Impaati system recently and they were using Harskan Corteks. Do you know anything about that?"

"Well, it wasn't one of ours," Jason said. "They may have been an independent group but we don't have any Harskan hardware."

"And you've never tried to buy any from any of the renegades operating out here?"

"We don't buy stolen merchandise," Janson told him. "And we can't ask the Harskan Elders for it ourselves. Your people are a little touchy about outsiders dropping in. Which is why, when I saw you, I thought you might stand a better chance. You would of course be given considerable remuneration in exchange for your help."

"No."

It wasn't quite the reaction Janson had been hoping for.

"I'm sorry," Drackson told him. "Returning to my home sector would be difficult."

"Why's that, if you don't mind me asking?"

Drackson sighed. "It's somewhat personal but as you're not a Harskan, I don't think you'd see any shame in it. Some time ago, my brothers were involved in a crime which disgraced my family and several others. Very prominent families too."

Janson nodded. He had heard about this. "So you're in exile?"

"Exile? Well, of a kind. In Corsidan, I suppose you'd call it self-imposed exile. I'd rather not live with the shame of my brothers' crime. In the Harskan sector, it followed me everywhere. Out here, I'm free of it."

Janson felt his heart sink. He had been so sure that this was the opportunity he'd been waiting for but now it seemed he'd delayed his trip to Bestira for nothing.

Drackson sighed and turned to the young captain. "Asten, what do you think?"

Or maybe not.

"I don't know," Asten told him. "I don't want to make you do anything you don't want to. We had enough of that when we were working for Big Blue."

"It would be for a good cause," Drackson admitted, though more to himself than either Asten or Carla. "And we don't like what Corinthe's doing in the Frontier either." He thought a little longer. "Perhaps I was too quick in my reply. The problem lies in convincing the Elders to listen to me now that I am among the dishonored. However, while I may not be able to present any request to them in person, I might be able to find someone who can." He turned to Janson. "How much compensation would you give us in return for this?"

"Eleven thousand," Janson replied. "Half up front and half when you get back, guaranteed whether the Elders help the Resistance or not."

"Make it twelve," Drackson told him, with a hint of a smile. "It's a tidier number."

3. Shadows

ADMIRAL ROTH'S FLAGSHIP THE *SENTINEL* drifted in the middle of nowhere, with the nearest star system twenty light-years away and the edge of the Federation's territories thirty-three. And somewhere beyond this vast sea of emptiness was the Harskan sector.

Commodore Hallyd scowled at the field of stars sprawling across the bridge viewscreen.

"Is this it?" he asked, turning to face Roth.

"We're here," Roth said, here being the planned position where the *Sentinel* would be able to establish a clear transmission to the Harskan leaders on El'aesi.

"About time," the commodore said. "With all the delays you've caused, you've kept me away from Corsida for three weeks now."

"I'm sure they've been able to manage," Roth told him. "Besides, would you have preferred it if I had allowed those pirates to continue disrupting that trade route? Left Saeban without fuel supplies for a few months, while letting a few hundred more innocent people get killed?"

"I would have preferred it," Commodore Hallyd replied, almost spitting the words out, "if you had sent another ship to deal with the problem. I find it hard to believe there weren't any ships closer to the Saeban system at the time. In fact, I wouldn't be at all surprised if your motivation in handling the situation yourself had been nothing more than a ruse to stall my address to the Harskans."

"Really, Commodore," Roth chided him. "I'm surprised at you. Do you sincerely believe I would deliberately delay a mission of such importance?"

The commodore turned away, glowering. "I wonder."

"Well, we're here now," the admiral said. "Ready to transmit when you are."

Two and a half hours later, Commodore Hallyd was hard at it, talking to a diplomatic representative who was handling the discussions on the behalf of the Harskan Elders. And his annoyance that he wouldn't be permitted to speak to anyone higher in the ranks could have been a bit more subtle.

From the other side of the bridge, Admiral Roth watched alongside the captain of the *Sentinel*.

"Well, Captain Merrick," he said. "It seems the proceedings are going smoothly, wouldn't you say?"

"What is he doing?" the younger man wondered. "Does he want to start a war with these people?"

"He's playing a power game," Roth explained. "And considering that's all he ever does, one can hardly expect anything else from the man. Let's hope the indifference the Harskans are famed for extends far enough to ignore his offence."

"They're not at all alarmed by his threats though, are they?"

Roth favored the captain with a smile. "You noticed that?"

"Well, they must have recognized the commodore's authority," Merrick pointed out. "They would certainly know he speaks on Corinthe's behalf. Yet, they made him wait two hours to talk to anyone. And I don't know for sure but it seems to me that Harskan representative is bored more than anything else. He seems to be agreeing with the commodore to... well..." He trailed off, not wishing to say something untoward about a superior officer.

"To shut him up?" Roth suggested, having no such reservations.

"Well, yes."

"I agree," the admiral said.

For a few moments, neither man spoke and the only sound on the bridge was the conversation between Commodore Hallyd and the Harskan on the monitor.

"Are you all right?" Merrick asked.

Roth frowned. "I was just thinking. The Harskans have some impressive resources at their disposal but nobody really knows the full extent of their capabilities. I'd like to find out."

"I take it this won't be a formal investigation?"

"No," Roth replied. "This is simply for my own curiosity. After all, it'd be fairly unlikely the Harskans would wage a war over an insult. I'll put my own men on the job. Besides, I don't want to leave the navy's intelligence network undermanned, do I?"

"No," Merrick agreed. "Although isn't mounting an investigation to simply satisfy your curiosity somewhat excessive?"

Roth glanced at Commodore Hallyd before replying. "You're right, Captain. There's more to it than that." He lowered his voice. "I know what my men will find. However, what they will provide me with is documentation, along with photographic evidence of just a sample of what the Harskans have at their disposal. Evidence that I can present to Corinthe and this glorified secretary of his if they decide to press this matter with the Harskans further. I believe I can put an end to this particular part of Corinthe's plans."

"And the rest of them?"

"That is the question."

"So, what's the plan?" Asten asked, leaning back as the ship shot off on its pre-programmed course.

"As I explained," Drackson said, "because it would be difficult for me to negotiate with the Harskan Elders, I need to find someone who can do so on my behalf but I have someone in mind. However, just leave everything to me. For the moment, you and Carla can sit back and relax."

Asten clasped his hands together. "Great."

Carla leaned forward from her seat behind them. "Are you sure there's nothing we can do, Drackson?"

"Actually, there really isn't," Drackson replied. "The less you two are involved, the better our chances. You know a number of Harskans don't really care for humans too much, or anybody who isn't Harskan."

"That's right," Asten said, turning around. "Anyway, what are you trying to do, Carla? If we don't have to do anything, we can look at this trip as a well-earned holiday."

Carla slapped his shoulder. "Don't be so lazy."

Asten laughed and climbed out of his seat. "Come on, let's go and get something to eat."

The others followed him out of the cockpit—although he ducked back in by himself to check something—then they all went to the galley, pulled out some containers and cutlery, grabbed some drinks and headed into the lounge area.

"What's this?" Carla asked, peeling back the lid of her container and inspecting the contents inside.

"Some local dish I picked up back on Palanami," Asten told her. "I've heard it's quite good. Gaerejash or something like that."

"Oh, Gaelejish," Drackson said. "Yes, I've heard it's good too."

Carla tried a bit. "Yeah, it's nice."

Asten took a sip of his drink. "Only the best for my crew."

For a little while, no one said anything as they all enjoyed their meal. Then Carla spoke up. "So, this is different. Working for the resistance movement."

"*A* resistance movement," Asten corrected her. "There must be at least a dozen of the things. Although our client seems to hold this one in high esteem."

"Well, if a lieutenant is able to hire mercenaries for rates like this without consulting higher authorities, then they must be a fairly large organization," Carla pointed out.

"Assuming Lieutenant Janson wasn't acting outside his boundaries," Asten countered. "But you're probably right."

"Anyway," Carla continued, unperturbed, "I think we could really do some good with this."

"Maybe," Asten said, his thoughts elsewhere.

"What's wrong?"

He shook his head. "Just before I left the cockpit, I thought I saw another ship on the radar. But if there was, it must have dropped off the scopes."

"Oh well," Carla murmured. "I'm sure it's all right. You know, it could have just been a glitch."

Asten shrugged. "Yeah, that's possible, I suppose." They finished their dinner and, with the ship on a pre-programmed course for the next twelve hours, turned in to get some sleep.

Khalin checked her instruments one more time just to be sure. There was no mistake. She turned around. "Epcar. What do you make of this?"

The man beside her leaned over. "That's interesting."

"We saw that same ship at our last refueling stop, didn't we?"

Epcar frowned. "Yeah. I wonder what they're up to."

"It could be a coincidence," Khalin conceded, "but I can't see why anyone else would be heading out this way."

"There's still one more system between us and the Harskan sector though. It's not much of a place and it's pretty far out of the way but maybe they're heading there."

"Dailas?" Khalin scoffed. "Possibly. But almost no one does any trading with the place and the locals never travel off-world. They're so isolated that if they seceded from the Federation, no one would even notice."

"Probably not," Epcar agreed. "Although you never know with Corinthe running the show. He might well send a fleet of cruisers to pummel their whole planet."

"True," Khalin replied. "Anyway, getting back to this mystery ship of ours, I think we should let Admiral Roth know..." She trailed off as something else took her attention. "Well well."

"What is it?"

"It seems we've picked up another traveling companion. Another small ship just popped onto the radar and I'd say whoever's flying it is trying hard not to be noticed."

"Do you think they're following us?"

"Us," Khalin said, "or our friends in the first ship."

"The mind boggles," Epcar muttered. "Well, I suppose I'd better contact the admiral."

Rain pelted against the sloping roofs of Dailas' one and only spaceport, gushing over the edges onto the streets below. It was night and coupled with the rain, it made for poor visibility but it wasn't a difficult landing for Asten. The wind wasn't too strong and the landing platforms were a lot more generous than some others he'd seen. Raised above the buildings on various pylons, they were wide enough to accommodate a good sized cargo hauler. Rather considerate for a place that didn't receive that many visitors.

"And we're down," he said cheerfully as he locked the landing gear into place. He switched off the main engines and climbed out of his seat. "All right. I'll get the fuel. Drackson, see if the local shops have anything worth stocking in the galley. Carla, stay here and keep an eye on the ship."

"Sure," Carla replied. "It looks like miserable weather for being outdoors anyway."

"Quite," Asten agreed as he and Drackson left.

Carla climbed out of her seat and sat in Asten's usual place at the helm. Watching the viewscreen, she smiled as Asten and Drackson made their way across the platform and stepped into the elevator that led to the buildings below. She hadn't known them for long but she'd grown fond of them. Ever since the three of them had left the *Feet First* and that stuffy, overbearing Big Blue, they'd been a close-knit group.

It had been good timing too—going into business for themselves—as small operators began to do very well due to drastic changes in shipping regulations around the time. Corinthe had made it practically mandatory for cargo haulers to use escort ships from the Shipping Guild, which Drackson had said would happen sooner or later, and a lot of the larger independent operators like Big Blue had been effectively shut down as a result. Although, Carla had heard the old captain was doing well in the outlying systems and along the Frontier.

However, given the exorbitant amounts the Shipping Guild charged for its services, a lot of smaller businesses appreciated equally smaller ships like the *Lady Hawk* that could escort their freighters under the radar for much lower fees.

As Carla mused over all of this, she grabbed a pad and pulled up some information on the Harskan sector. Thanks to Drackson, there was a fair bit of it in the *Lady Hawk*'s data banks.

After ten minutes of reading, Asten reappeared with a man in the uniform of a Dailas spaceport employee. This uniform was one of their protective wet weather versions, better suited to the evening's conditions than Asten's soaked clothes.

Asten pointed out the fuel valve on the *Lady Hawk* and led the way, with the man walking behind him.

Carla sat up as she got a better look at the man; he was now a few steps behind Asten, who was explaining something about the valve set up, but he didn't seem to be paying attention. He just stared at the back of Asten's head and tightened his grip on a large wrench.

Carla bolted out of the cockpit, racing downstairs to the hatchway. If Asten wasn't already grateful to have her services, he was sure going to be now. She hit the release for the hatchway and it shot open with a loud hiss. Outside, the man was raising the wrench above Asten's head.

"Asten, look out!"

The man brought the wrench down but Asten was too fast for him. Rather than turning around to get a front row view of the wrench right before it cracked his skull, he jumped to the left. Unable to stop the momentum of his swing, his assailant stumbled forward and Asten socked him in the jaw. The man swung the wrench around again and Asten kicked him in the chest, knocking him to the ground.

Asten then reached for the gun that was holstered on his right hip but thought the better of it. His assailant could have taken him out with a gun too but had decided against it. Perhaps the authorities on Dailas were a little faster than most when it came to slamming down on firefights.

The man climbed to his feet again and Asten took a few steps back. He wasn't sure what to do now but he kept his hand on his weapon just in case. If the worst came to the worst, he could always explain it to the spaceport officials. However, as his assailant came at him again, Drackson stepped onto the platform with a few boxes of supplies.

He dropped them immediately and charged Asten's assailant, locking both his arms in one motion, dislocating his shoulder and making him drop the weapon. Then he grabbed the man's head, snapped his neck and dropped the limp body.

"Thanks," Asten said, his relief evident in his voice. He turned to Drackson, who was standing motionless. "Are you all right?"

"Yeah," Drackson nodded. "That was just a messy business, that's all."

Carla came over and stared at the body. "Oh my… "

"It's okay," Asten told her. It wasn't of course but he couldn't think of anything else to say.

Drackson tapped the dead man with his foot, rolling him onto his back to get a look at the face. "I wonder who he was. I'll get a picture and run it through the computer."

Asten grimaced. "Good idea. Now, we've just got to work out how we're going to get our fuel without raising any suspicions."

"What do you mean?" Carla asked him.

"I mean, I was just down there and they sent me back with this guy. Am I supposed to go back and ask for someone else?"

Carla shrugged. "Just tell them that you don't know where the guy's got to. Say you got separated and ask them if they've seen him. They'll try to contact him and when they can't get in touch, they should just send you up with another man."

"Worth a shot, I guess," Asten muttered. "But if they don't buy it, we might have to get out of here in a hurry. Drackson, do you think you can hide this guy somewhere while I'm gone?"

Drackson shook his head. "This place is too open. I'll put him in a cargo hold and we can jettison him in space." He turned around and sniffed the air.

"What's wrong?" Asten asked.

"I'm not sure," Drackson said. "I thought I saw someone by the elevator but I can't see anyone now. Maybe I was imagining things."

"Maybe. All right, I'll go and see those guys downstairs again. Think you can manage this guy without me?

Drackson glanced at the dead man on the landing platform. He was a large man but he wouldn't be too heavy for him. Harskans were considerably stronger than humans.

"No, I think I can manage."

"Good," Asten replied. "The sooner we get out of here, the better."

4. Tracking the *Lady Hawk*

"WELL," EPCAR ANNOUNCED AS THE COCKPIT door slid shut behind him. "We won't have to worry about keeping an eye on the second ship anymore."

Khalin stared at him. "What do you mean?"

Epcar planted himself in his chair, slinging his arm over the side. "Well, it looks like it got here ahead of the bigger ship too. Or at least it was cleared for landing first. Anyway, the pilot went down to the service areas under the landing platforms and got himself decked up as a spaceport worker. Then when our friends in the bigger ship landed, he latched onto the captain, pretending he was going to refuel his ship. Then, when he and the captain got up to the landing platform, he tried to kill him with a wrench."

"You're joking."

"It gets weirder. The captain managed to get out of the way in time. And then his first mate or someone saw the whole thing, ran over and snapped the other guy's neck."

"Snapped his *neck*?"

"That's what I said."

Khalin leaned back in her chair. "Hard to believe."

"Well," Epcar said, "the guy was a Harskan."

Khalin let out a long breath. So their mystery ship was heading to the Harskan sector and they had a Harskan on board.

"I've never heard of a renegade Harskan returning to their home sector," she said. "They're up to something and I intend to find out what it is. Do you have any idea who their attacker was?"

Epcar shook his head. "Not really. I didn't get a good look at the guy. And by the way the crew of the ship were scratching their heads over him, I don't think they recognized him either."

"Which means he's probably some gun for hire," Khalin muttered. "Whoever he was though, he's done us a big disservice. Now our friends are going to be looking over their shoulders for the rest of the trip." She rapped the control board in annoyance. "You didn't get anything that could tell us who this guy was?"

"I might have something," Epcar said, pulling out a small surveillance recorder. "I got a little bit of the fight on this. The resolution's pretty good."

Khalin checked out the footage. "Yeah. I can probably pull a decent still image from this and run it through the system."

"All right," Epcar said. "You do that and I'll see if I can pull the name of our other mystery ship from the landing records here."

It took about twenty minutes for the *Lady Hawk* to be refueled. It took just two minutes afterwards to high-tail it out of there.

"There's no need to hurry," Carla said, trying to calm Asten's nerves.

"Maybe not," he replied. "But I don't want to stick around either."

He watched as the hue of the planet fell beneath them on the viewscreen, giving way to the darkness of space. Then he glanced at the switch that would, with a small flick, open the rear cargo hold to the vacuum of space and suck the body of their would-be-assailant into the void. However, as keen as he was to get rid of it, it was better to wait until the *Lady Hawk* was clear of the planet's gravity well. He pulled his hand back.

Beside him, Drackson sat up. "I've got him."

"Who was he?" Asten asked.

"A bounty hunter called Tath. There's not a great deal on him. And he didn't have any criminal convictions, although he was wanted for questioning by several authorities around the Federation core worlds. But the reasons aren't specified here."

"Doesn't matter," Asten told him. "I'm more concerned with why he was trying to kill me. Because unless that guy was after me for some past indiscretion that I've clean forgotten, the only thing I can think of is that he somehow knew we were doing this job for the Resistance. And if he thought it was worth his time to track us down, then there must have been a nice reward in it for him."

"And who would offer such a reward?" Drackson suggested.

"Exactly. Now, I don't know how badly we've been compromised. I think since we've come this far, we may as well stick at it. And we'll be safe enough once we reach the Harskan sector. At least from any Federation nonsense. But we might have some trouble when we get back to the rendezvous."

"We might," Drackson agreed. "But there's no point in worrying about it now though."

"No," Asten conceded. He flicked the switch and jettisoned Tath's remains into oblivion. It didn't lift his spirits as much as he'd hoped.

. . .

Admiral Roth left the bridge of the *Sentinel*, satisfied there was no pressing business there requiring his attention. Commodore Hallyd, much to his chagrin, had been placed on a shuttle several days ago and taken back to Corsida and things had been quiet since.

When Hallyd had complained about the haste of his forced departure, the admiral by way of explanation had offered none, save that an urgent matter had arisen. No doubt Hallyd had his own opinion on that and was possibly telling Corinthe all about it right then. Admiral Roth however couldn't care less. And right now, something *had* come up.

He crossed another hallway and entered his private quarters. As the door slid shut behind him, he hit the lock and made his way over to a small communication console. He checked the recognition code and flicked it on.

"Proceed."

"Pilot of second vessel a known bounty hunter named Tath. Jumped the mystery ship crew at the last stopover. Unsuccessfully. Harskan crew member took him out. Ship still outbound. Landing records identify it as the *Lady Hawk*. Keeping our distance."

"Understood. Carry on."

"Over and out."

With that, the transmission was ended.

For a moment, Roth didn't move. This was not a wholly welcome turn of events. The quarry would now be paranoid and this was going to make the task more difficult for his unit.

He conducted a brief search through the records for any mention of the *Lady Hawk* and the results of his query confirmed what he'd already suspected. There were no orders anywhere in relation to the ship, which meant it had either been targeted by a private organization somewhere or that the bounty hunter had been acting on his own volition.

Despite the inherent absurdity of it, Roth's instinct leaned towards the latter. The *Lady Hawk* was heading for the Harskan sector, that was certain, and that wasn't considered a place of refuge for people on the run. It also struck him that jumping the ship's crew hadn't been Tath's end goal but rather a step towards it. And if that was the case, then the *Lady Hawk* could be a lead to something quite valuable. Tath wasn't in a position to follow the trail any more but Roth was.

Epcar watched the viewscreen of their disguised gunboat as the computer calculated possible course projections for the *Lady Hawk*. And as they left the familiarity of the Federation behind and headed into the void that lay between it and the Harskan sector, he wondered if any of the toys the admiral had provided him and Khalin with would be up to the task ahead. Finding what types of ships and miscellaneous military hardware the Harskans had at their disposal would be straightforward enough but the *Lady Hawk* was another matter.

"What do you think about this ship of ours?" he asked Khalin.

"I'm not sure," she replied. "Following it is one thing but I'd like to see what happens when the crew disembarks at some of their stopovers. I want to know who they talk to and what they talk about."

"Me too," Epcar said. "The question is how."

Khalin thought about it. "Well, the *Lady Hawk*'s going to land somewhere sooner or later and I've got a hunch that it's not going to be on any of the more heavily populated worlds. I doubt it'd be on El'aesi."

Which made sense, Epcar knew. Humans aside, the Harskan leaders weren't too keen on rogue Harskans who'd left the sector either. So whatever their intentions, the crew of the *Lady Hawk* would have to play things safe to start with.

"When it does make its first landing," Khalin continued, "it'll probably be somewhere quiet with minimal, possibly non-existent, security. When that happens, we'll land as close as we can and one of us will stowaway on the ship."

"That could be dangerous," Epcar said.

"It could be," Khalin agreed. "Which is why *I'm* going to do it."

"You?"

Khalin smiled. "Well, it's my crazy plan, isn't it?"

Epcar shrugged. "Fair enough. So I guess I'll be documenting Harskan hardware all by myself then. But how will I find you after I'm done?"

"You'll still be tailing this ship, won't you?"

"Yes."

"I'll take a beacon signal with me. Once I've found out what I want to know, and it's safe to do so, I'll get off the ship and activate it. Then you can come and pick me up."

"All right then," Epcar said. "Now since there's nothing but empty space from here to the Harskan sector, let's go and get some sleep. I doubt the *Lady Hawk* will be making any more stopovers today."

5. Raptors over Ipaatid

ABOVE THE PLANET OF IPAATID, A DOZEN Federation warships loomed in orbit. With each ship five hundred meters in length and carrying twenty gun emplacements, it amounted to a frightening amount of power. From his vantage point two hundred kilometers away, Commander Zak Materson of the Resistance forces certainly thought so.

With their systems powered down to keep their Raptor-7s from showing up on the enemy's radar, he and a small reconnaissance group were observing, and recording, everything that was taking place.

His communication console crackled to life. "They're broadcasting, Commander." That was Ja'is, his starboard wingman.

"Patch it through," Zak told him.

There was a flicker as their short-range communication frequency shut off and the Federation broadcast came through the speakers. "... your planetary shield and await further instructions. Repeat, this is a Federation task force. Please lower your planetary shield and await further instructions."

There was a long pause.

"Federation task force, this is Governor Savic," a mature voice stated. "Please state your intentions."

"Governor Savic, this is General Kellahav of the *Adjudicator*," an abrupt military type responded. "As of now, it is my duty to bring your system under Federation protection."

Kellahav, Zak reflected. That was a familiar name. For the past few years, Kellahav had been the commander of a dirty little secret of Corinthe's known as the Blackguard squadron. Initially, this had been Rear Admiral Calaom's baby but he had then handed it over to Kellahav, along with a general's rank. There was supposedly some controversy about that promotion as well, although Zak wasn't sure what it was about. Since then, the Blackguard squadron had been involved in a number of special operations along the Frontier. Operations like this one.

"General Kellahav," the governor of Ipaatid replied. "However charitable your intentions, we have not requested any such protection."

There was another pause and a flicker of static erupted from Zak's speakers. He contemplated switching to a long-range frequency but decided against it. They were pushing their luck as it was since it wouldn't take too much for an observant communications officer on board one of the warships to notice there was a third party listening in.

"Nonetheless, you must submit to it," Kellahav said. "Every system along the Frontier is under threat from the Minstrahn Empire, our own worlds as well. United, we will be able to ward off any attacks by this aggressor. Independent systems such as your own however would not stand a chance."

"In other words," Savic replied, "in order to prevent being annexed by one cluster of systems, we must allow ourselves to be annexed by another?"

"You twist my words," the general told him. "Although I see there's some truth in what you say. However, let me assure you, Ipaatid will fare far better under Federation jurisdiction than it would under the Minstrahn."

"Perhaps," Savic said. "But maybe we should ask the Minstrahn. The people of Ipaatid have eyes and ears, General. We are well aware how Corinthe is stirring panic in the Federation over this so-called threat from the Minstrahn and we have seen no evidence to back his statements. What we *have* seen is a series of incidents in which Federation warships have overrun independent worlds along the Frontier. And I tell you, we will not idly allow Ipaatid to be added to this list."

"Have a care, Governor," Kellahav warned. "We have twelve warships in orbit and more can be readily called in if I request it."

For a few moments, Savic was silent. He understood what that meant all right. "I need some time to discuss the situation with my cabinet," he said at last. "I will contact you in two hours and inform you of our decision."

With that, the transmission ended.

Zak smiled to himself. Governor Savic had already surrendered of course but he had done so on his terms. And by terminating the transmission when he had, he had given General Kellahav no chance to respond.

He leaned back and flicked the comm switch over to Sigma squadron's encrypted frequency. "You heard all that, ladies and gentlemen? We've got two hours to kill so get yourselves comfortable. Maintain present status but keep your engines in standby mode. If something goes wrong, we may need to get out of here in a hurry."

His eight squadmates acknowledged the order and he turned the comm off and sighed. This was *not* his favorite past time. If he could sleep for the next two hours, it might not be that bad but he didn't have that luxury. If he didn't stay alert, he could well wake up in a Federation detention facility or, more likely, not wake up at all. And for a brief moment, the astronomers of Ipaatid would be treated to the brilliance of the Materson constellation.

He watched the dozen Federation ships orbiting the planet but they remained where they were. No fighters left their hangars and it seemed while Governor Savic had undoubtedly wounded his pride, General Kellahav had agreed to the two hour wait. Whether he decided to make an issue of it later remained to be seen of course but Zak didn't think he would. He doubted Kellahav would want to put the population any further offside than he had already.

The next two hours passed by with treacle slowness but Zak managed to stay alert.

"All right, guys," he said, switching the comm on again. "We're back on." He switched it over to the frequency that Ja'is had given everyone earlier so they could listen in on the communications between the Federation task force and the planet.

"... no choice, we submit the planet of Ipaatid to the protection of the Federation."

"Very well," Kellahav's voice came through. "Please lower your planetary shield and await the arrival of our ambassador's shuttle. We will speak again soon."

"Understood, General Kellahav. We are lowering our shield now."

Zak sat bolt upright in his seat as he saw the scene unfolding in front of him. So that was what the governor had done with those two hours.

"Governor Savic! What are you doing?" Kellahav barked.

"I'm sorry, General," the governor replied. "I don't understand what you mean. We have simply lowered the planetary shield in line with your request."

The swarm of transport ships coming out of the atmosphere was now *very* impressive. One of the Federation cruisers started moving to intercept them, its captain not waiting for any orders. With this imminent threat, the ships scattered into smaller groups, throwing the larger vessel off.

"You orchestrated this." That was Kellahav again.

"I had nothing to do with it," Savic said. "These ships are civilian transports. They must have formed their own conclusions as to what was going on and decided to take their chances on their own."

"Have it your way," Kellahav told him. "But if you won't do something about these ships then I will."

The transmission was cut short and within moments, the Federation ships were maneuvering to block the escaping transports and scrambling their fighters.

"Sigma squadron," Zak commanded. "Power up. Our reconnaissance mission is over."

"Are we heading out then?" Ja'is asked.

Zak hesitated. The others weren't going to like this. "We're heading out but not just yet. I think we can help some of these transports get away."

"With all respect, Commander, the general's orders were pretty clear on this subject."

"When he gave us those orders, he had no idea this was going to happen," Zak countered. "And I'm not going to leave these people if there's a chance we can help them."

"All right."

"Besides, if there's any trouble, I'll take the rap for it," Zak added. "Let's go. There's a squad of Wasps heading out twenty degrees to the portside. *Kharmin shake*."

With that their Raptor-7 fighters came to life, with brilliant flares of blue from their rear engine thrusters, and they shot towards the incoming enemy ships. Between them, three large transport ships were heading straight across their flight line, gunning for the edge of the planet's gravity well for all they were worth... and Zak saw on his viewscreen the squadron of Wasps pursuing them.

The Wasps were small ships, designed with cheap mass production in mind, and were little more than triangular twin stabilizers with inbuilt weapons placements and a cockpit-engine compartment jammed between them. Inside those basic fighters, Zak knew the pilots would now see his group too. For a moment, he wished he could have seen the looks on their faces when they saw his Raptor-7s arrive out of nowhere.

The Raptor-7 was the star of the Novatech Systems fleet, a sleek fighter capable of incredible speed and manoeuvrability and although it was widely used throughout the Federation, it was increasingly recognized as one of the favored fighters of the Resistance. In the case of Sigma squadron, the blue markings on the noses and wings of their ships would leave little doubt. The Resistance command had been adamant on this point. It was an ongoing concern that the Federation might punish innocent third parties for Resistance strikes so in any situation where open combat with Federation forces was possible, all Resistance ships involved had to carry clearly identifiable markings. Yes, the Wasp pilots would know who they were dealing with today.

Zak fired a salvo of blasts into the midst of the Wasps and had the satisfaction of seeing one disintegrate in a billowing cloud of gas. He had the edge of surprise and it worked. The Wasps, which had been hunting down defenseless transports moments earlier, scattered out of the way. In wings of three, six of his squad mates veered off to port and starboard to close the enemy in an entrapment formation. He and his own wing however went straight through the group, ready for a vertical loop.

For a few frightening moments, they were beyond the cluster of enemy fighters with nothing between them and four large Federation warships coming to investigate. A volley of heavy blasts shot past him and his wingmen but went wide. The main batteries on those ships were designed for use against other capital warships and were never intended for anything as small as their Raptor-7s. It was possible for an experienced gunner to hit small fast moving targets with them of course—and the point-defense cannons could be pretty damn accurate—but Zak wasn't going to give them that chance. A split second after they'd come under fire, they pulled into their vertical loop and came back behind the enemy fighters. They'd pulled off their *Kharmin Shake* maneuver and now all nine ships in Sigma squadron were between the Wasps and their carriers, herding them away.

Some of the hot shots in the enemy squad appeared to pay no notice to them though, still heading straight for the escaping transports.

"Ja'is?" Zak shouted. "Twenty degrees, starboard side!"

"I see them."

"I'll cover you," Zak said. "Layson, Adaria. Watch my back."

"Got it, Commander," Adaria replied, her voice confident and controlled.

Ja'is accelerated ahead and immediately a pair of Wasps was on his tail. But before they got a single shot off, Zak blew them out of the sky. A split-second later, his viewscreen lit up as a blast clipped his fighter across the nose.

"Are you all right, Commander?" That was Layson.

"I'm fine. They just scratched the paint."

Ahead, Ja'is took out three Wasps with a succession of quick blasts and the escaping transports cleared the planet's gravity well and made the jump to lightspeed.

"Good shooting, Ja'is," Zak said.

"Thanks."

"Commander," Adaria's voice cut in. "The remaining Wasps are veering off to port. They've got two squads of reinforcements coming in on the same vector."

"Commander." That was Deacon. "Fourteen transports have managed to leave the system. I think we've done all we can."

Zak sighed. They'd done well all things considered. And that was fourteen more transports than there would have been if Sigma squadron had done nothing. Still, a lot more transports weren't going to make it.

"You're right, Deacon. Okay, Sigma squadron. Let's go home."

. . .

The Harskan sector was a mysterious and frightening place in the minds of most people who lived within the Federation. Little was known about what went on inside its borders and the people who called it their home. And the fact that most of the Harskans people encountered in Federation space were dangerous renegades did nothing to sway this popular conception. For Asten and Carla, that fear and awe was still hard to shake, even though Drackson was with them. And the pair of Harskan Corteks coming straight for the *Lady Hawk* didn't help.

The communicator came alive with surprisingly clear Corsidan speech.

"Unidentified ship, you are in Harskan territory. Respond or be destroyed."

"Drackson," Asten said. "You're on."

Drackson leaned over the communicator. "All right. Just one thing. While I'm talking to them, keep quiet. They may do a scan and discover I have passengers on board of course. And if they've got the right gear, they could find out you're not Harskans. However, if I play my cards right, as you say in Corsidan, they'll let us pass without any trouble."

"Unidentified ship, you are in Harskan territory. Respond or be destroyed," the voice came again.

"Kallajai'es, saherai jaehl'adaesol," Drackson responded. *"Gael jea Drackson fei Araujion eliman. Cha jea est jeraes est tae'is alaesu."*

Although he didn't understand a word of Harskan, Asten recognized Drackson's name and his family name 'Araujion'. Drackson couldn't have identified himself any more clearly to the pilots in those vessels.

"Drackson?" came the reply. *"Saes jea kerimach est chara. Araujion eliman haelim jea-dra esj'aerae-tach omajen. Benisa, jor-esch dechae jea-tach leseia-tach saes-esch amon'gaetol, saes-dra. Harim'fae, saes e'lisas laie'fron."*

"Helaeshi." Drackson switched the communicator off.

Asten looked surprised. "That was quick. Is everything all right?"

Drackson smiled. "Actually, I'd say it is. I identified myself and told them I was on an important errand. They recognized my name and that of my family but fortunately, while my family's shame is well known, it is equally well known that I was not directly involved with the actions of my brothers. The pilot I was speaking to acknowledged as much and gave me permission to proceed. As it is also his duty to report any ships entering the sector, I think it is safe to assume other authorities will be informed and we won't be hindered any further."

"Glad to hear it," Asten told him. "All right. Let's go and see this friend of yours."

"Right."

Drackson climbed out of his seat. "Sorry, Carla. We're going to have to swap for a moment."

"No worries," Carla said, making room.

She sat down in the copilot's seat next to Asten while Drackson busied himself at the navigation controls. Officially at least, nobody from Federation space had ever been within the borders of the Harskan sector so there were no charts for the area on any of the commercial navigation computers produced there. For this reason, Drackson had to find the coordinates another way. Under normal circumstances, it would be an impossible task, guesswork that would have them hopping blindly all over the sector until they ran out of fuel or flew into a star. Fortunately though, the Harskans had established an enormous network of communication satellites throughout the sector which provided navigation data, among many other things, that pilots could access through shipboard communicators. Drackson accessed this network now and soon had the coordinates for their next destination.

"All right," he announced. "I'm done. And you now have the navigation charts for the entire Harskan sector as well."

· · ·

Epcar stared at Khalin in disbelief. "What do you mean we've lost them?"

"I think the phrase is self-explanatory," Khalin replied. "But look, we *had* to keep our distance. There's no way we could have sat right behind them with those Harskan Corteks there."

"All right," Epcar sighed. "But what are we going to do now?"

"Well," Khalin said, "I was able to tap into the conversation and it's not all bad news. That Harskan identified himself as Drackson of the Araujion family and from the sound of things, he's been living outside the sector in voluntary exile because of a crime his brothers committed.

"Now I think it's likely that other Harskans will inquire about him as he travels through the sector so I've set up the computer to flag any mention of him on the long-range communication network."

Epcar nodded. "Good thinking."

"And in the meantime," Khalin finished, "we'll just do our best to make sure the *Lady Hawk* doesn't get too far ahead of us. It'll take some speculation but we have her last trajectory so it shouldn't be too hard to guess where she's off to next."

. . .

It was the better part of a day and a half's travel for the *Lady Hawk* to reach its first stop in the Harskan sector, a planet that looked like at least a dozen others that Asten had seen except it wasn't in Frontier or Federation territory.

"Well, here we are," he said, turning to Drackson. "Lamas'ca."

"It seems rather quiet out there," Carla observed. "Shouldn't there be a welcoming committee or something?"

"No," Drackson said. "It's a quiet world."

"All right then," Carla said. "Now, are you going to introduce us to your friend or do we have to hide on the ship?"

Drackson shrugged. "I honestly don't know. I don't habitually bring humans to my home sector. I'm sure you'll be fine but I'll talk to my friend alone first."

"Fair enough," Asten said. "I was wondering though, if we do end up meeting this guy... does he speak Corsidan?"

"Yes. In fact, since it's so widely spoken, most Harskans do. Although not on a regular basis of course."

"Why would Harskans who have no interest in anything outside their territory want to learn a language that they'd never use themselves?" Carla asked.

"Despite their isolation, Harskans keep a *constant* eye on what goes on outside our sector," Drackson told her. "And Corinthe's activities in the Frontier won't have gone unnoticed."

"That's good," Carla said. "If the Harskan leaders are already concerned about it, they might be more willing to help the resistance."

"Maybe," Drackson said. "We'll find out."

Asten then brought the ship in on a course for atmospheric entry. "Shall we?"

"Yes, but not too quickly," Drackson told him. "We should wait until we are hailed before we go in. I imagine that will be any second now."

"Will you be handling it again?"

"Have you miraculously mastered the Harskan language during the trip in?"

Asten smiled and shook his head. "All yours then."

A few moments later, the expected inquiry from what counted as the farming planet's flight control came through.

"Elas'maie-ensa ch'aj, gael jea Lamas'ca fae'ra haledaes. Amaeris memans saes-tal, haelim est saes-esch ch'aj del saes-esch je'sari."

Drackson flicked on the communicator. *"Lamas'ca fae'ra haledaes, gael jea Drackson fei Araujion eliman est* Lady Hawk. *Cha jea talist-ensa est neraji est Ha'jaest in'fael'jion Cha he'laemi si da'frae afra'jae aleia."*

There was a pause and then the Lamas'can controller spoke again. *"Edae'saritach, Drackson. Amaeris ja'haiel esen'fae chara de'trahal kalam-ensa tra'ja."*

"Edue'saritach," Drackson replied. The communicator went silent. Asten looked at him questioningly but Drackson waved his hand in a dismissive gesture.

A few moments later, the controller came back on. *"Habrast ularcach si kalam est tra'ja heil-daes jeic."*

"Helaeshi," Drackson replied and switched the communicator off. "We've been given permission to land in the main city on platform sixty-three," he told Asten and Carla. "Now, I'll let my friend know we're coming."

6. A Reunion on Lamas'ca

THE MAIN CITY ON LAMAS'CA WAS LITTLE MORE than a scattered group of low set buildings surrounded by farmland and small mountains, and the spaceport sat on its outskirts. As the *Lady Hawk* landed, the sun was sinking below the horizon with scattered gray clouds reflecting the last of its fiery light.

By the time the ship was powered down, evening had fallen and a lone Harskan waited outside. He was much darker than Drackson, taller and of more slender build but unmistakably Harskan.

"Your friend?" Asten asked, looking at him on the viewscreen.

"Yes," Drackson replied. "Braesk. Wait here. I'll be back as soon as I can."

"Is Drackson okay?" Carla asked Asten once he had left. "He looked… sad."

"I think coming here's stirring up a lot of painful memories," Asten replied. "I'm not sure how long Harskans live but Drackson'd be quite a lot older than us. He's never told me much about this thing with his brothers but I'd say that it's been a *very* long time since he was here last."

"Maybe he'd like to talk about it. Do you think—?"

"Absolutely not. If he wanted to talk about it, he'd tell us. We don't want to open up old wounds."

"But you always joke about with him trying to guess his age."

Asten shrugged. "That's different. I started that up to ease him out of his shell a bit. You remember what he was like. Anyway, he enjoys it."

He leaned back in his chair, getting comfortable.

"Do you think we'll be able to leave the ship?" Carla asked after a while.

"I don't know," Asten said. He hated the idea of being cooped up inside for days on end but it was better than some of the other possibilities that were swimming through his head. "You heard what Drackson said."

They waited about half an hour more then Drackson returned.

"Well?" Carla asked.

"It's all right," he told them. "Come outside and I'll introduce you to my friend."

As they emerged from the hatchway, Drackson's friend smiled at them.

"You must be Asten and Carla," he said in clear Corsidan. "Welcome to Lamas'ca. I am Braesk."

"It's a pleasure to meet you," Carla replied.

"Yes," Asten said, shaking his hand.

"And you likewise," Braesk told them. "Drackson speaks most highly of you." He turned to his friend. "Come. My home is not far," he said, still speaking in Corsidan out of courtesy for the two humans.

"Is it okay if we're seen with you?" Carla asked him as they walked towards the city.

"It is no problem," Braesk assured her. "People will undoubtedly be curious and it's safe to assume there will be a lot of staring but there's nothing to worry about. And while some people may look hostile, they will not harm you. Even though you are not Harskans, there would be heavy penalties if they did so."

"Although if you caused any trouble of your own first," he added, "that would be a different story. However, since you are friends of Drackson, I doubt you would do any such thing."

"No," Carla agreed. "Besides, if we caused any trouble here, we would hardly be able to ask the Harskan Elders for any help in keeping Corinthe out of the Frontier."

"Quite so," Braesk concurred. "Although, to be honest, I'm not sure what assistance you hope the Harskan Elders will provide."

Carla looked at him in surprise. "Drackson seemed to think you'd be able to help."

Braesk glanced back at his friend. "Drackson's confidence is very assuring. Yes, I'll be able to help. However, I don't know if I can persuade the elders to grant your request."

Carla nodded. It was true that whatever decision the Harskan Elders made was out of their hands.

They passed a few more landing platforms, all little more than well-flattened earth surrounded by low whitewashed walls. Carla got the impression that interstellar trade and travel were distant secondary concerns to the locals. Everything appeared to be well made and in good condition but it was all very basic.

As they walked, they saw a few other Harskans but not many. As Braesk had anticipated, some stared but none gave them any trouble.

Soon, they had left the landing platforms behind them. "We don't have to pay a landing fee?" Carla asked Braesk.

The tall Harskan laughed. "The consensus on Lamas'ca is that if you want to land here, you're welcome to."

They then came to a small vehicle.

"Ah, here we are," Braesk announced, opening the left rear passenger door. "Make yourselves comfortable. There's plenty of room."

Carla and Asten climbed in, while Braesk went round the other side and sat in the driver's seat. Drackson sat beside him.

"Is everyone comfortable?" Braesk asked.

"Yes, thanks," Carla replied, strapping herself in with the seat harness.

"Yeah, we're good," Asten told him, doing the same.

Then with a whirring of engines, the vehicle came to life and lifted off the ground. It hovered where it was for a moment then climbed several meters at a time until the city was about thirty meters below.

"Where are we going?" Asten asked.

"To the mountains over there," Braesk told him, pointing ahead. "Can you see them?"

Asten couldn't at first but when he leaned forward a bit, he made out their silhouettes through the forward windshield. It was strange but the night sky was deep purple, not blue like it was on most planets he'd been on. He'd seen skies like it before but he still found it intriguing.

"I thought you said your home wasn't far," Carla said to Braesk, interrupting Asten's private reverie.

"It isn't," Braesk told her. "Some of the locals live up to three hundred kilometers away. Anyway, we're almost there. It's closer than you think.

Under a minute later, hovering directly above the mountains, they saw Braesk's home nestled on the ridge below with a small landing platform jutting out beside it, bridging a narrow crevice. A little ship sat on the platform and between it and the homestead, there was some space for the atmospheric speeder they were in. As Braesk brought them down, they saw several similar structures along the ridge in the distance.

"Here we are," Braesk announced as he shut down the engines.

They stepped out and headed into the house. Asten whistled. It was a fine piece of real estate. A circular building with large windows and panoramic views. Below, he made out the lights of the city on the darkened plains.

"Nice place you've got here," he said.

"Thank you," Braesk replied, hitting the latch to the main entrance. "Come in."

He led them to a large lounge room that naturally had the best view in the house and everyone sat down.

"All right," he announced. "Let me appraise your situation. You are acting as emissaries on the behalf of a resistance organization that has formed against Corinthe."

"That's right," Asten replied.

"What's their end objective?" Braesk asked. "How do they plan to stop Corinthe annexing the worlds along the Frontier? Are they planning to take over the Federation?"

The questions threw Asten. He hesitated for a moment, his mouth opening while he tried to think up an answer. However, Carla saved him the trouble.

"No. I don't think the leaders of the Resistance are anarchists," she said.

"Anarchists?"

"*Basa'javol,*" Drackson translated.

"Ah," Braesk murmured, turning back to Carla. "I'm sorry. Please continue."

Carla glanced at Asten before replying but he didn't seem bothered that she'd jumped in. He looked more relieved than anything.

"The aim of the Resistance is to halt the Federation's aggressive expansion policies, you're right," Carla told Braesk. "But I don't think they'd want a large scale war with the Federation if they could avoid it. I'd say they'd like to stop Corinthe with as little loss of life as possible but given the nature of the situation on the Frontier right now, confrontations are probably inevitable. And that's why the Resistance needs aid."

Braesk nodded. "I see."

As he listened to the conversation, Asten glanced at Drackson. His friend was strangely quiet.

"Do you think the Elders might help?" Carla asked Braesk.

The tall Harskan hesitated. "That's the question, isn't it?"

"What's the problem?"

"The problem is that the Harskan leaders will not give us a fair hearing," Braesk explained. "In Corsidan, you might say they'd be 'prejudiced'."

"I don't understand," Carla said.

"It's because of Drackson," Asten said, turning to his friend.

With a sigh, Drackson stirred. "He's right. I don't know if you noticed or not but I'm rather well known here. Without a doubt, the Elders will have already received word of my return and it doesn't matter whether I'm present with Braesk or not when he speaks to them. They'll *know* I'm involved."

Carla grimaced as the problem became all too clear. Drackson had been rather strange about the whole thing right from the moment Lieutenant Janson asked them for their aid. At first, he'd been pessimistic about their chances. Then he'd found new resolve and confidence. And since then, he'd swung between both extremes like a pendulum. Right at that moment however, he looked about as despondent as she'd seen him. She sighed. "Is there any way around the problem? I mean, where does this culture of communal shame come from?"

"There are several reasons for it," Drackson tried to explain. "One is a deterrent."

"I see," Asten said. "If you know that by committing a crime, you will shame your family as well, it might make you think twice."

"Pretty much," Drackson said. "But we also have a concept of shared responsibility and in our eyes, a wayward Harskan is a Harskan whose family has failed to raise that individual properly." He looked at Carla. "Does that make sense?"

She nodded. "Yeah, I understand."

"Don't despair though," Braesk said with some encouragement. "I think there's a way around this problem."

"What's that?" Drackson asked.

"Well," the other Harskan said, "one of the members on the council of Elders, Arasil, is an old friend of my family."

"So he may be more inclined to listen to you?" Carla asked him.

"He may be," Braesk answered. "But that's not why I mention him. Besides, even though he'd be inclined to listen, I think he'd be afraid to say so in front of the other Elders, especially Caeras. He is very forceful and is used to getting his way. No, I bring up Arasil because he carries a secret the other Elders do not know about but I *do*. I see you are aware of the *incident* which ruined Drackson's family name. As you may also know, Drackson's brothers weren't the only Harskans involved in that crime. Sixteen individuals were directly involved and so a number of families suffered the same shame as his. One of Arasil's closest friends also suffered that shame as well, though he carries it in secret."

"So we appeal to Arasil," Drackson said, sitting up.

Carla smiled. The pendulum was swinging back.

"That's right," Braesk told his friend. "Except 'we' will not be going. You should remain here with your companions. I will go. You are my friend and you helped me in the past. Therefore, it is only right that I should help you now."

"I believe the balance is in your favor in terms of what is owed between us," Drackson told him.

Braesk smiled. "I doubt that but, even if that's so, how can there be any debt between friends? I help you now, Drackson, because it is my wish to do so."

"Then I am grateful, believe me," Drackson replied, his manner changing yet again. "But what have we just been discussing? The council of Elders will know you are speaking on my behalf and we know this will make them almost deaf to reason. So much so that you already plan to expose the fact that the close friend of one has also suffered the shame I have. Therefore, it would be pointless attempting to hide my hand in this affair. In fact, doing so could well do more harm than good."

Braesk sighed. "You're right, my friend. We will go together." He looked pointedly at Asten and Carla. "However, you two must remain here. Your presence we *can* keep hidden from the Elders."

"No," Carla told him, realizing the original plan had been flawed all along. "We must come as well. This request for aid is from people who live beyond the Harskan sector. I may not be an expert on the ways of your people, Braesk, but I'd imagine your Elders would not be impressed if we sent you and Drackson to make a request on our behalf without being there in person."

"You forget that Harskans are not really accustomed to dealing with non-Harskans," Braesk reminded her.

"True. But this is a request from *a lot* of non-Harskans. Besides, according to Drackson, they'd already know what's going on in the Frontier. So you're going to be dealing with their prejudices against non-Harskans whether we're with you or not."

"What you say is true," Braesk replied after a considered pause. "Very well. We will go together."

Zak waited as General Draedon finished reviewing the surveillance footage Ja'is had taken at Ipaatid. Once again, he heard the conversation between General Kellahav and Governor Savic play out. It sounded macabre the second time, knowing that since he'd returned to the Therah asteroid base, Ipaatid had been overrun.

The recording stopped and the general leaned back, his eyes still fixed on the now dark monitor. "Thank you, Commander. You are to be commended."

"Thank you, sir."

"We can use this footage," the general told him. "In the face of Corinthe's ceaseless propaganda, we need all the evidence of the truth we can get."

"If we circulate it though," Zak pointed out, "Corinthe's associates will dismiss it as forgery."

"Of course they will. However, we've dealt with that before. You can't convince everybody, we know that, but there are ways of determining if footage is authentic or not so I'm sure we'll get the truth out to *some* people."

"Now," he continued, "there's another matter we need to discuss, Commander, isn't there?"

Zak braced himself. "Yes, sir."

"You know why you were instructed not to intervene, regardless of what you saw?"

"I didn't question the order, sir. It was simply that an unforeseen complication arose."

"It wasn't unforeseen," Draedon said. "It was a possibility and we'd both considered it or at least something very much like it, hadn't we?"

"Yes, sir."

"And although, as you so mechanically stated, you didn't question the order, you knew why I'd given it."

"The success of the mission was our first priority," Zak told him, knowing it was pointless to feign ignorance. The general knew him too well for that. "Engaging in combat with the enemy, unless we were fired upon first, could have jeopardized that, as well as our lives. And if we got ourselves killed, then not only would the mission have been a failure, the Resistance would have been down nine pilots."

"And as awful as it is to say it, that would have been a far greater loss in the grand scheme of things than the loss of some civilian transports," Draedon said. "I know you don't think in those terms, and to be honest, a part of me is glad you don't. It's bad enough that even *one* of us has to. However, I'm afraid it's necessary when you're on these kinds of missions."

The general then favored him with a smile. "Having said that though, you also did a brave thing. You made a difficult decision under pressure, saved a number of lives and brought all the pilots under your command back safely."

"Thank you, sir," Zak replied. He got up to leave... and stopped.

"Sir, there's something I was wondering about."

"What's that?"

"The planetary shield. I don't know why they didn't leave it up. If it wasn't strong enough to repel an attack from the Federation cruisers, why have it in the first place?"

"I don't imagine they were counting on Federation cruisers attacking them when they designed it," Draedon said, a touch of sadness in his voice. "I've seen the schematics of some of those shields and while they would keep out pirates and even a number of smaller assault frigates, the batteries on a large Federation warship would punch right through them. But by circulating the footage your squad took of the takeover, we may be able to convince other independent systems to upgrade their defenses."

"And perhaps convince them they need to stand together much more if they want to defend themselves from Corinthe's expansionary task forces as well?"

General Draedon smiled. "That's the premise of our whole movement really, isn't it? United we stand, divided we fall, as the old adage goes. Unfortunately though, it's turning out to be a long slow process. There's all too much self-interest and willful ignorance of the 'well, we don't have to worry about that' variety throughout these systems. Anyway, you should get some rest, Commander. You look tired."

7. The Harskan Elders

THE SPACEPORT OF DANNERI WOULD NOT make it onto anybody's list of places to visit. It was old, run-down, hot and dusty with insulation tubing and other miscellaneous junk strewn over the dirty streets and landing platforms. But for Terrac Nenmais, crouching behind an empty crate, it was ideal for his work.

Terrac was a stern looking man. The lines in his face had hardened over the years and there'd already been many. Now, he was well into his fifties but he still had the strength and physical stamina that had kept him alive through all of them. During those years, he'd worked for several prominent criminal organizations, collecting debts, infiltrating rival organizations and taking out people who put their noses where they didn't belong. Now though, he had a new job. The money was better, he had a lot more resources to work with and he no longer had to look over his shoulders for the authorities. Now he was one of them.

He couldn't use his own name in the field any more though. Corinthe had been adamant about that since if word got out that his favorite field agent was wanted on a dozen worlds, he'd be brought up on more charges than he'd care to imagine. Furthermore, according to the official records, Terrac Nenmais was interred in a high-facility prison on Corsida anyway. So to everyone he dealt with now, he was known only by a mediocre pseudonym he'd made up: Vendon.

Keeping himself out of sight, he watched a nondescript freighter on the other side of the crate. The crew had gone aboard and he was waiting for it to take off. Once it did, his job would be finished and he could get out of there.

In reality, he would have preferred to blow the crew away but he had to keep the bigger picture in mind. If he was right about these guys, they were involved in supplying food and essential equipment to a division of the largest resistance organization that had formed against Corinthe, the one the analysts said might actually pose a threat. And so he remained where he was, forcing down the feelings of aggression he had carried all his life. Vendon was well aware he was psychotic but because of that self-awareness, he could control his violent urges. Which was just as well since nobody would have anything to do with him if he didn't, Corinthe included.

After a few more minutes passed, the ship still hadn't taken off and Vendon grew impatient. He couldn't work out why a crew of professional field operatives was taking so long to prep a ship for launch unless they were up to something else.

Then one of them emerged carrying a compact blaster. Vendon knew it was possible the man was just following a hunch but it was soon clear he wasn't leaping at shadows. He walked around the hull of the ship very deliberately and stopped by the housing of the main thrusters. Then, after producing a small tool, he pried a small metal object off the ship and crushed it under the heel of his boot.

As the man returned to the ship, Vendon bit back a curse. He'd just removed the homing beacon that had been placed on the ship several hours earlier with quite a lot of difficulty.

Moments later, the hatchway slid shut and the ship came to life, lifting off the ground with a loud whine from its engines.

All this time, Vendon had been carrying a light field pack with him and now, he slung its strap off his shoulder and pulled it open. Inside, there was an assortment of tools, supplies and several weapons, including a compact version of a sniper assault rifle that could be folded in half for storage. He pulled it out and extended it, the two halves locking together with a satisfying click, then pushed the scope into place.

With the homing beacon removed, he was no longer able to track the ship, which had been his primary objective. However, with the loss of that opportunity, a new one had arisen. One that while not as useful in the larger scheme of things was immensely more satisfying.

Peering through the scope, he found what he was looking for, a thin piece of conduit leading into the engine compartment. He took aim and fired. The conduit ruptured and a dark gray gas gushed from the ship. Then he fired again, igniting the gas and setting the surrounding section of the hull alight. Several moments later, something underneath the plating there overheated and the whole section exploded. Vendon smiled.

The ship was now coming down for a forced emergency landing and he pulled another weapon from the pack, a high powered rifle with a rapid repeating action. As the ship touched down, the hatchway opened and a crew member came running out for oxygen, coughing as thick black smoke poured out from inside. Vendon blew him away with a quick succession of blasts and got into a better position.

Corinthe would most likely want him to take some of the crew members alive, he knew, but that was all right. He'd just have to doctor his report a little.

As the edge of El'aesi filled the *Lady Hawk's* viewscreen, a glowing hemisphere of light turquoise blue, Carla marveled at how a planet seen from space never lost its beauty or the majesty of its vast scale.

As they entered the atmosphere and felt the slight jolt as the ship was subjected to atmospheric conditions once again, Asten emerged from wherever he'd been hiding.

"Hey Asten," Drackson said as they all strapped in for the ride down.

"Hi," he said, a little surprised at his friend's casual greeting. As far as he was aware, Drackson had never used a casual expression like 'hey' before. At least not *casually*. He glanced at Carla. Maybe their influence was taking effect.

"Sorry, I dozed off for a bit there," he said. "I think my body's been running on Palanami time this whole trip."

"Relax," Drackson replied. "Don't worry about it."

Asten smiled. He hadn't been keen on handing control of his ship to someone else—it made him feel a bit useless and also a little nervous—but Drackson and

Braesk had handled everything so well, he hadn't fretted over it for long.

"Do they know we're coming?" he asked.

"Yes," Braesk said. "They're waiting for us now."

"Oh."

"Well, there's no need for unnecessary formalities," the other responded. "They know why we're coming and they have time. At least enough to listen to our request."

Below, a shallow ocean appeared to race below them, dotted with scattered islands. Then it looked as though they were flying over one of the world's larger continents. There were great swathes of forest, amongst which Asten discerned long chains of mountains. Vast deserts also stretched across the interior and there were other areas that seemed strange to him, patches of something that glistened in the sun.

"What are those areas?" he asked Braesk. "Cities?"

"No," the Harskan told him. "They're the famed crystal forests of El'aesi."

"I've never heard of a crystal forest."

"The crystals are formed when the molten rock under El'aesi's surface comes into contact with certain rock sediment of a different type," Braesk explained. "When it heats up, it expands and then it forms crystal pillars as it cools down again, hard as steel. And these pillars break through the surface in clusters of spears.

And when there are many all together, it really does look like a forest."

"I'd love to see that," Carla said.

"I don't think we'll have the chance, sadly," Braesk said. "As I understand it, time's something of an issue."

He was right, Carla remembered. The rendezvous with Lieutenant Janson at Palanami was only about a week and a half away now.

"However," Braesk added, "you will still get to see the crystal as some of the more significant buildings on El'aesi are made from it."

"Including where we're going?" Carla asked him.

"Exactly."

She turned to the viewscreen again and saw they were nearing the western edge of the continent. As it rushed underneath them, she saw vast plains running between more mountain ranges, over which numerous blue rivers flowed. Along their edges, there were several large cities but as they shot overhead, it was clear they were going somewhere else.

They saw more forests and some fjords, and then they were over the ocean again. Carla noticed that while it had seemed like the middle of the day just before, it now appeared to be much later.

Ahead, bathed in the serene light of El'aesi's sun as it fell behind them through distant rain clouds and sea mist, a large pillar of rock rose out of the sea. And built into its crest was a series of interlinked towers shaped like spires of coral and made from the same crystal they'd seen before. They were not transparent but they were definitely translucent. At certain points, Carla saw stone sections built into the overall structure and she guessed the living quarters and other rooms were inside them.

From several of the towers, landing platforms shaped like sea shells fanned out and Braesk brought them down on one of the highest ones.

"We're here," he announced. "Come. The Elders are waiting."

Outside, there were three Harskans. Two males and one female, distinguished by her different shape and the fact she was wearing a gown that any human woman would be glad to have in their wardrobe. For an older female of a somewhat reptilian people, Carla was surprised by just how feminine she was.

When they emerged from the hatchway, they were welcomed by the roar of gale force winds sweeping overhead, thankfully forced up by a protective barrier around the landing platform. They looked at the Harskans, who watched them in silence but did not approach. Asten and Carla stayed back, while Braesk walked over and bowed his head.

"Kallajai'es, Braesk fei Helas'jar eliman," one of them announced.

"Kallajai'es, cha-esch nemo'liatol Caeras del Arasil," Braesk responded, nodding now to each of the three in turn. *"Kallajai'es, cha-esch nemo'lowae Ramani."*

"Kallajai'es, Drackson fei Araujion eliman," the Harskan who had spoken before said, now turning to Drackson.

"Kallajai'es, cha-esch nemo'liatol Caeras del Arasil," Drackson replied, greeting them in the same manner as Braesk had. *"Kallajai'es, cha-esch nemo'lowae Ramani."*

The Harskan then looked at Carla and Asten.

"Del mia jea saes-esch nes'paratol?" he asked.

"Hae'jia jea Carla Casdan del gae'jia jea Kalai Asten Korr fei Lady Hawk," Drackson explained.

"Cha bes'iam Lady Hawk *jea ch'aj gael jea onai heia chara?"* the Harskan inquired, nodding towards the ship.

"Gael jea vasara."

"Cha karai'es," the Harskan said, nodding to himself. *"Draes, aji Cha besiam gael Carla del Asten hes'para Corsidan?"*

"Gael jea heli vasara," Drackson confirmed.

"Ka'hai," the Harskan said. *"Esen'fae jera jea elesa'ia, galia chara jea chara-esch milash est Corsidan."*

He walked past Drackson and inspected Carla and Asten. Finally he spoke to them. "Welcome to El'aesi.

Your friend Drackson has given me your names. You may call me Caeras."

"It is an honor to meet you," Carla said, bowing a little.

"Yes," Asten said, not knowing how he was supposed to act. Remembering Braesk's warnings about Caeras, he felt a little apprehensive. He hadn't realized he'd be meeting the Elder the moment he disembarked from the ship. Also, he had secretly hoped the Elders didn't speak Corsidan so he could sit out all the proceedings and leave everything to more persuasive speakers. However, Drackson *had* said that most Harskans were familiar with the language. Asten tried to focus but there were no two ways about it. He was out of his depth.

"Come," Caeras said, turning away and striding to the tower entrance.

It was a bit warmer as they stepped inside the tower, which was a relief, but Asten was more interested in the layout of the place. He had expected something sparse and lifeless, cold with great high ceilings, and what he got instead was more akin to a fine hotel. Lush crimson carpet covered the floor with a large emblem of some description sewn into it and the walls were covered in polished wood panels. To his right, the first flight of a wide staircase disappeared around a corner and ahead, the room became much larger with a floor to ceiling window that offered the occupants an unspoiled view of the ocean.

Caeras and the other Elders led them up the stairs where they came to a small balcony that looked over the larger room below. There, seven chairs faced each other with three on one side of the balcony and four on the other. The Elders took their seats and the others followed.

"So Drackson," Caeras began, "It has been quite a while since I saw you last. Have you spoken to your mother since your return?"

"I have not," Drackson replied. "I have not been here long. Nor can I stay long. However, I think it is better this way. She has already gone through the grief of parting with me once. I wouldn't want to put her through it again."

"That is a good answer," the older Harskan said with approval. "I thought as much myself in fact and so while I was informed of your arrival shortly after you met with that border patrol, I made sure that your presence here was known only to those who needed to be informed."

"Thank you, Caeras, for your discretion. You are most considerate."

"Perhaps," Caeras told him. "However, you may wish to save your gratitude for I was not so concerned for you as for the Lady Araujion. She has suffered enough shame already from the actions of your brothers. Imagine the disgrace she would bear if it were to be known that after all of that, you had the audacity to return to our sector, bringing outsiders with you."

Sitting to Drackson's left, Asten stirred with sudden anger at the old Harskan for talking about Carla and himself as if they weren't there. And the fact he was doing this in Corsidan so they could understand every word was shameless. Carla, ever the diplomat, put a hand on his knee to calm him.

"There was no arrogance in Drackson's act," said Braesk, coming to his friend's defense. "He came here because he realizes how important it is to stop Corinthe before he brings about a full-scale war."

"Is that what you would have me believe, Braesk?" Caeras asked. "This request you spoke to me about comes on the behalf of a resistance movement that has formed along the borders of the Federation. Now, tell me truly, do you honestly believe our friends here are selfless resistance fighters?"

Braesk did not reply.

"Drackson and his two companions here are the crew of the *Lady Hawk*," Caeras told him. "At first, I suspected they were independent haulers but their ship seems too small. The more likely explanation, I feel, is that they are mercenaries. Honest enough, I am sure—perhaps even honorable in their way—but not devoted supporters of a resistance movement." He turned to Asten. "Am I correct, Captain Korr?"

Asten took a deep breath. This was not what he had signed up for. "Yes, that's right. We're just being paid to deliver a request on the resistance's behalf."

"I thought as much," Caeras said, but the brief coldness in his voice had gone. "And they gave this job to you because they thought with Drackson, you might stand a better chance than they would on their own and this is true. However, there is more. Drackson, knowing that the shame his brothers brought upon his family might hurt his chances of receiving a fair hearing, enlisted Braesk to make the request instead. Then someone among you realized how absurd it would appear for a lone Harskan who had never lived on the Frontier to come to us, asking for aid on the behalf of a group of people he had never met. And so now you are all here."

Nobody replied.

"And now," Caeras told them, "you can return to the Frontier and tell your clients that you have passed on their request."

8. The Elders' Decision

"WAIT," BRAESK SAID, "LET US BE REASONABLE.

It seems that the only reason you wish to send us away as quickly and quietly as possible is because you wish to avoid any further embarrassment from the Araujion family."

"It is one of my reasons, yes," Caeras admitted. "Although not my main one."

"Still, would you not agree that it's somewhat tenuous to shun Drackson for the actions of his brothers? He committed no crime."

"I agree," Caeras replied, "but I am not the only one you would need to convince. Many still wonder why Drackson left as well and there are some who believe he was in league with his brothers."

"They could not be more wrong."

The strength with which Braesk had spoken took Caeras aback. However, he saw in his poise that the younger Harskan had spoken in passion rather than disrespect. He saw a flash of pain in Drackson's eyes, a resurgence of buried grief. He reached his own conclusions as to how the affair of Drackson's brothers had closed but did not voice them to find out if he was right.

"I apologize," he murmured.

Braesk bowed his head in acceptance.

For a moment, no one said a word. Asten, for his part, held his breath, not even daring to glance at Carla for reassurance.

Finally, Braesk turned to the other Elders, his gaze coming to rest on Arasil. "My lord Arasil, surely you would see it is wrong to shun the Araujion family for the actions of a few individual members."

Caeras glanced at his companion. "What does he mean by this?"

Arasil's eyes fell downward. "He has called me out."

The other Elder, the woman who Braesk and Drackson had addressed as Ramani, leaned forward. "Arasil, we do not understand."

The Elder smiled sadly. "Sixteen Harskans took part in the terrible crime that ruined the name of the Araujion family. Sixteen individuals from eleven families. I do not wish to name him but one of my closest friends, a Harskan who I admire as much as any among us here is the head of one of those families. He carries his shame in silence but it is no less painful to bear than it would be if it were known to others. And I can tell you both that he does *not* deserve the burden he has carried all these years."

"Ah." Ramani nodded in understanding, gazing downwards.

Once again, silence fell over everyone present and this time, Caeras was the one to end it. "This makes something clear that has troubled me for many years. Why could you not have told me this in confidence?"

Arasil shook his head. "It was not my place to say."

Tears welled in Caeras's eyes. "Yet you tell me now?"

Whoever this friend of Arasil's was, Asten realized, he had been close to the other Elders as well.

Arasil sighed. "Now, it *is* my place to say. Braesk was quite right to bring it to light under the present circumstances."

"I see," Caeras said as he regained his composure. If he was angry with Braesk, he didn't show it.

"It would be hypocritical of me to judge Drackson by the actions of his brothers," Arasil continued, "when I believe in my heart it is wrong to do so." He looked at both Caeras and Ramani with equal measure. "Of course, you are not in my position and there would be no hypocrisy if you were to do so but nonetheless, I implore you not to judge Drackson either."

"I will not judge him," Ramani said. "Although, having said that, the judgment of families for the crimes of individual members is something that is widespread among our people and it has been for many centuries. It is not something that is easy to change and it does serve some purpose."

"Nobody in this room is asking us to change all that," Arasil pointed out. "I believe that Braesk brought this up so we may consider Drackson's request on its own merits, not on personal prejudices."

"That is all well and good," Caeras argued, "but personal prejudices aside, what merit does this request actually have? Our human friends here have freely admitted that this is simply a job for them."

"Yes, for us it is," Carla spoke up, bringing all eyes on her. "However, as the request doesn't come from us, our own motives should be immaterial surely?"

Ramani smiled at her. "Well spoken, my young lady. By your conviction though, I see this means more to you than you confess. You fear the direction Corinthe is taking the Federation too, don't you?"

"I do, my lady," Carla replied. "And from what I've heard from Braesk and Drackson, you have been watching the events along the Frontier with concern as well."

Caeras locked his eyes with hers before Ramani could respond. "You are well-informed. However, unless Braesk and Drackson have been particularly selective in what they have told you, you must also know that we do not directly involve ourselves with the affairs of others. I do not wish to bring my people into conflict with Corinthe's forces. If he attacks us then we will wipe him from the pages of history. But only if he attacks first."

"Wait a minute," Asten said. "You're certain that if Corinthe attacked the Harskan sector, he would come off second best."

"Without a doubt," the old Harskan told him. "And I don't say this out of pride or arrogance. Ask the Levarc."

"Then you could help, surely? You must feel something for the people on the Frontier whose worlds are being overrun."

"I don't know if you believe me or not," Caeras confessed with a weariness in his voice that hadn't been there before, "but I do. However, as much as I care for the people out there, I care most strongly for the people who are under my protection here and it is my duty to do so. And as you must surely know, there is one thing all wars have in common."

Asten nodded as he understood. "People die."

"People die," the old Harskan repeated. "And I could not bear to send any Harskan to their death unless I absolutely had to."

The last feelings of frustration drained from Asten's body and now that he understood Caeras, he fell into silence.

"Perhaps," Ramani suggested, "there is another way in which we can help."

Everyone turned to her.

"It seems that while this resistance group must have many willing fighters, it is at a distinct disadvantage in terms of its military hardware. All the evidence suggests that it doesn't have enough ships to pose any serious threat against Corinthe and this is where I believe we may be able to help."

"Wait a moment," Arasil interrupted. "If you are about to suggest what I think you are going to suggest, then should we not consult the rest of the council?"

Ramani shook her head. "We do not have time. Our friends have already told us they can't stay long and even if they could, I believe this resistance group is going to need an infusion of new ships as soon as possible."

"Ah," the other said, leaning back with a knowing expression on his worn face.

"What do you mean?" Asten asked.

Ramani looked taken aback. "You mean to tell me you don't know?"

Beside her, Caeras smiled. "Of course he doesn't. They are not members of the resistance, remember?"

"I'm surprised the contact who gave them the job neglected to mention it though," Ramani said.

"Maybe he didn't know himself. Either that or he didn't think it was something he wanted to trust our friends with," Caeras suggested before turning to his guests. "You see, my friends, Corinthe's military might is still growing and I'm not talking about his occupation of the independent worlds along the Frontier. I am talking about the arsenal he has at his disposal. Right at this very moment, he is constructing new warships, in secret, to compliment the armada he already has. And our sources inform us they're near completion."

"Then the resistance group could be in dire straits," Asten said.

"Is that some Corsidan idiom pertaining to trouble?"

"Um, yeah. Sorry about that."

"No apology necessary," the Harskan waved it off. "You were speaking in the manner that is natural to you. However, you are quite right. If the Federation completes the construction of these ships, then the balance of power will be too great and the resistance will be unable to prevent further annexations."

"So what was the plan you were going to suggest?" Asten asked Ramani.

"My plan, if Caeras and Arasil agree to it, is to provide this resistance group with a few wings of Corteks and some light assault ships."

"And how would you propose to do that?" Caeras wondered. "If we gave ships to this group, for all intents and purposes, it would be the same as declaring war against the Federation." He smiled. "And we already told Corinthe's pompous aide we had no interest in that."

"You're right," Ramani agreed, also smiling at the reminder. "If we gave ships to this group, it *would* be a declaration of war. But if a group of renegade Harskans stole a large cargo vessel with the ships inside and took it into the Frontier or Federation with the intention of selling their stolen merchandise... and if was then stolen from *them*..."

Caeras considered it. "That could work. I wouldn't have any grievances with such an arrangement."

"Neither would I," Arasil said.

"However," Caeras added, facing the crew of the *Lady Hawk*, "I have a condition I would ask of our friends first."

"Anything," Carla said before the others had a chance to reply. Asten shot her a quick glance but it was too late. Besides, when he saw how much she cared about this, he realized he couldn't go against her even if he wanted to.

"I want you to handle the supposed theft," Caeras told them, "as a token of good faith to us." If he saw Asten's glance, he wasn't making an issue of it.

Asten stirred. Carla and Drackson were now watching him, as were the Elders. He wished he were back in the lounge on the *Lady Hawk*. Already, he felt he was being sucked into the whole resistance thing against his will and he wondered if Carla had signed them all up behind his back. On the other hand though, the con job they were describing didn't sound too bad. In fact, it almost sounded fun.

"Sure," he said, giving in. He had officially thrown in his lot.

"Thank you," Caeras replied, rising. "Come. Let us adjourn and discuss our plan further over dinner. I am sure you will find Harskan food to your liking."

During the next few hours, they ate well and the details of Ramani's plan to supply the ships to the resistance organization were finalized. Then it was time for the travelers to set off, to take Braesk back to his home on Lamas'ca and to get back for their rendezvous with Lieutenant Janson.

"Take care and may fortune smile on your efforts," Caeras told them as he saw them off on the landing platform. He turned to Drackson. "And before you go, Drackson, there is something I would like to say to you. There are many sadly who will always associate the name of the Araujion family with the shameful actions of your brothers. However, I want you to know that *I* will always think of you and your mother with respect. There is grace and honor in you, my friend, and those who oppose Corinthe will fare better for having you among them. The circumstances that drove you to live in the Federation were unfortunate but out of them, a new opportunity has arisen for you. A chance for you to do great good and show all the worlds that there is valor in the Araujion family."

It was late morning in the main city of Lamas'ca when the *Lady Hawk* landed there again, although there wasn't much more to see. Still, the group was sorry they couldn't stay longer.

Asten was the first out of cockpit once they'd powered down the engines and the first to the hatchway. He flicked the latch as he always did but he hesitated before he went outside. For a moment, he stared at the lock for the pressure seal. The hatch couldn't be opened unless the seal was released first but he couldn't recall flicking the switch. He shrugged. Maybe he was just going mad.

"Well, Braesk," he said once they were outside, "thank you for everything. It was an honor to meet you."

"Likewise," the tall Harskan replied. "This has turned out to be quite a remarkable experience. I did not expect the Elders would help us as they did."

Carla smiled. "People can surprise you."

Braesk smiled back. "Indeed. Well, I think you had better be on your way. I'm sorry our time together was so brief but perhaps we can meet again under less hurried circumstances."

"I'd like that," Carla told him.

"Take care of yourselves," he said in farewell. "Carla. Asten." He turned to Drackson. "Goodbye for now, my friend. I will say nothing to your mother of what you have told me but I think it would bring her much relief and comfort to know you are alive and well, despite what you and Caeras say."

Drackson nodded. "You're right. You can tell her I was here. And tell her I shall be restoring the honor of our family in the distant worlds of the Federation and the Frontier."

"That would bring her much joy."

"Thank you, Braesk. For everything."

"You are my friend, Drackson. I would do it all again if I had to."

Drackson tried to smile.

"You were gone a long time," Braesk told him, "and I think that living amongst the peoples of the Frontier and the Federation has made it easier to live with the pain your brothers brought you. You do not feel the shame as strongly now as you did before, do you?"

"No," Drackson confessed, "for I am no longer fully Harskan."

"Then it seems to me you are free to be whoever who wish," Braesk told him. "And to *go* wherever you wish."

"Yes." This time, Drackson did manage a smile.

"Then I hope you can stay longer when you next come. And the next time, you will see your mother?"

"I will," Drackson said. "I promise."

Braesk smiled. "I look forward to seeing you again."

"As do I," Drackson replied. "Farewell, Braesk."

"Farewell, Drackson."

Everyone felt a little sad as they took their stations on the *Lady Hawk*. Despite their apprehension when they'd first arrived, Asten and Carla had grown rather fond of the Harskan Sector. For Drackson though, it was a somber farewell. Until this moment, he hadn't realized how much he'd missed it. Now he was leaving once more, old feelings of loss awakened again. But this time, things were different. This time, he knew he would return.

Flanked by four other warships of the Federation fleet, the *Sentinel* drifted towards a floating field of debris, the scattered remains of what had once been a number of medium sized transport ships.

"What do you make of it?" Admiral Roth asked an officer analyzing the wreckage.

"Well, as you can see, there's not much left," the man replied. "However, a lot of the pieces look like they're from the standard S-7 cargo carriers that Corsidan Heavy Industries churn out."

"Non-military," the admiral said. "They should never have been this close to unpatrolled space without an escort. Is there anything out there to suggest they had at least some type of protection?"

"Nothing," the other told him, shaking his head.

"Then I can only deduce two possibilities. Either this was a congregation of people without one shred of common sense among them or they didn't have much time to prepare before they set off to wherever they were trying to go."

"What do you mean by that, sir?"

Roth pointed at the black void that presently filled the bridge viewscreen. "About twelve light-years that way lies the Ipaatid system. It was recently annexed by the Blackguard squadron under the command of General Kellahav. I'd wager that the people who died here were trying to get away from the system when it happened. Then they were either attacked by pirates or..."

He trailed off. He knew what had happened all too clearly. Equally clear to him was the fact Kellahav would get away with it. Scattered wreckage in the middle of nowhere did not constitute hard evidence and even if it did, Corinthe wouldn't act on it. Especially if Kellahav had been acting under his orders or Rear Admiral Calaom's. No, Corinthe would sweep it out of sight and there'd be nowhere else for Roth to take it.

Besides, even though he was the Supreme Commander of the Federation Navy, Roth had no jurisdiction over the operations along the Frontier. Thanks to Corinthe, Calaom had free reign there. A much older man, Calaom had stayed on as a rear admiral when his contemporaries had retired and there was no doubt he resented Roth's promotion to supreme command. It was therefore no surprise that Calaom had quickly fallen in with Corinthe and his new direction for the Federation.

Perhaps, Roth reflected, it might have ended there— having a few men on Corsida with dangerous ideas but without the means to carry them out—because despite his rank, Calaom was no commander.

But Calaom wasn't stupid. He knew his limitations and, knowing he didn't have what it took to subdue the more powerful independent systems of the Frontier, he'd brought in people who did. Now, in

General Kellahav, Corinthe and Rear Admiral Calaom may have found the man to champion their cause. And that *was* reason for concern.

"Admiral."

Roth turned and saw Captain Merrick.

"Yes, Captain?"

Merrick straightened his back. "Code gray. Priority two."

Roth nodded. "Thank you, Captain." He turned to the young officer beside him. "That'll be all, Lieutenant. Thank you."

If the lieutenant had any burning desire to find out what a code gray was, he didn't show it.

Leaving Captain Merrick on the bridge, Roth headed aft to his private quarters. Inside, he locked the door as he always did and went straight to the communication console in the center. He checked the recognition code and flicked on the communicator. "Proceed."

"Reconnaissance summary. Primary ship yards and two of the five regional defense fleets. Substantial. Quite substantial."

"Go on."

"Additional incoming."

Some transmitted data appeared on the console monitor. Roth glanced at the sophisticated alien letters.

Learning the Harskan language had turned out to be very useful for his intelligence network.

"Received," he said. "I will contact you again momentarily."

He terminated the transmission and began mentally translating the Harskan. He hesitated over one section.

"...*dreish'na kaer'dai-dres ch'ajol del Harskan Cortekol...*" he murmured. "Light assault ships and Harskan Corteks."

He called his agent back. "Do you read?"

"We read you," she replied.

"Good. Tail the *Lady Hawk* and determine its next rendezvous point."

"Understood."

"Over and out." Roth ended the transmission and contacted the bridge.

"Yes, sir?" the voice of a young man came through the communicator.

"Ask Captain Merrick to join me in my quarters."

"Right away, sir."

With a click, the communicator was silent again. The admiral went back to the door and released the lock, then paced about the room while he waited for the captain. He didn't have to wait long.

"You wanted to see me, Admiral?" Merrick asked, coming through the door just moments later.

"Yes, come in," Roth told him. "Lock the door behind you. It seems that that bounty hunter who got himself killed pursuing the *Lady Hawk* was on to more than he may have suspected. Gamma-Five reports that the crew of the ship reached an audience with the Harskan Elders on El'aesi and struck a deal to acquire light assault ships and Harskan Corteks for one of the resistance movements."

"I can't believe it," Merrick replied.

"I can hardly believe it myself," Roth told him, "but a member of Gamma-Five managed to stow away on the ship and spy on the crew for several days while her partner tailed the ship to El'aesi and back. It all checks out."

"That's neat work, sir. What about the Harskans' military capability though? Did you get your documentation?"

"I did. However, as it turns out, the matter with the *Lady Hawk* is far more interesting. Now the bounty hunter Tath, I suspect, had no way of knowing what he'd stumbled onto. But I believe, at the least, he must have overheard a conversation between the crew and a member of this resistance group back on Palanami and in tracking the ship, he was trying to get a lead on the group."

"What makes you so sure of that, sir?"

"Well, it's the only explanation that makes sense," Roth explained. "There was no bounty on the ship itself as you remember, yet the bounty hunter risked his life trying to track it."

"But why did he attack the crew?"

The admiral smiled. "I think he wasn't that bright. Possibly he thought he could get the location of a resistance base by coercing the crew and that *would* be something he could get a reward for."

"I suppose that's as good an explanation as any," the captain conceded. "Where's the *Lady Hawk* now? Is it still in the Harskan sector?"

"No, it's back in Federation space now," Roth replied, "and I think the crew are planning to rendezvous with their resistance contact. Now as you can imagine, this is potentially very useful for us. The transfer of the Harskan ships is scheduled to take place three weeks from now at the Adari refueling station but this resistance group currently has no knowledge of the arrangement. *That* will only happen when their representative can meet with the crew of the *Lady Hawk* again. I think you follow me."

Merrick nodded. "Yes, sir." There could be a lot of benefits, he realized. They could prevent this group from obtaining new ships, possibly get some leads on some of their bases and maybe even obtain the ships for themselves. The Federation for the most part used standard vessels in its navy but the admiral was not averse to using other ships just because they didn't come off their own assembly lines.

Roth smiled. "And I believe Gamma-Five will be able to provide us with a projected time and location for the rendezvous shortly."

The captain thought for a moment. "May I ask, Admiral, what you plan to do if you do learn the location of a resistance base?"

"I'm not sure, Captain. It is a dilemma certainly. Clearly, we don't want this resistance group reaching any position where it would be able to attack more Federation ships and endanger the lives of any of the men aboard them. But on the other hand, while we go about reaching them in two very different ways, their goals and my own are not dissimilar. In the meantime though, what we can do is buy more time to make such decisions by keeping this matter between ourselves. The fewer who know about it, the better. If word of it reached Corinthe, things could get messy."

"I understand," Merrick replied.

"Good. Now let's adjourn to the bridge. It's time to leave."

"What course shall we set? Are we returning to Corsida to report what we've found here?"

"That can wait," Roth said. "First, we'll set a course for Palanami. That was where our late friend Tath, failed bounty hunter extraordinaire, decided to track the *Lady Hawk*. Now, Gamma-Five might find otherwise but it will almost certainly be the rendezvous point."

9. The *Lady Hawk* Returns

As HE LOOKED AT THE CHRONOMETER ON THE far wall, Commodore Hallyd took a deep breath. It was time for his scheduled meeting with General Kellahav and he always found him a little intimidating. Kellahav was a career military man and like Admiral Roth, had quite an impressive record going back to the Levarc War, the war that had almost ripped the Federation apart. Since he'd been too young to enlist, and exempt from conscription, Hallyd had been lucky enough to miss the worst of it. However, those who'd been more directly involved and had survived were a tougher breed and it was no surprise that many of the ones who'd stayed in the military had risen to prominent positions.

Unlike Admiral Roth though, Kellahav wasn't just a hardened old war horse. He had a cold edge the admiral lacked and while Roth's record was almost suspiciously clean, Kellahav's was rather questionable. It was the man's great failing. He was too vicious and easily swayed by passion in the heat of battle. But when he wasn't aggravating volatile situations or launching strikes without authorization, he was a good commander and more importantly, one of the few senior officers in the navy who followed Corinthe's directives without giving him a whole lot of backchat first. It made Hallyd grit his teeth just thinking about the attitudes of the other officers in the fleet, the ones who took their cues from Admiral Roth. You couldn't get them to do anything without them complaining every step of the way. In the past, he'd tried to explain there was a difference between giving them a directive and telling them how to do their jobs but now he'd given up. Thankfully, General Kellahav gave him no such trouble.

A short chime sounded and Hallyd switched the remote release for the door to his office. He rose as Kellahav entered.

"General," he said, waving a hand towards the other side of his desk. "Good to see you. Have a seat."

"Thank you," Kellahav replied as they both sat.

He looked a little younger than Admiral Roth, Hallyd thought, and although his hair was also gray, it was darker and he had more of it. His facial features were well preserved too and apparently, there were a number of women out there who considered him handsome. Although since the man was all business,

Hallyd had a hard time picturing him in any scenario where he could meet his female admirers.

"So," he said, "let's talk about this proposal of yours. First of all, I should say Corinthe is interested. However, he wants to know a little more about it before he gives it a green light."

"Of course," Kellahav replied with an understanding smile.

"Now, you're suggesting we make a move against the Phalamkian system," Hallyd said, bringing up a report Kellahav had sent him earlier and checking he had the name right. "And this would involve some alteration to the schedule of our operations along the Frontier."

"It would but not as much as you think. However, my sources recommended we start the groundwork for this particular operation sooner rather than later. The Phalamkian system is not like Ipaatid. These people have seen a lot of action in the past. They've got a strong navy and some pretty impressive merchandise to go with it. Even you must have heard of Phalamkian Battle Titans, surely?"

"I have but only a little. Enlighten me."

"You wouldn't take one on lightly," Kellahav told him. "A Phalamkian Battle Titan is quite capable of taking out one of our Class-A cruisers and a frigate wouldn't stand a chance."

"Formidable ships then. And do they have a lot of these?"

"They appear to. My sources are compiling stock lists on everything they've got as we speak. I should be able to get some hard data to you by the end of the week."

Hallyd nodded, typing up a note on it. "These sources you refer to… Standard intelligence?"

"Yes," Kellahav replied. "And if you're going to ask, no, I don't have access to Admiral Roth's secret network."

Hallyd smiled politely. Whether it was true or not, this was the standard line from everyone he talked to. If Admiral Roth allowed other people access to his sources, they weren't forthcoming about it.

"Trust me," Kellahav told him. "If I had anything on where he was getting all his information, I'd be the first to let Corinthe know. All I know is that whoever his sources are, they're damn good and the information the admiral has passed on from them has proven accurate. However, our guys are pretty sharp too and I think Admiral Roth underestimates them."

"Well, I'd hate to think our own heavily funded intelligence network was so ineffective that people felt it necessary to use independent sources."

"No, they're good," Kellahav told him, getting back on track. "And I've done some cross checking on the

Phalamkian thing and the information looks solid. They've got a very impressive armada and *this* is the part I think you and Corinthe should pay attention to. The Phalamkians assist in the defense of a number of neighboring systems as well, not just their own. Unconditionally as well, it would seem."

"That's very noble of them," Hallyd remarked.

"Indeed," Kellahav said. "And while they don't place any obligations on other systems for assisting them, their neighborliness has made them rather popular."

"So basically, we're looking at a bastion on the Frontier. We've got a potential rallying point for a number of systems and you want to take it out before these systems can make a united front." Hallyd clasped his hands. "I see where you're coming from. So how do you plan to go about this?"

"Well, I think you can see this is going to require a little tact," Kellahav told him. "It's also going to take some time. The first thing we need to do is to take care of its strongest neighbors. I've identified three nearby systems we'll need to take out of the game before we can make any move on the Phalamkians and I'd suggest we get started on these straightaway."

"Now," he said, pulling out a card and sliding it across the desk to Hallyd, "I don't mind who Corinthe assigns to take care of the other two but I'd prefer to handle Kordan myself."

Hallyd frowned as he picked up the card and put it into his pad. "I've never heard of it."

General Kellahav smiled. "With respect, Commodore, you don't spend much time on the Frontier."

"Yes, I'm aware of that," Hallyd replied, trying not to scowl. "Still, is there some reason you want to handle this one particularly?"

"It's the most heavily defended of the three," Kellahav told him. "And I've already spent some time analyzing their weaknesses. I'd hate for my hard work go to waste."

"Very well," Hallyd said. "I'll relay the request when I see Corinthe."

"Please do," Kellahav said, rising to leave. "And I trust you will present my proposal to the security minister with your most emphatic support, Commodore."

Over the next two days, the *Sentinel* made its return from the Frontier. Two of the other warships accompanying it set off on the second day to do a sweep of a nearby sector, while the remaining ships continued on at a good cruising speed towards

Palanami. For most of this time, Admiral Roth stayed in his quarters and was hardly seen on the bridge. And he was in his quarters at the start of the third day, when Captain Merrick came to find him.

"Come in, Captain," the admiral said as the door opened. Seeing Merrick's expression, he frowned. "What is it?"

"We've had a security breach," Merrick told him. "Lieutenant Ardel's informed me that someone outside this ship has hacked into the computer system and accessed your communications log. I took the liberty of asking him to bring up any files the intruder may have accessed and one of them was a log of your last conversation with your agent from Gamma Five."

To his surprise, Admiral Roth wasn't angry.

"It is a problem," Roth told him, "but it's not as big a security breach as you may believe. You see, the only reason that conversation was logged was because Corinthe had his technicians put a mechanism in the system to log all my communications automatically. As a way of keeping track of me. So our intruder was either Corinthe himself or one of his lackeys."

"Commodore Hallyd perhaps?" Merrick suggested.

"I don't think so," Roth said. "Corinthe wouldn't give him access to something like that. No, I'd say it was his other pet."

"Vendon?"

"Vendon. An unfortunate occurrence really. If he had waited another week to pull this stunt, this whole business would have been wrapped up."

"What do you think he'll do now?" the captain asked.

Roth shrugged. "I'm not sure. It would depend on whether he was acting under Corinthe's orders or his own volition. I imagine it's the latter. However, that doesn't matter at the moment. And as for finding out what he plans to do next, why don't we just ask him?"

"Ask him?"

"Why not?" Roth said, a little smile playing on his lips. "The simplest way is often the best."

He switched on his communication console and keyed in the frequency for Vendon's private transport ship.

"This is Admiral Roth," he announced. "Come in, Vendon."

There was a slight pause. The monitor flickered to life and a stern looking man appeared. At the sight of him, Captain Merrick took a step back. It didn't matter how many times he saw that face. It still gave him the shivers.

"I read you, Admiral," Vendon said. "How may I be of service?"

"Actually, I was wondering if I could help you," Roth replied, his manner courteous and friendly. "It seems you've been searching through my communications log. Perhaps I could help you find what you were looking for."

"Thanks, but I've already found it," Vendon told him. "It appears you've been going outside the standard channels again."

"That's a rather odd thing to say, coming from you," Admiral Roth pointed out, "but go on."

Vendon gave him a cold look, perhaps wondering how much he knew about him.

Actually, the admiral knew almost everything about his sordid little history. His intelligence network had made fast work finding out where Corinthe's favorite field operative had come from. However, he kept the knowledge to himself for the time being, filing it away for future use. Corinthe would deny it if it were brought to light but there was enough there to put them both away for a very long time.

"Anyway, Corinthe's not happy about it," Vendon continued. "You know he doesn't like you using sources the rest of us don't know about and he doesn't like you keeping secrets from him. And now, I find out you've got a lead on what appears to be the largest resistance organization within the Federation and the Frontier regions. And you haven't said a word about it to anyone."

"If I haven't said anything, it's because the lead isn't certain at this stage," Roth replied, remaining civil. "So I don't require any assistance with it just yet. However, if it turns out it's genuine, I'll certainly let you know."

Vendon scowled. "You know, with an attitude like that, it's no wonder Corinthe finds it necessary to check up on you all the time. Also, you will have assistance, whether you want it or not. As soon as you know the rendezvous point, I am to be informed immediately, by direct order from Corinthe himself. I will then bring in a team, along with some orbital support, and take over the operation."

"I think that would be a mistake," Roth told him. "You have very little information about the ship we've been tracking, while my people have been on this for several weeks."

"Good for them," Vendon replied before terminating the transmission.

Several days later, the *Lady Hawk* arrived at the Palanami system.

"Well," Asten announced, "here we are. Anything on the radar?"

Carla shook her head. "No."

Drackson placed a hand on Asten's shoulder. "Listen, that bounty hunter we met on Dailas may have seen us talking to Lieutenant Janson down there when we were in the bar but he could not have possibly heard what we were talking about on this ship. And that includes the details of our rendezvous."

Asten sighed. "I suppose you're right but I can't shake the feeling there's something wrong."

"All right then," Drackson conceded. "Maybe your hunch is right. But unless something's happened to him, Lieutenant Janson is waiting for us down at that spaceport with six thousand credits. And my people are arranging a delivery of a lot of expensive hardware that depends on us. Risky or not, we've got to go through with this. Besides, haven't we all agreed to stick to the plan?"

"True but that doesn't mean we can't change our minds," Asten pointed out.

"Well, speaking for myself, I still want to go ahead with it. But it's your ship."

"Don't worry," Asten replied. "We'll stick to the plan. But I think someone ought to stay behind and guard the ship, just to play it safe. If there are any Federation agents down there, they could have it impounded in a heartbeat."

"I can stay with the ship," Drackson told him, fastening his safety belt for the descent.

"All right," Asten said. He hit the communicator. "Palanami spaceport control. This is the *Drifter's Folly*, requesting a landing platform."

"We read you," a bored voice responded. "One moment..." There was a short pause. "Okay, you are cleared for landing platform 67 and it'll be the usual rate of thirty credits a day."

"Understood. *Drifter's Folly* out." Asten flicked off the communicator with a scowl. "The usual rate? Wasn't it twenty-five the last time we were here?"

"I think so," Drackson said. "However, I'd say we've got more pressing things to think about. Nice name by the way. Do you have a trick ID responder to go with it?"

"No," Asten replied, playing along. "I just assume that spaceport authorities don't bother checking these things. Right then. Here we go." He hit the controls and they descended into the stratosphere of the planet.

"Don't go too slowly," Drackson cautioned him. "The ground staff down there will wonder what you're up to."

"I wasn't going slowly."

"You were. You were trying to scope what was on the other landing platforms."

"Okay, I was having a look." Asten sighed. "Although knowing Federation agents, it's probably pointless. They wouldn't leave anything noticeable lying around."

"Probably not," Drackson agreed. "Um, Asten? You're still doing it."

"What? Oh, sorry." Asten increased their rate of descent and brought the ship in to a smooth landing. "Well, this is it."

"Now Drackson, you'd better stay well out of sight," he said as he got out of his seat. "If there *are* Federation agents about, we don't want them to know you're aboard."

"Sensible enough," the Harskan replied. "Lock the hatch on the way out."

"Will do," Asten said. "Carla, bring a blaster."

"I've never used a blaster in my life," she protested.

"I don't like them much myself," Asten told her with some empathy. "But if anyone decides to take shots at us, I'd prefer it if we could shoot back."

"All right."

Soon, the two of them stepped out on the landing platform.

"Well," Carla said after a cursory glance, "I don't see any Federation types waiting to arrest us or anything like that."

"Who says they'd arrest us?" Asten asked.

"Well, they wouldn't shoot us here," Carla argued. "It's too public."

"They'd be in civs," Asten countered. "Then after they'd killed us, they'd all scramble onto their nondescript freighters and disappear. And the Federation would tell the locals they were doing everything in their power to find the people responsible."

Carla shook her head. "You're always ready to assume the worst."

Asten shrugged. "It's good to be prepared. Anyway, I don't think we'll have to worry about running into any Federation thugs until we reach the bar. They want our contact, not us."

"True," Carla agreed. She sighed. "You know, I can't help feeling a little guilty about putting him in danger like this."

"You shouldn't feel guilty," Asten told her. "We're helping him. Besides, it goes with the territory."

Outside the landing platform, there were a few people about the dusty streets and they couldn't be sure there weren't any Federation agents walking incognito among them. Asten took in his surroundings as they headed for the bar where Lieutenant Janson would hopefully be waiting for them. Among other things, he saw there were just two side streets between the landing platform and the bar and they connected with another street running parallel to the one they were on. If they were cut off coming out of the bar, both of them offered alternative routes back to the landing platform. As long as they weren't blocked by Federation commandos.

On the other side of the street was a canyon that Asten remembered from their previous visit but he didn't give it much consideration. It wouldn't be any use as a possible escape route. Its sides were steep and while it wasn't a long way to the bottom, it was long enough to sort out anyone stupid enough to take the plunge.

Then before he knew it, he and Carla were at the bar. He tried to act nonchalant.

Inside, there were enough patrons around to provide a little anonymity but nowhere near enough to make the kind of crowd someone could disappear in. Giving the whole place a quick scan, Asten saw Lieutenant Janson sitting against the far wall. To all appearances, he was just another customer, probably tired from a long cargo haul, relaxing with a nice cold drink and minding his own business. If he had seen him and Carla come in, he didn't show it.

Returning the favor, Asten didn't give him a second glance either and bought a drink for Carla and himself. For a second, he looked at his with regret. He had instinctively bought one of his favorites but since he wasn't going to be drinking it, he should have bought something cheap and nasty instead.

For a couple of minutes or so, he and Carla didn't move. Then, seeing some vacant seats at the table next to Lieutenant Janson, he gave her a nod and they went on over.

As he and Carla sat down, he raised his glass to his lips to conceal them. "We've been compromised," he muttered just loud enough for the lieutenant to hear.

"I know," the other man murmured, his eyes cast down on a card he was fidgeting with to give him an air of unconcern. "Several disguised Federation shuttles landed here a few hours ago."

Asten grimaced. "Are we being watched now?"

Lieutenant Janson didn't look up. "There are five agents blocking the exits."

"Where?" Asten whispered.

"There are two at a table by the doorway you came through," Janson told him. "Another standing across from them at the bar... and there are two dodgy looking characters standing next to the exit on my right."

"Any idea how we'll get past them?" Carla asked him. She glanced at each of the men. None of them were moving but they were all looking her way now and they weren't trying to hide it. Then she noticed something else, possibly the thing that had given them away to Lieutenant Janson as well. All of them wore blasters on their hips, not that uncommon, but they also had smaller blasters up their sleeves. And once Carla knew what to look for, she saw they had other nasty things hidden on them.

"Don't worry," Lieutenant Janson replied. "They wouldn't want to start a firefight in here unless they had to."

"Still though, they're not just going to let us walk out of here," Asten told him. "I think we're going to have to start a little firefight of our own."

"Are you crazy?" Carla hissed, hoping none of their observers had overheard the remark.

"Well, we've got to get past them somehow."

Janson grimaced. "Asten's right, Carla." He turned to the young captain. "But once we're clear, what next?"

"You come with us and we'll give you a ride to wherever you need to go," Asten told him. "We can talk more once we're out of here."

"What about my ship?"

"You can send someone to pick it up later. These guys don't know what it looks like. However, it looks like they've had their eyes on the *Lady Hawk* from the moment we landed. So if we don't take it, they will and I'll never see it again. Besides, Drackson's waiting for us on board."

Janson smiled. "I guess that settles that then. Although I think we'd have had to leave one ship behind anyway."

"All right," Carla said. "Now, have either of you got a plan for getting out of here?"

"I do," Asten replied, lowering his voice. "Get ready to run out the exit by the bar."

"The one on the right's closer," Janson pointed out.

"I'm aware of that," Asten told him. "But that's the one they'd expect us to take."

"All right," Janson replied. "We'll do things your way."

"But if they see us running for the other one..." Carla said.

"If this works, we'll have some cover," Asten told her. "Trust me. Then once we're outside, head down the first side street. That oughta throw them off our trail long enough to get to the landing platform. And lastly, keep your blasters ready."

Well aware that all five of the Federation agents had their eyes fixed on him now, Asten braced himself. They knew he was about to try something. He just hoped they wouldn't guess what it was. And despite Janson's earlier assurances they wouldn't start a firefight inside the bar, several of them looked like they were seriously considering it.

Keeping his eyes on them, Asten drew his blaster, moving his shoulder as little as possible. Across the bar, two of the Federation agents pulled out their own guns. Beads of sweat trickled down his brow. He counted to three in his head, dropped to the floor, pointed his blaster at the wall and blew away an electrical circuit board. Across the bar, tiny ceiling sprinklers started up, spraying light mist over the room.

Bewildered patrons leapt up, people shouted over one another and it was perfect chaos.

Using the end of a table to pull himself up, Asten looked around. The three Federation agents at the other end of the bar were out of sight but the guys on their right were still in full view. Before they could train their weapons on them, Janson blasted one and he collapsed, going down without a fight.

His friend wasn't so obliging though and shot several blasts their way. Asten pulled Carla to the floor, while Janson crouched down several feet to their right, the agent pinning him down. Asten knew the other three commandos were only moments away so he had to act quickly. Bracing himself again, he rolled out from under the table and shot the agent through the chest.

"Come on!" he shouted.

Carla and Janson climbed to their feet and they made a run for it with the crowd. Through the mass of bodies heading past the bar, Asten saw two men heading the other way. Then two quick shots rang out and they dropped.

He glanced behind him for a moment. He couldn't see who'd taken them out but it was clear now that Janson had brought his own back-up.

Then, with the way clear, he followed Carla and Janson out onto the sandy street.

"Come on," he told them, running to the first side street.

Carla followed with Janson taking up the rear. Another shot rang through the air and several meters to their left, a small chunk was taken out of a sandstone wall. They'd been spotted again.

Taking cover behind the building on the corner of the side street, Lieutenant Janson fired a few shots in return.

Asten pulled out his communicator. "Drackson, you there?"

"I read you," came the reply.

"We're heading back now… as fast as we can."

"Glad to hear it 'cause we've got company."

"Fire up the engines and take them out," Asten replied. "We're getting out of here."

Up ahead, a succession of loud blasts, shouts and screams echoed between the buildings. Asten led the others around the last corner on the left and they came out onto the landing platform through a small entrance.

Several men lay dead about the place but two were still standing, shooting at the *Lady Hawk* while a cannon on the underside of the ship swiveled towards them, sputtering short bursts of fire. Before the men realized they'd arrived, Asten shot one in the back, dropping him like a stone, and Janson got the other one as he was turning around.

Then the hatch slid open and Asten motioned Carla and Janson aboard. As he went inside himself, he took one last look back and saw a large man charging at the ship and bringing a nasty looking assault rifle to bear.

"Drackson!" he called out.

"I see him," his friend replied from the cockpit and a moment later, a blast from another one of the ship's gun emplacements hit the entranceway, leaving a pile of rubble and dust right in the man's path.

Asten shut the hatch and breathed a sigh of relief. With a familiar whine of the engines, the ship took off.

With Carla and Lieutenant Janson at his heels, he jogged to the cockpit and sat next to Drackson.

"Nice work back there," he said, taking over the flight controls.

"Thanks."

Janson whistled. "You guys are brave having all those illegal weapons modifications on your ship. What if Corinthe found out you were taking business from the Shipping Guild?"

Asten made a face. "Don't get me started on the Shipping Guild." He glanced at his instruments and saw a warning light. At least *one* of the commandos from the landing platform hadn't been firing blindly because one of the cooling lines to the rear stabilizer was leaking. Thinking quickly, he cut the line off and powered the stabilizer down to run on half capacity. It wasn't ideal, and he and Drackson would have to fix it later but there wasn't much sense in worrying about it right then.

"By the way," he asked the lieutenant, "who was that guy at the landing platform?"

Janson grimaced. "You noticed him, huh?"

Asten nodded. "That man's killed before, that's for sure. And I'd bet he's done it so many times, he doesn't give it a second thought."

"Yeah, he's a killer all right," Janson told him. "Remember that face. That was Corinthe's personal field agent, Vendon. Head of the Federation's special operations."

"Special operations like that one?" Carla asked.

"Right."

For a moment, there wasn't a sound in the cockpit. Then a short series of beeps emitted from the control panel.

"Uh oh," Asten said. "Incoming Wasps on our six. And there's another flight coming in from the port side."

"There's a Federation cruiser out there too," Drackson told him, powering up the guns. "Looks like we're not out of this yet."

10. A Near Escape

"THESE GUYS ARE GOING TO CUT US OFF before we can clear the gravity well," Asten muttered, getting ready for some evasive maneuvers. "Carla, you and Drackson are on the guns."

Lieutenant Janson pulled out a small communicator. "Sigma squadron. Red alert."

Asten whirled around. "You've got back up out *here*?"

"They'll be here soon enough," Janson replied. "And since I escorted them in, I'd say it's quite fitting that they escort us out."

His little joke, while Asten wasn't in on it, actually made sense. Down at the spaceport was a rather large bulk freighter that he'd 'escorted' to Palanami in his own ship, a Galleon Light Class gunboat he'd stolen from the Shipping Guild. And the moment he'd called for backup, an explosion had blown open the freighter's hull and through the gaping wound left behind, several Raptor 7s glided out one after the other then shot into space.

Ahead, three Wasps came straight for the *Lady Hawk*, firing a short salvo of blasts. Drackson took one out with the forward cannons, one flew past the ship and the third was ripped apart by a volley of fire from the starboard side of the ship.

A moment later, Asten nearly flipped the *Lady Hawk* into a steep dive as a Raptor-7 shot straight past the ship into a group of oncoming Wasps.

"Don't worry," Janson assured him. "These are some of our best pilots. They know what they're doing."

In the distance, the Raptor-7 took out two Wasps in the middle of the cluster then corkscrewed its way behind the group and took out another one. The remaining Wasps accelerated away and scattered when they were blindsided by two more Raptor-7s that had come over the equator of the planet below.

"That pilot is amazing," Asten said, indicating the first of the Raptor-7s they'd seen.

Janson smiled. "That's Zak Materson. He's the squadron commander."

"An old hand then?"

"Actually, no," the other replied. "He's only been flying a few years."

"The boy's got a lot of promise, that's for sure."

"Maybe I can introduce you when we get back to the base," the lieutenant suggested.

"Speaking of that," Carla chimed in, "where are heading?"

"The Therah system," Janson told her.

"Never heard of it."

The lieutenant smiled. "That's kind of the point with a good hide-out. But I take it you'd like some coordinates." He thumbed on his communicator. "Sigma squadron. Well done. Head back to base as soon as we're clear."

"Understood," a voice replied.

"All right, Lieutenant," Asten called back, "ready when you are. Have you got the coordinates handy?"

"Yeah but I'll need to punch them in your nav computer myself. I only carry these things in my head."

"How in the hell can you remember *navigation coordinates*?" Asten asked. Then he shook his head. "Never mind. Carla, you'd better swap with the lieutenant."

"Sure," Carla replied, swinging herself out of the navigator's place. She and Lieutenant Janson changed over and a moment later, Asten had the coordinates.

"Well," he said as they accelerated to lightspeed, "that's another planet we'll never be able to show our faces on again."

Drackson grinned. "I'll put it on the nav chart with the rest of them."

On the small viewscreen in his Raptor-7, Zak watched the *Lady Hawk* disappear. However, he couldn't break out the drinks yet. He and his wing still had a few Wasps to contend with before they could get out of there.

Focusing on the job at hand, he locked his targeting system onto a Wasp he'd been tailing and pulled the trigger. As the twin blasts from his cannons ripped the small fighter apart, he felt a brief twinge of sympathy for the pilot inside. The men who flew these things were both faceless and nameless to him but they probably weren't that different from him. They were just pawns in whatever game it was that Corinthe was playing. Briefly, he remembered his conversation with General Draedon. The general probably thought about these things all the time.

He glanced at his scopes. "Deacon, there's one on your six. Go starboard. Adaria?"

"I see him," the young woman's voice came back.

Off to the side, Deacon cut across Adaria's flight path but the Wasp that had been behind him didn't fall into the trap, veering off at the last moment. Adaria turned to track it but Zak stopped her. "Let him go, Adaria. Let's head back to base."

"Copy, Commander."

He waited as Adaria and the others went to lightspeed and when the last of them had gone, he left too.

It felt good to be in action, General Kellahav thought as he paced along the bridge. The government of Kordan had been most obliging. They had demanded he turn his ships around and leave their system and had then set about establishing a defense blockade. After which, Kellahav had simply signaled the second half of his task force.

It was risky of course, having Class-A Cruisers pull out of lightspeed so close to the planet. As well as the danger of a rather high-speed impact with the planet itself, there was the added risk of plowing right through that blockade.

However, they had planned it all down to the last detail and their efforts were paying off handsomely. He smiled in grim satisfaction as a Kordani gunboat shot across the bridge viewscreen, spiraling out of control before erupting in a blaze of burning gas and fading away. Closer to the planet, the enemy frigates were being decimated. Trapped between his main group and the group that had ambushed them so expertly from behind, they were being systematically ripped apart.

He glanced at a nearby radar display. "Squadron one. Pull back. Those frigates are badly damaged and they're leaving the fighting. They'll make good eyewitnesses."

"Copy, General."

"General!"

Kellahav turned to the second officer who had called out. "What is it, Lieutenant?"

"Three Phalamkian Battle Titans coming in at eleven."

"Move our ships behind the Kordani blockade," he said, quickly devising a plan. "That way, they won't be able to fire and we will."

With the slightest jolt, the *Adjudicator* began to turn and Kellahav felt the engines kick in as it accelerated. He switched on his communicator. "Bravo group, there are three Phalamkian Battle Titans coming in on your twelve. They're your primary targets. Proceed to intercept. We'll cover you from behind their main picket line."

The new arrivals appeared to have spotted the trap that Kellahav had laid out for them but were unable to move out of it fast enough. Soon, the guns of a dozen Class-A Cruisers ripped through the remaining Kordani frigates and pummeled the Battle Titans.

"The Battle Titans are leaving!" one of the radar officers exclaimed after just a few moments of this.

Kellahav gave the radar display closest to him another glance to confirm it.

"Are they abandoning Kordan?" the captain of the *Adjudicator* asked him. He sounded as staggered by the sudden retreat as the radar officer was.

"They are but it's not the cowardly retreat you think it is," Kellahav told him. "I'd say the Kordani probably told them to leave. All they could do here is throw away three good warships on a lost cause. I'd say they're heading back to the Phalamkian system where they might do a bit more good. And if I'm right, the Kordani should be contacting us at any moment to cut their losses."

He switched the communicator frequency so he could address his whole task force. "All ships, hold your fire. All fighters, return to your cruisers."

The crew on the bridge waited to see what would happen next but the tattered remains of the Kordani defense forces were dormant.

A beep that sounded louder than it really was broke the silence.

"General," the communications officer called out. "The Kordani are hailing us."

Kellahav smiled. "Good. Hopefully, they'll be more agreeable now."

The journey to the Therah system took the better part of two and a half days. During that time, Zak and the other pilots in Sigma squadron went into transit trances, a type of technologically induced hibernation pilots of small ships used for long journeys. As long as the period of hibernation wasn't too long, or too short, it was quite safe and ships with the technology installed woke pilots automatically once they reached their destination or earlier if there were problems en route.

Asten, Drackson and Carla in the meantime told Lieutenant Janson about the ships the Harskans would provide and then regaled him with stories of their trip.

When they arrived at the asteroid base and stepped out into the hangar, Asten took a deep breath.

"This is incredible. You built all of this in the middle of an asteroid?"

The hangar was huge, accommodating a full fighter squadron and several transports.

The fighters were those of Sigma squadron and Zak and his squadmates were presently climbing out of them and stretching their legs to shake off the effects of hibernation. Meanwhile, ground staff set about doing maintenance checks on the ships and refueling them.

"Come on," Janson said to his new companions. "I'll introduce you to Commander Materson before we head into the base. He's just over there."

He pointed out a young man talking to one of the technicians about something and once their little conference was over, he walked over to him.

"Commander Materson," he said, shaking his hand. "Thank you for your help back there."

"Not a problem, Lieutenant," Zak smiled. "Still, it's always nice to be appreciated."

Janson put a hand on his shoulder and guided him over to the others. "Here, I have some people who want to meet you. Commander, this Captain Asten Korr of the *Lady Hawk* and his crew, Drackson and Carla." He turned to Asten and the others. "And this is Commander Zak Materson, leader of Sigma squadron."

"Nice to meet you," Asten said, extending a hand.

"And you," Zak replied, shaking all their hands in turn.

"That was some fancy flying back there," Asten told him.

Zak shrugged. "Just doing my job."

"Well, if every pilot in your Resistance group can fly as well as you, then Corinthe should just hand in his resignation right now."

The younger man laughed. "Thanks."

"Anyway, we'd better let you and your squadron go and refresh yourselves," Janson told him. "We'll see you later."

"Sure thing," Zak replied and turned to the crew of the *Lady Hawk* before leaving. "Well, it was nice to meet you all."

"Now," Janson said once they'd said goodbye, "we'd better go and see the general. And get you the rest of your compensation."

"So they're providing us with a shipment of light assault ships and Harskan Corteks," General Draedon said, not for the first time. Asten got the impression he was repeating it just to remind himself it was true. "And they asked you to handle the transfer from our end?"

Asten twitched. There was something about official types, even courteous ones like General Draedon, that always put him on his guard.

"As a show of good faith," Drackson said.

Asten glanced at him. If his friend felt a little ill at ease, he didn't show it.

The general considered this for a moment. "Have you got any experience in this sort of thing?"

"Not really," Asten admitted. "But the Harskan Elders gave us an outline of how the operation should proceed and I don't think it should be too difficult."

"Well, I guess it's their operation," Draedon said. "And their ships. Very well. We'll keep to the arrangement. Now, is there anything we can do to help?"

At this, Carla raised her eyebrows and gave Asten a look.

"Actually, there is one thing we'd like," Asten said. "Just in case we run into any unexpected trouble, I'd like to have Commander Materson and his squadron with us."

"I believe that could be arranged," Draedon said. "So you've seen Sigma squadron at work, have you?"

"Yeah."

"They're a talented group of pilots," Draedon told them with unmistakable pride. "All the more remarkable for the fact that there's not a single one among them with more than five years experience in the cockpit. I've got a few more seasoned groups that I would trust to the end of the galaxy and back but these new pilots are the real future of the Resistance."

"Assuming you can't put Corinthe out of office in the next month or so?" Asten asked.

"That would be nice, wouldn't it?" Draedon replied. "Sadly, I don't think Corinthe will be easy to get rid of. He's been the security minister for thirteen years, and he's been working in the Department of Security and Defense since well... before they even *called* it the Department. Back when it was still the Bureau. From what we've been able to gather on him, he's been involved with the Federation government for over thirty years now. And all the time he was hiding in the woodwork, he was busy laying down the foundations for this grand scheme of his."

"However," he said, smiling, "we've got a few things we can look forward to soon and the acquisition of these new ships is one of them. Now, when is this operation scheduled to take place?"

"In three weeks' time," Drackson told him. "Which should give your pilots enough time to familiarize themselves with the new fighters. That is if you want them ready to demolish those new warship's Corinthe's working on under the table before they're finished."

The general stared at him for a moment. "You're rather well informed," he said after he found his voice again. He shot a sideways glance at Lieutenant Janson but the younger man just shrugged.

"I am," Drackson said. "My people keep a close eye on the goings on of the Federation and they told us about the new ships. I assume you want to destroy those ships before Corinthe can turn them on you."

Draedon considered the implications of this. That a secluded people in another region of space knew something about Corinthe's plans that the Resistance had only just discovered themselves. He was glad the Harksans were on his side.

On board the *Sentinel*, Admiral Roth braced himself for a conversation with his favorite underworld assassin turned Federation special operative. He already knew the Palanami operation had been blown and he also knew Vendon was going to place the blame on him, although he didn't need his field teams to tell him that.

He flicked on the communicator and Vendon's face appeared on the screen on cue. Roth felt an urge to hit it, which surprised him as he never really had violent impulses. However, since giving in to the impulse would only damage a good piece of hardware, he resisted.

"Vendon," he said, putting on a pleasant smile. "I trust the operation was a success?"

"Shove it, Admiral," the other man replied. "You know it wasn't. I imagine you're enjoying this, aren't you? Knowing I failed."

"No," Roth told him. "I'm not. I wanted you to succeed just as much as you did."

Which wasn't true. While he wanted to know where some of the Resistance's outposts were, he didn't want that knowledge falling into Corinthe's hands.

"However, the past is past," he added. "There will be other opportunities."

"You mean the transfer of Harskan ships into the hands of resistance fighters?" Vendon asked, undoubtedly accusing him for not sharing that particular information.

"I was speaking in general terms," Roth replied.

"Well, it's too late for that," Vendon said with a smug grin. "I found that part of the message as well. It was clever putting it in Harskan but Corinthe and I were one step ahead of you."

"Corinthe hired a rogue Harskan to translate it," the admiral told him, venturing a guess. Vendon would never have worked that one out by himself. It had to have been Corinthe or someone else on his staff. Secretly, Roth hoped it was the latter. Corinthe was cunning enough as it was.

"In fact," Vendon went on, letting the comment slide, "in light of this most recent development with our neighbors in the Harskan sector, we may now have sufficient grounds to declare war."

Roth pursed his lips. For all of Corinthe and Hallyd's posturing regarding the Harskans, he was fairly certain that the security minister wouldn't be that stupid and *mostly* certain that Vendon wasn't either. However, the man did have a rather cavalier attitude towards life as well as a self-destructive urge.

"I wouldn't suggest that to Corinthe if I were you," he cautioned him just to be on the safe side.

Vendon raised his eyebrows in an expression that Roth knew was intended to be intimidating. However, the theatrics were wasted on him. "And why's that exactly?"

"Because unlike you, my men have seen the resources the Harskans have at their disposal," the admiral told him. "And they vastly outnumber our own. We would be decimated and as a general rule, it's not good practice to start wars you know you will lose."

Corinthe wouldn't start a war with the Harskans on purpose, of course. Admiral Roth knew it was just another part of his overall scheme, creating the sense of a crisis so he could continue to militarize the Federation and annex worlds under the pretence of strengthening its borders.

"Furthermore, Corinthe is stretching the trust of ordinary citizens far enough as it is.," he added. "Surely, you understand this."

"All right," the other man conceded. "Still though, you sent me in unprepared to Palanami."

So he was back on Palanami again. He had a rather erratic mind. "Sent you? Interesting choice of words. Anyway, what do you mean by 'unprepared'?"

"That ship had hidden weapons emplacements," Vendon replied. "It would have been nice to have known about them."

"I didn't know about them either," Roth said, not bothering to raise the point that if Vendon hadn't hacked into his private communication records, none of this would have happened. "Besides, I don't know why you went in with your guns blazing. Why didn't you just put a homing beacon on that ship instead so we could track it later?"

"I would have but someone stayed behind with it," Vendon replied, feeling on guard. He wondered if Roth knew about that recent failure of his with a resistance lead. "Besides, we didn't think they'd go back to it."

"Why's that?" Roth asked him. "Since you couldn't know which ship their resistance contact flew in with, they could leave that one and pick it up another time. So they were almost *bound* to go back to their ship."

He looked at the man with veiled disbelief. "You didn't happen to find that other ship by any chance, did you?"

Vendon glowered. "We did as a matter of fact but I don't imagine anyone will be coming back for it. It was a bulk freighter and it was used to smuggle in a wing of Raptor-7s."

"What happened with those?" the admiral asked with sudden interest, although he believed he had a fair idea.

"That's none of your concern," the other man replied. "From here on in, Corinthe is relieving you of this operation entirely."

Roth mustered the last dregs of his patience. If he wanted Vendon and Corinthe to cooperate with him, he had to play nice. Although for a moment, he was distracted by the nagging fact that the bulk freighter Vendon referred to must have been escorted to Palanami by another ship to avoid suspicion. And that the resistance contact would have had back-up on the ground as well. Vendon and his men should have checked those things out. However, given the mess they'd made of the whole operation, that was now neither here nor there.

"So Corinthe has a plan regarding the transfer of these Harskan ships?" he asked.

"Yeah," Vendon said. "He's putting me in charge. To obtain the ships for ourselves and arrest anyone we find who's involved in the conspiracy."

To dope them up on drugs and ask them question after question in the hope of finding a lead on any of the resistance groups. Which would be illegal but at this stage, Roth wouldn't put it past Corinthe. Again, he wondered why Vendon couldn't simply put a homing beacon on something and the only explanation he could think of was that the man just preferred the more destructive approach. Despite Vendon's anxieties on the subject, he really didn't know about the incident on Danneri.

"I think we might have more success if we tried a quieter approach," he suggested. "Understand I'm not trying to compete with you for Corinthe's favor, Vendon. You have your talents and I have mine. And I think in our respective fields, we're both very good at what we do."

Vendon nodded. "And this is more in your respective field, I take it?"

Roth smiled. Perhaps the man was coming around. "Exactly."

However, his relief was short-lived. When Vendon spoke again, his tone was dark. "I know what you think of me, Admiral, because everyone I deal with in the Federation thinks the same thing, including

Corinthe. You believe my only talent lies in taking lives. Well, there are numerous other skills that go with that trade, including those subtle skills you think I'm incapable of."

"I never suggested you were incapable of anything," Roth said.

Vendon ignored him. "Now, I admit I slipped up at Palanami but it won't happen again. I don't make the same mistakes twice. However, this isn't about me. It's about you, Admiral. This job is more in your field of expertise than mine, you're quite right. And if that was the only thing Corinthe was concerned with, he'd give you the responsibility for the operation without question. But what he needs, Admiral, is someone he can trust, not a renegade whose loyalties are unclear. And until this crisis can be resolved, Corinthe's authority supersedes yours." His lips curled in a thin smile. "He has therefore given instructions that you are to pass on all the information you have about this ship transfer to me."

"Well, if Corinthe has translated all the data I received in confidence," Roth told him, emphasizing the last part, "then I have nothing further to give you. Goodbye, Vendon."

11. The Heist

"CALLING THAT THING THE ADARI REFUELING station is a joke, right?" Asten said to anyone who was listening. "Sure if you turn a few clicks starboard and head along that vector for a day, you'll hit the Adari system... but honestly."

Carla shook her head. "You do talk rubbish sometimes."

"Thanks."

"Don't mention it." She looked at the radar scopes. "Well, I can't see Zak and the rest of Sigma squadron so I guess they're already on the station. And there's nothing out here."

"I can't imagine why," Asten said.

They were in the middle of nowhere. There were no planets of any kind, no nearby stars or even asteroids.

The station however was quite the hotspot. Large and surprisingly lively. During the three weeks that had passed since their arrival at the Therah asteroid base, Asten and the others had made two trips to the place to familiarize themselves with it at Lieutenant Janson's suggestion and there were enough hangars in the station to rival an average spaceport, large enough to accommodate anything up to a mid-sized bulk freighter and pylons underneath for larger vessels to dock with.

The whole thing was constructed in an open ring shape with one large shaft spanning its diameter that braced the structure and also allowed people to travel between both ends of the station without having to walk around the outer rim. Although if they wanted to, there was a generous walkway for that as well, with large viewing windows where people could look at the stars or watch ships coming and going. And along the walkway were a number of shops, bars and cafes too. Asten remembered one of the latter quite fondly, although he doubted he'd have a chance to get a hot drink there this time.

"Now," he said, "our friends from the Harskan sector... Hangar forty-three?"

Drackson nodded. "Forty-three."

"All right then. Let's wait a few minutes and head in."

On board the station, Vendon gazed about the central control room. He had several plain clothed commandos outside and a handful of technicians with him, while in another part of the station, a large division of shock troopers were waiting on standby alert. He wasn't taking any chance of a repeat of the Palanami debacle.

Across the room, the station chief supervisor eyed him warily. Having been expecting another uneventful shift, he hadn't been happy when Vendon and his men had come in and requisitioned his control room.

"Well," Vendon said, "our Harskan friends are no doubt here already and whoever this resistance group is sending can't be far off. I think it's time we got started."

The technician nearest him nodded. "All right." He started keying in some sequences that would seal off various sections of the station, preventing anybody but authorized security staff from moving between them.

"I hope your men are up to scratch," Vendon told the chief supervisor but there wasn't any warning in his voice. He'd already taken the liberty of assuming they weren't and with the commandos and the shock troopers, he was confident they had enough men to handle the job.

"We're ready for the lock-down," the technician beside him said.

Vendon nodded to the chief supervisor. "You can make the announcement. Say we believe there are ship thieves operating in the area. I'm sure you know the drill."

"I'll do my best," the man replied, stepping over to the communicator but keeping Vendon in sight the whole time.

"Attention," he said into the speaker. "Attention. All pilots, crews and passengers are requested to return to their vessels. Ship thieves are operating on the station. Please return to your vessels and remain there until the all clear is given. Repeat. Ship thieves are operating on the station. Please return to your vessels and remain there until the all clear is given."

Satisfied, Vendon headed for the door. "Good. Repeat the message a few more times."

The man considered telling him that he knew how to do his job but decided against it.

Outside, Vendon saw red lights flashing while, every five seconds, an automated message broadcast the fact that a lock-down was in progress. Groups of people were running about the place, hopefully heading back to their ships, although there were of course a number of people who seemed to think they were above running for some reason. He wondered if they might get a move on if he fired a few shots at their feet.

Curbing the impulse, he went back inside the control room to look at the surveillance cameras.

. . .

Moments later, the communicator aboard the *Lady Hawk* came to life with a short series of beeps and a blinking light.

"Someone's hailing us," Asten said. He checked the display. "It's not Zak's signal. It might be our Harskan friends."

"I think you're right," Drackson agreed, fiddling with the controls. "Let's see if we can get a clearer signal..."

He broke off as a clear Harskan voice came through. "...*sa ch'aj, hesj'on. Elas'maie-ensa ch'aj, hesj'on.*"

"*Cha laej'ast saes,*" Drackson replied and waited. Something wasn't right.

"*Laie'fron elstae tralaesta,*" came the voice of the other Harskan. "*Sevaerai haledaesol est basaec neravast-ach laherst. Jera hesta aleia jea chaj braecol anestalensa est mei del a'estra jea ilae taleshem si jea tae'laes.*"

"*Karai'esach,*" Drackson told him and flicked the communicator off.

Asten raised his eyebrows. "Trouble?"

"He told me that Federation authorities have ordered a lock-down as there are ship thieves operating in the area."

"How does he know Federation authorities are there?" Carla asked. "I've been in a lock-down before.

These stations have their own security staff who handle these things."

Drackson shrugged. "I don't know. And it's entirely possible he might have been wrong. But he also said he thinks the timing is too convenient to be a coincidence and I think he's got a point."

"I agree," Asten said. He eyed the station and fidgeted. "Let's hold position for a moment. I want to see what's going on before we head in. And decide if we still want to go ahead with this."

"But you promised—" Carla started.

"I know what I said."

"What was that?" Vendon demanded.

"Someone sent a transmission from the station," the technician at the workstation beside him said, tapping some keys to bring it up. "And it looks like they got through to someone."

He paused. "Well, that wasn't long."

"What?"

"The transmission's finished already," the technician told him. "Anyway, here it is."

Vendon listened as it played out.

"That must have been the Harskans we're looking for," he said after it had finished.

"You recognize the language?" the technician asked him.

"No. But who else would risk sending a private transmission in the middle of a lock-down?" Vendon reasoned. "Where did it come from?"

The other man backtracked it, while glancing over the landing records. "Hangar forty-three. There's one large freighter listed there that landed four hours ago."

"That's them." Vendon faced everyone in the room. "All right, keep your eyes on the scopes for incoming ships. I don't think we'll have long to wait."

For a few moments, the control room was silent. Then there was a short beep from one of the control panels and one of the technicians turned around. "Something's just come in radar range now, sir."

Asten was still deciding what to do when he saw it: a mid-sized frigate that dropped out of lightspeed on their portside before heading towards the station. It didn't look like a Galleon or anything from Novatech Systems or Aurora Prime and he was wondering what it might be when a worrying thought crossed his mind.

"Oh no," he muttered.

"What's wrong?" Carla asked, while Drackson looked at the disappearing frigate with concern as well.

"If there *are* Federation agents aboard the station and they're expecting resistance fighters to turn up at any minute, then they're going to swarm on that frigate the moment it lands," Asten told her. "We've just placed some innocent people in a very dangerous situation."

"But even if they swam that ship," Carla replied, "they'll realize the crew aren't members of a resistance group, surely." The suggestion was made more in hope than anything else.

"How?" Asten asked her.

Carla didn't answer, and she could already picture the crew of the ship declaring their innocence to a cynical Federation officer as they were hauled away.

"We've got to go in, Asten," Drackson said.

"All right," Asten muttered. He hit the controls to fire up the weapons emplacements. "Get ready for some fancy flying."

He kicked the engines into gear and they accelerated towards the frigate, which was already slowing down to land in the hangar it had been allocated... which Asten noticed was forty-one.

"Damn it," he muttered.

Drackson saw it as well. "That's *definitely* too close to be a coincidence. They're onto the Harskans as well."

Asten decelerated. They were right in front of the hangar now and the frigate's landing pads were locking in place. It had landed on the left side of the hangar, leaving a generous space around it. And that space was filling up as men in gray blast armor moved in to flank the frigate. Every one of them wore a protective face concealing helmet and even from a distance, their appearance was distinctive enough that neither Asten, Drackson nor Carla had any trouble recognizing them.

"Federation shock troopers," Carla said.

Asten felt a sudden rush of bravado. He even smiled. "That's all right. These guys are ground troops. They've got nothing on us."

Carla let out a nervous laugh. "Um... I think firing on the Federation's finest from the air might permanently tie us in with our resistance friends, don't you think?"

Asten sighed. The moment they'd taken that job with Lieutenant Janson, they had settled that issue. "I think we're past that now."

"All right, ready when you are," Drackson told him, gripping the firing controls.

"One moment," Asten replied and punched in the encrypted frequency he had set up with Sigma squadron before they had left the base. "Zak? You there?"

"I read you, Asten," the younger man replied.

"We've got trouble. Shock troopers all over a frigate in hangar forty-one. We're heading in but we'll keep you posted."

"Understood."

Asten switched off the communicator. "Somehow."

"All right, here we go," he said as they accelerated towards the hangar. There was a slight jerk as they cut through the atmospheric seal and Asten realized he had never come through one this quickly before. He hoped he hadn't done any permanent damage to the ship but it seemed okay. And right now, there were more pressing things to think about.

On the deck, the shock troopers were thinking the same thing as they heard the roar of engines and looked up to see some type of private gunboat coming straight for them.

"Watch out!" one of them shouted, right before a volley of blasts blew chunks of metal all over the deck. Several troopers were thrown through the air by the explosions and rolled across the deck, dead or concussed.

The ship meanwhile looked as if it were about to crash into the hangar but at the last second, it veered away, disappearing out of sight.

"Nice shooting there, Drackson," Asten commended his copilot. He swung out of his chair. "Carla, take over. Now's your chance to fly this baby."

"What?"

"If we still want to pull this job off, I've got to go down there. Come on."

Carla climbed up and settled herself into the pilot's seat. "I'm not sure about this."

"Relax, you'll be fine," Asten told her. "Just head back into the hangar, but slowly this time, and get nice and close to the deck so I can jump out. Then the moment I'm gone, turn around and get the hell out. I'll call you on the communicator as soon as I can."

Drackson leaned back. "You be careful out there, Asten."

"I'll be fine," Asten replied.

The *Lady Hawk* turned towards the station in a graceful arc and glided into the hangar. There were still a handful of shock troopers standing and a couple of them fired at the ship, one of them using some type of portable missile launcher instead of the more conventional blaster rifle. He hit the port stabilizer wing, blowing out a chunk of metal and exposing some scorched wiring underneath but, before he could celebrate, Drackson blew him halfway across the hangar.

Asten leapt out a moment later, rolling as he hit the deck from a little higher than he'd have liked but he picked himself up straightaway.

He watched the ship for a split second as it turned and shot away and he saw the damage to the port stabilizer. Most of it was cosmetic but it still ticked him off.

Just then, a shot sizzled past much too close for comfort and he dropped to the deck and shuffled behind some large boxes.

"How many did you see?"

Asten frowned. That wasn't a shock trooper. They always sounded a little mechanical because of their helmet filters. He wondered whether the man was an officer type but that didn't fit either. The voice was too harsh and not cultured enough.

"Just one." That was a shock trooper. "Behind the boxes over there."

"Leave him to me," the other man replied. "Take your men over to hangar forty-three and wait for me there."

"Right, sir. Let's go, men."

Asten listened as the surviving shock troopers left, trying to separate the sounds of their boots on the deck from anything that might give away the position of the other man. However, it was an exercise in futility and once the troopers had gone, he had no more clue to where the man was than he had before.

For a moment, he panicked. His common sense briefly deserting him, he put his head out and nearly had it blown off. The shot missed him by a hair's breadth, scorching the wall behind him, and he ducked back after getting a split second glance at his assailant. It was the man from Palanami.

He pulled out his blaster and mentally counted to three. Then he leapt to the right side of the boxes, firing several shots as he did, and crouched back behind them. He hadn't hit Vendon but he had forced him to retreat behind one of the frigate's landing pads, giving himself a little more room to breathe.

Asten then looked at the ship and wondered what the occupants were thinking right then. No doubt, this was a little more drama than they'd anticipated when they had approached the station. There was also a small part of him that hoped they might come down and help him and he wondered why they weren't doing anything.

Then he saw something he'd missed earlier. A large ramp had been lowered to the ground and, above it, a few wisps of vapor lingered in the air, which meant the shock troopers must have lobbed something nasty up there. Asten hoped its effects weren't fatal.

Above him, one of the boxes exploded. He winced as a smoldering chunk of metal bounced off his shoulder. Clearly, Vendon had a pretty serious blaster.

Asten leaned out and fired a couple of more shots and saw Vendon duck back behind the landing gear again. Then he ran to his own right, getting some distance between them and hiding behind some more crates. He hoped they were sturdier than the first lot.

Then a glimmer of hope emerged. A familiar face appeared at the far end of the hangar and unlike Vendon, it was someone he was happy to see.

"Zak, get down!" he shouted and not a moment too soon.

Vendon fired several blasts at his friend and Zak only just managed to dive out of the way, ducking behind the frigate's forward landing pads. The shots hit the wall right where he'd been standing a split second before. Momentarily out of danger, he made a small hand gesture and Asten nodded. Now there were two of them, they could flank Vendon and converge on him.

Working in tandem, they made their way down the length of the frigate, firing as they went and forcing Vendon into the corner of the hangar. Then Asten got a lucky shot in. He didn't hit Vendon but he got the next best thing and he smiled as Vendon's blaster cartridge exploded in his face, throwing him back a few steps at the same time.

With a surge of adrenaline, Asten rushed forward to finish him off but he'd underestimated his opponent. Vendon jumped him as he was still bringing his blaster to bear, gripping his wrist and flinging his weapon six meters across the deck. Vendon then brought him between himself and Zak, using him as a human shield.

Zak ran to help his friend but Vendon was already ahead of him. Grabbing Asten by the scruff of the neck, he slammed his head into the deck, dazing him, and dragged him over to where his blaster lay. But as he reached down to grab the weapon, his head was in front of Asten's body for just a moment and with an amount of precision that would leave most gunslingers to shame, Zak shot him through the temple.

Asten shook Vendon's lifeless arm off him and stretched his shoulders before bending back down to retrieve his blaster. Then Zak walked over, inspecting his work. "I actually got him?"

"You got him all right," Asten said. "And you saved my life. You know that?"

"Well, you can buy me a drink sometime." Zak leaned over the body at his feet. "I wonder who he was."

"I have no idea what his real name was," Asten said, "but his field name was Vendon. Head of Corinthe's special operations."

"Hm."

"Yeah," Asten said, turning away. "Now…"

He trailed off as the sounds of footsteps echoed through the hangar. "It sounds like the shock troopers are coming back."

Zak heard them too and the two of them tried to keep out of sight. A moment later, five gray armored figures appeared. Trying to be as quiet as he could, Asten pulled out his communicator, thumbed it on and whispered into it. "Drackson. Our friends are back."

"Right," one of the shock troopers announced, his filtered voice filling the hangar. "The game's up. Come out with your hands above your heads."

"Give me a good reason," Asten muttered.

"You have ten seconds," the shock trooper warned and began counting them down. As he did, he and his men moved under the frigate. They weren't going to get caught out in the open again.

When they were too close for comfort, Asten leaned out and gunned one of them down. Then the rest of them trained their weapons on him and he set about testing the limits of a landing pad's capability as a shield barrier. It stopped the blasts quite well but didn't provide much cover and as he huddled to keep himself behind it, he really missed the crates he'd been hiding behind earlier.

Zak then jumped out and, with the advantage of surprise, got two of them. Clearly the shock troopers had thought there was only one person hiding under the frigate. The remaining two whirled about to aim at Zak, which was a fatal mistake because it provided Asten with the perfect chance to get another shot in and Zak put the last one out of his misery a moment later.

"Nice shooting," Asten complimented him.

"You too," Zak said, stepping out into the open again.

"Drackson, you there?" Asten asked, holding his communicator up again. There was a short static reply. "Good. You can stay back for the time being. We've got everything under control." He thumbed the communicator off and gave Zak a smile. "He says that's good."

"Well, I'm glad to hear it," the younger man replied. "Come on. Let's check on the crew of this thing."

They headed up the ramp where they saw several dazed figures climbing to their feet. All of them had black hair that they wore in long braided tails and had bluish skin with large eyes that were reminiscent of glazed black marble. However, their most distinguishing feature had to be the additional pair of arms they all had.

"Phalamkians," Zak murmured. "That explains the ship design."

"Yeah," Asten agreed. He offered a hand to one of them. "Here. You okay?"

The man accepted the assistance and pulled himself up to an impressive seven-foot height. It was only then that he seemed to register what was going on and he looked at both Asten and Zak quizzically. "You're not shock troopers."

"No, we took care of the shock troopers," Asten told him.

"They threw up some kind of stun grenade or something…" the man said. "I thought we were dead. Why… What were they doing? I don't understand why they surrounded our ship like that."

"It's a good point," came a new voice.

Asten looked up to see two women appear. Neither of them looked like the rest of the crew. The first had eyes like the Phalamkians but while her skin had a bluish hue, it looked more human. She also had golden red hair like Carla's and only had the one pair of arms.

Her companion, who only had two arms as well, looked entirely different again with dark blue hair and skin that was somewhere between light blue and green. Her eyes were red, featureless, without even pupils, and while it may have been a trick of the light, they rather gave the impression that they glowed.

The first woman looked at Zak for a moment before turning to Asten. "You seemed to be expecting these soldiers."

"Expecting, no," Asten told her with a shake of his head. "Perhaps 'anticipating' is a better word."

"You're with one of the resistance groups, aren't you?"

"Well, uh…" Asten stumbled, trying hard to think on his feet. All the running around with Vendon and the shock troopers had taken it out of him.

"A resistance group?" Zak asked in a puzzled manner, covering him.

The woman smiled. "You don't need to pretend. Do you think after Federation troops tried to attack my crew that I would turn my rescuers over to them?"

Asten exchanged a glance with Zak. "Yeah, you've got a point there."

"My name's Selina," the woman introduced herself before nodding to her glowing eyed companion and the Phalamkians. "This is Maia and this is my crew."

Asten raised his eyebrows. "Your crew? You're the captain of this ship?"

Selina gave him a curious look in return. "Why should that surprise you?"

"Well, you don't really look like a Phalamkian."

Selina chuckled. "I don't really look like a human either though, wouldn't you agree?"

Asten shrugged.

"I'm half Phalamkian, half human," Selina explained. "And my father is rather highly ranked in the Phalamkian defense forces. Anyway, that's enough about me. What about you? I didn't get your names."

"I'm Asten and my friend here is Zak."

"Well, it's a pleasure to meet you both," Selina said. "And we are *all* in your debt." She waved her arm in an expansive gesture to indicate herself and her crew. "And it is the custom of my people to reward those who help us."

Zak waved his hand, feeling a little embarrassed. "There's no need, really. Besides, if it hadn't been for us, you wouldn't have been in trouble in the first place."

"That's right," Asten pointed out. "Those shock troopers only jumped you because they thought you were us."

Selina didn't budge on the subject. "Well, that's all well and good but you still risked your lives to save ours and I'd be grateful if you'd give me the opportunity to show my appreciation. I can see you're in a hurry now but if you come to the Phalamkian system, I will make it worth your while." She paused again for emphasis. "Well worth your while. And I would urge you to ask the leaders of your resistance movement for leave to visit my system because what I have in mind is in their best interests too."

"What do you mean?"

Selina smiled. "I think you follow me. Go and do whatever it is you've got to do. But don't forget what I said. When you have the time, come to the Phalamkian system."

"So we just turn up and ask for you?" Asten asked her.

Selina laughed, and the last traces of her earlier intensity vanished. "Well, tell them who you are as well. However, I'll let the spaceport authorities know to expect you. Sooner or later."

"All right," Asten said. "Maybe I'll see you there."

"Wait a minute," Zak interrupted, turning to Selina. "Are you guys going to be all right for fuel?"

"What do you mean?" Selina asked.

"I mean I seriously doubt they'll let you refuel here now. That gunfight down there would have well and truly tied you in with us."

"Don't worry," Selina assured him. "We have plenty of fuel. We were just picking up some food supplies. However, I'm sure we can manage a couple of more days with what we've got."

"All right," Zak told her, not entirely convinced but knowing better than to argue with this woman about how she managed her own ship. "Then you should get out of here as fast as you can. Maybe we'll see you again but I'll have to talk to my superior officers." He gave Asten a nod and they said goodbye to their new friends.

"All right," Zak said as they left the hangar. "I'm heading back to my ship to make sure everything's all right outside. I'll also disable the cameras until I'm back on my ship. The techs gave me something for that back at the base."

"Right."

"So wait at least three minutes before putting on your show. We wouldn't want our friends upstairs to miss it now, would we?"

Asten grinned. "No, we wouldn't want that."

It was quiet on the bridge of the *Sentinel* but there was no shortage of personnel about. Captain Merrick looked at his chronometer. Nineteen hundred hours standard time. He grimaced. They were supposed to have been in the Taeia system eight hours ago. Admiral Roth however wasn't concerned and he already had his report on their fictional engine failure ready to file with Commodore Hallyd as soon as they got back.

Just then, the communications console next to the admiral's chair came alive. "... *Harrier*. We need assistance."

"So General Navaast is in on this," Admiral Roth murmured, more to himself than to Captain Merrick. "Interesting."

"We read you," another voice replied. "What happened?"

"Vendon's dead. Our shock trooper squad is not responding. Also, someone's scrambled the internal surveillance systems and the cameras are down. Wait. They're back again."

There was a slight pause. "Amateurs," the other scoffed. "Keep watching that hangar."

Admiral Roth flicked off the communicator without waiting to hear the rest of the conversation and turned to Captain Merrick. "That's that then. Take the *Sentinel* in, Captain, and have our fighters ready to launch in ten minutes."

12. A Nearer Escape

IN HANGAR FORTY-THREE, A LARGE CARGO carrier sat with its loading ramp down. One of the crew members, a Harskan, came down it seemingly to check a fuel line then disconnected it from the ship and went back inside.

About half a minute passed before some kind of gunboat drifted into the hangar and landed next to the bigger ship. As its landing gear locked in place, a large figure emerged wearing an enclosed black hazard suit and carrying a nasty looking grenade in one hand.

Then from one of the hangar's two internal entrances, a man came running in with a blaster. The figure in the hazard suit threw the man a spare gas mask and then lobbed his grenade up the cargo carrier's loading ramp. It exploded on contact and a thick black cloud of gas poured out of the ship and into the hangar.

The pair charged into the ship, firing several blasts, then the shorter of the two re-emerged for a moment.

He nodded in the direction of the gunboat and it lifted off. Then he went back up the loading ramp and hit the switch to close it.

From within the station, the sound of boots on metal echoed towards the hangar, getting louder and louder until several commandos with large blaster rifles burst onto the deck, firing at specific points on the ship, hoping to hit something that would disable it. However, the great engines of the cargo carrier were already groaning as they lifted its bulky weight off the deck and rotated it towards the airlock. The commandos fired a few more shots, more to vent their frustration than out of any hope of stopping it, and watched as the carrier cleared the hangar.

One of them groaned. "We're dead."

Asten dropped the gas mask on the ground, while Drackson pulled off his helmet. It wasn't very comfortable, having been made with someone of smaller stature in mind, but it had been necessary. If the cameras had recorded a Harskan making off with the cargo carrier then their phony heist would have been pointless.

"Drackson, Asten," one of the other Harskans aboard greeted them. "I am Eraehast. I am the captain of this vessel."

"A pleasure," Asten said, shaking his hand before Drackson had a chance to reply. He wasn't sure why he'd felt the urge to get the first word in but he suspected it may have been a reaction to the impotence he'd felt the entire time they'd been in the Harskan sector.

"It's an honor to meet you," Drackson told him.

"So," Eraehast asked, "did our charade go well?"

"I think so," Drackson replied. "Of course, we can only guess what it looked like on the surveillance cameras but I imagine it was convincing enough."

"Good."

Just then, Asten's communicator beeped. He pulled it out and thumbed it on. "Go, Carla."

"Asten," Carla replied, sounding rather panicked. "A Federation warship's just arrived."

"Okay. Um... has that other frigate gone yet?"

"Yeah, it made the jump a couple of minutes ago."

"All right then. You can't do anything from where you are. Head back to the base and we'll see you there."

"You be careful," Carla replied. With a click, the communicator went silent.

"It seems we've got company," Asten said, turning to Eraehast.

"*Sevaerai jaehl-ch'aj laie'fron est chara!*" a Harskan shouted from the other end of the ship.

"*Karai'esach*," Eraehast called back before looking Asten's way again. "The pilots have seen it too." In frustration, he eyed the Harskan Corteks around them. "It is a pity we cannot use these ships. This carrier has little in the way of maneuverability. If we—"

"Don't worry," Asten told him with a slight smile. "We're not exactly alone out here."

"There they are," Captain Merrick said.

"Launch squadron one," Admiral Roth said.

He watched the viewscreen as the fighters shot towards the cargo carrier. "Flank them but don't fire on them yet," he instructed. "They may surrender without a fight and I'd like to take that ship with all its cargo intact."

The communication console beeped and Captain Merrick reached for it.

"Ignore it," Admiral Roth told him.

"It's from the *Harrier*," Merrick pointed out.

Admiral Roth nodded. "Yes, I thought it might be. However, I'll talk to General Navaast later."

He turned back to the cargo carrier, which was now flanked on both sides by his fighters. "They've been rather quiet, haven't they?"

"Yes, sir," Captain Merrick agreed.

"What's the name of the vessel?"

The captain checked his display. "The *Nemo'lowae Braec*."

Admiral Roth chuckled.

"What's that?" Merrick asked him.

"I think our Harskan friends made that up for this mission as a bit of a joke."

"Oh," Merrick murmured. Without knowing any Harskan, it was lost on him. "Well, shall I hail them?"

The admiral leaned forward. "Allow me." He flicked on a communication channel. "This is Admiral Roth of the *Sentinel* calling the *Nemo'lowae Braec*. Please respond."

Hearing no reply, he repeated his message but got the same result.

"Keep a sharp eye on the radars," he told the bridge crew. "Our friends are not surrendering yet, despite the fact they're sitting ducks. They must have an ace up their sleeves that we don't know about."

"Raptor-7s coming in at three o'clock," a crew member called out a moment later. "Twelve of them."

"Alert squadron one to intercept them," Admiral Roth commanded. "And launch squadron two."

"Another group's heading out to greet us," Ja'is said over the communicator.

Zak eyed the new fighters warily. They were moving pretty fast and they were breaking off into small groups.

"I see them," he replied. "Ja'is, see if you can distract them while I go after the first group. Adaria and Layson, cover him."

The other pilots acknowledged the order and headed off.

Zak shook his head. He'd overheard the transmission from the warship to the carrier and was still somewhat in shock over the fact that the admiral of the Federation navy was out here. He wondered how badly they'd been compromised then shelved the train of thought. The way Asten had told it, the whole charade had been for the benefit of the Harskan leaders so they could at least officially maintain their neutrality. Whether the Federation believed they had any hand in it or not wasn't his concern.

"Deacon, get behind those three fighters that are pulling away from the carrier," he said as he noticed the original group of Wasp pilots weren't just idly waiting for him.

Then the Wasps scattered. Zak tried to track them but they were giving him and his squadron a hard time. Then there was a burst of static over the communicator and he saw a bright explosion on the viewscreen.

"We've lost Charis!"

The voice disappeared in the residual static caused by the explosion and close by, a piece of fuselage tumbled end over end into the dark void.

Zak gritted his teeth, feeling an equal measure of grief and angst with a slight sensation of nausea. This wasn't the first time he'd lost someone under his command but that didn't make it easier.

"Zak." The voice was somewhat distorted but he could still recognize it as belonging to Ja'is. "My quarry is fraternizing with yours and you've got one on your tail."

"I read you," Zak replied, toggling the image on his viewscreen. "I see him."

"All right," Ja'is said with deliberate care. "When I say, break off hard to your starboard side. Ready... go!"

Zak did and a moment later, a piece of debris shot past his port side, flaring briefly before the cold airless vacuum outside extinguished the flames around it.

"Thanks, Ja'is."

"Impressive, these pilots, aren't they?" Admiral Roth commented.

"I think our own are still performing very well," Captain Merrick replied.

The admiral smiled. "Really, Captain. I haven't wounded your pride, have I? Yes, our own pilots are performing very well indeed, as you so rightly point out. However, these resistance pilots have a natural flair which is a rare commodity."

"Although, those Raptor-7s give them something of an advantage too," Captain Merrick pointed out. "If they had as many pilots to find ships for as we did, they wouldn't be able to afford them."

"Yes," Admiral Roth conceded. "You're right of course, Captain."

"Still though, they've got a good number of them as it is, don't they?" Merrick mused. "I wonder how a group of militias formed by deposed Frontier governments can be so well equipped."

"Some of those Frontier governments were well equipped to begin with," Roth told him. "And other worlds along the Frontier that haven't been annexed would be assisting them too, I imagine. At least the ones with enough sense to realize it's in their interests, at any rate."

Merrick nodded. Then he saw something on the viewscreen.

"The carrier's getting away," he said.

"Yes," the admiral replied. "Once those fighters appeared, we didn't really have much chance of stopping it. It's rather difficult getting a boarding crew through that kind of fighting. And we weren't really close enough to hinder them ourselves."

"Well, on the bright side, at least we won't have to worry about Vendon any more," Merrick said, quietly enough that no one else on the bridge could hear.

"Yes," Admiral Roth agreed. "There is that."

Several light-years from the station, the *Nemo'lowae Braec* dropped out of lightspeed and Asten turned to Eraehast. "Well, this is it. Thanks for all your help."

The Harskan smiled. "That's all right. We were, as you say in Corsidan, 'just doing our job.'" He nodded to his companions, who were now leaving the bridge and making their way to the small shuttle that would take them back to the Harskan sector.

"Drackson. Asten," he said. "Farewell."

"*Helaeshi*," Drackson replied with a slight bow.

He and Asten then went to the bridge.

"Well," he said as he sat down in the pilot's chair and looked over the controls, "this doesn't appear too complicated." He looked over his shoulder to make sure all the necessary pressure seals were operating; he didn't want all their new ships to be sucked out into space when the shuttle left.

Just like the airlocks back at the refueling station, the atmospheric seals only gave way to something of appropriate mass that applied enough force, allowing ships to break through but nothing else. However, all ships and stations had the additional support of pressure seals that could be applied anywhere their designers wanted and could prevent anything sliding out accidentally. In the *Nemo'lowae Braec*, the pressure seals were placed just back from the main launch airlock to create an effective second barrier around the cargo area. While they were in place, anything that slipped through the atmospheric seal would be pushed straight back in again.

Once Drackson was satisfied the seals were all running at optimal capacity, he hit the release for the airlock's external shield door. There was a hiss from the hydraulics as it slid open and he saw the shuttle flying away on the viewscreen.

Asten gave a sigh of relief. "We did it."

"Yeah," Drackson replied. "All right. Let's head back to the base."

13. Selina

WHEN THEY ARRIVED BACK AT THE THERAH asteroid base, Asten and Drackson were surprised by the size of their reception. Zak and his squadron were standing in front of a large crowd of technicians and mechanics who were no doubt assembled to look over the new Harskan ships, while standing a few feet away, General Draedon waited with a broad smile.

As they came down the loading ramp of the Harskan cargo carrier, Carla emerged from the crowd and gave Asten a big hug. "You made it."

"Yeah," Asten said with a sheepish grin.

Carla then hugged Drackson. "Hey."

Drackson smiled. "Hey."

"That's quite the crowd out there," Asten said, looking around.

"They're all waiting to get a look at the new fighters," Carla said. "Now, come on. General Draedon wants to see you. Zak told him everything. Including what happened in that other hangar with those Phalamkians."

"Impressed the general, did we?" Asten asked her.

"Well, right now, the Phalamkians are the most powerful group on the Frontier," Carla told him. "And you've just established ties with the daughter of a highly ranked member of their defense force."

She stepped aside as they reached the older man.

"Well, I've got to hand it to you," Draedon said, shaking Asten's hand and then Drackson's. "You've done us proud. I'll let Lieutenant Janson know the good news as soon as he gets back from his latest assignment."

"We couldn't have done it without Commander Materson and his squadron," Drackson told him.

"Well, I'm glad you brought them along," Draedon replied.

"Me too," Asten agreed. "Speaking of which, I was wondering if perhaps Commander Materson might be entitled to a little R and R."

The general raised an eyebrow. "Oh?"

"I think he's making an obscure reference to an envoy mission to the Phalamkian system, sir," Zak said, appearing by Draedon's side.

"I see. So you'd like Commander Materson to accompany you?"

"Yes sir," Asten replied, falling into the more official manner of the other two men. "I don't know what our newfound friends have in mind for us exactly but I think if it's anything that could benefit the Resistance, it'd be better to have a representative along."

General Draedon's gaze flicked down for a moment. "Yes, of course," he murmured. He turned to Zak. "Commander, it's your call. If you don't want to do it, I can always send someone else."

"I'll go," Zak said.

"All right then," the general said, turning back to Asten. "Are you taking the *Lady Hawk*?"

The younger man shrugged. "Our friends would recognize it and I'd be much more comfortable bringing it along than leaving it behind."

"You keep it in good condition, I assume?"

"The best," Asten assured him, not taking offence as he knew what the general was driving at. "Don't worry. I'll take good care of Zak. He saved my life back at the station."

It was ridiculous, Admiral Roth thought. Ridiculous and more than a little insulting that he had to return to Corsida for a dressing down from Commodore Hallyd over the incident at the Adari refueling station. Hallyd and Corinthe had no one to blame but themselves for what had happened.

He wondered what his father would have done in his stead. When *he* had been Admiral, the Federation had actually been under threat, having been held under siege by the vast forces of the Levarc. The ruthless warriors had almost brought the Federation to its knees by the time his father had taken supreme command but he had driven them back and given the Federation the time it needed to rebuild its defenses. It was hard to imagine the decorated war hero would have put up with a self-centered upstart like Corinthe, let alone a pathetic yes-man like Hallyd.

However, Admiral Roth was not his father and nor could he dismiss the amount of support Corinthe enjoyed among some of the more well-positioned interest groups in the Federation. These were different days from the Levarc War and they required a different tack. They also required a lot of patience and at this moment more than usual.

"It seems you just have to involve yourself in everything these days, doesn't it?"

Roth blinked, turning his thoughts back to the conversation at hand and he focused on Hallyd sitting across the table from him. "I'm sorry?"

"Well, it was a remarkable coincidence, wasn't it? You *just happened* to be near the Adari refueling station at the time of a major covert operation. What are the chances?"

"I was fortunate," Roth replied. "Now, surely you didn't request me to come all the way here just to talk about the fascinating subject of probability?"

"Well, since you mentioned it, there *are* more important matters for us to discuss," Hallyd told him with a faint trace of disappointment in his voice. Clearly, he'd been hoping for more of an argument. "The incident at the Adari refueling station, while regrettable, has passed and there's no real sense in dwelling on it. However, in his capacity as security minister, Corinthe has outlined a new directive regarding this resistance organization we've been dealing with. All the evidence suggests this is a very large and sophisticated operation. From the markings on their fighters and a range of reports from various units across the Federation, we've been able to ascertain this is an organization with several divisions. They appear to operate independently for the most part but it looks as though they liaise with each other and trade supplies and hardware. We believe this business with the Harskans and the Adari refueling station involved just *one* division but there may be four or five in total, possibly more. So, as I'm sure you can appreciate, this warrants some attention. The other little resistance groups we've been hearing about are neither here nor there but this group is the big one. And Corinthe has a plan for handling this organization and he's asked me to go over it with you."

"Let me guess. He wants me out of the way?"

The younger man flinched. Evidently, he didn't like the fact the admiral read him like a book.

"He wants you," Hallyd said, emphasizing the words, "to scout the Federation and our border with the Frontier for resistance hide-outs. And he's asked me to provide you with a list of possible locations that intelligence has suggested, if you take any stock in their abilities."

"Intelligence is quite reliable," Roth said.

"Maybe you should use them once in a while then."

"I do."

"Including the divisions that Corinthe's established himself?"

At this, the admiral just smiled, not giving Hallyd anything. "Well, he thinks highly of them, doesn't he?"

"Well, despite your preference for that little sideshow operation of yours, you will investigate the locations on this list. Corinthe's orders."

One of these days, Roth thought, Corinthe was going to lose the special mandate the Federation had given him and the day that happened, he was going to have a nice long celebratory drink.

"Very well."

"You will investigate them, Admiral," Hallyd repeated for good measure.

"I heard you," Roth replied, rising to his feet. "Will that be all?"

"Yes," Hallyd told him, trying to sound officious. "I believe that's everything for the time-being."

"Good," Roth said. "I'd better make a start on these locations of Corinthe's. Good evening, Commodore."

He strode out of the office and returned to his shuttle by the most direct route.

"That was quick," his pilot remarked.

There were others, Roth knew, who would be offended by the notion of someone speaking in such a casual manner to a superior officer. He wasn't one of them.

"As it turned out, we didn't have that much to talk about," he replied.

After a short flight, he was back aboard the *Sentinel*, where Captain Merrick was waiting for him. "Well, Admiral. How did the meeting go?"

"Wonderful. We're being relegated to scouting backwaters."

"What a surprise."

"Did our men pull up the rest of Corinthe's new directives?" Roth asked him.

"Yes," Merrick hesitated. "Although, I imagine he won't be too pleased about that."

Roth shrugged. "Well, there wouldn't be anything there I'm not entitled to see now, would there?"

"Not if you're the commander of the Federation navy."

"Good. So was there anything I should be aware of?"

"Well, sir," Merrick hesitated, "yes. If Commodore Hallyd only mentioned *your* duties, then he *hasn't* told you everything."

"What has he neglected to let me know?"

"Corinthe's given him a special duty as well."

"And what does that mean?"

Merrick grimaced. "He's to be stationed at the Usile shipyards to oversee the completion of the new fleet."

"You're joking."

"I wish I were." Merrick looked at the admiral with renewed concern. He hadn't expected him to be elated by the news but the look on his face had him worried. "Are you all right, Admiral?"

Roth glanced at the other men in the vicinity but they appeared to be out of earshot for the moment. "I was just thinking, Captain, that nobody—and I include myself—has considered the possibility that the Resistance might be aware of our new warships and their location. And when you consider that possibility, you must surely see what a tempting target these ships would be. There would be of course be an impetus for the Resistance to prevent their completion before they could be used against them. But there would also be the sure knowledge that their destruction would be a heavy blow against the Federation's infrastructure as well."

Merrick raised his eyebrows. "And then one must consider how well Commodore Hallyd would handle things if a group of Resistance fighters swarmed into the place?"

"Exactly."

"However," Merrick said, trying to alleviate the admiral's fears, "the chances that the Resistance knows about these new ships would be rather slim, wouldn't they? I mean, there aren't even that many people in the fleet who know about them."

"True," Roth agreed. "But as a general rule, the worst case scenario is always easier to deal with if you're prepared for it."

"I suppose you're right. However, given Corinthe's new orders, what can we do about it?"

"Corinthe's orders," Roth replied, turning towards the bridge, "are only to investigate that list of locations he's provided. He doesn't specify anything beyond that. I say we visit the places on his list but do so in an order of our choosing. With a little forward planning, we should be able to chart a course that will bring us very close to the Usile system around the time those ships are nearly completed. And the closer to completion they are when the Resistance destroys them, the more expensive it'll be for the Federation. So an attack around that time seems most likely."

"I don't think Commodore Hallyd would be impressed if he found out about your plan though," Merrick replied.

"With any luck, the Resistance won't go near the shipyards and we won't be forced to head in ourselves," Roth told him. "However, if we do have to intervene, I'm sure I can handle another one of his tirades. Believe me, I've had plenty of practice."

Over the four days it took to travel from the Therah base to the Phalamkian system, Zak got to know the *Lady Hawk* pretty well. A cozy little vessel, while a damn good gunboat at the same time.

"Where did you find this ship?" he asked Asten.

"Tanem. When we wanted to go into business for ourselves, Drackson recommended the place. We got lucky, I think." Asten was quiet for a moment. "You know, since you're such a natural at all the controls, I almost feel like taking on a whole squadron of Wasps. We've never had a full crew on the *Lady Hawk* before."

"Could be fun," Zak said. "But I don't think General Draedon would be too thrilled if we went off risking life and limb for the fun of it."

"True. Although, I doubt we'll get into any trouble here anyway."

"We shouldn't, no," Zak said. "The general asked me if I trusted our Phalamkian friends but I told him not to worry."

"Why would he worry? I thought the Resistance has been trying to bring them in for some time."

"We have," Zak said. "And although they've been fighting the good fight from their end, they're definitely interested in joint operations and the like but we don't know much about Selina and her crew. I mean, personally. What were they doing so far away from Phalamki for starters?"

"Most Phalamkians I've met have been honorable people," Drackson assured him.

"You haven't me any with *me*," Asten said.

"No," Drackson said with a hint of a grin, "but I was hanging around the Federation and the Frontier for quite a while before I ran into you."

At this, Carla laughed.

"How long?" Asten tried.

"What's so funny?" Zak asked, looking around the cockpit.

"It's just an ongoing joke of Drackson's," Carla explained with a wave of her hand. "Drackson won't tell Asten his age and Asten's always trying to figure it out."

"Well, if Drackson's around retirement age, I'd like to know," Asten said. "I don't want to pay him a pension for a measly two years of service."

Drackson laughed. "I told you, for a Harskan, I'm the equivalent of a forty year old human."

"Yeah," Asten replied, "but is that thirty standard years or a hundred?"

Drackson chuckled. "You tell me and I'll tell you if you're right."

"Hey, look," Carla said. "We're nearly there."

The others looked at the planet looming larger on the viewscreen. Soon, they were hailed.

"Hello, incoming vessel. It's Selina. I see you there."

"Selina?" Asten replied. "This is a surprise. I thought we'd have to go through traffic control or the spaceport authorities—"

"The spaceport authorities," Selina said, sounding quite happy that she'd got the jump on them. "But I just happened to be out here... and here you are."

"What, are you on a pleasure cruise or something?"

"Why? Can't a woman relax once in a while?"

Asten laughed. "I don't see why not. So, what now?"

"Just follow me in," she instructed him. "I'll clear you with the spaceport authorities myself. Then I'll take you to see my father."

"Your father?"

"From the Phalamkian defense force, remember?"

"I remember," Asten said, looking over his instruments. Rather highly ranked as well, she'd said. "So is your ship that private yacht over there?"

"That's me. Shall we?"

Without further formalities, Asten followed Selina in. She cleared them as promised and soon they were soaring through the atmosphere of Phalamki. Actually, there were two other inhabitable planets in the system, which was a statistical miracle, but the Phalamkians left them alone so as not to spoil them. Besides, the planet they claimed for themselves was more than adequate enough.

It was a jewel of a place, with large turquoise seas and vast continents of varied landscapes. It had everything from glaciated mountain peaks to deep desert canyons, forests of all kinds and plains with numerous rivers winding every which way.

It was also on the plains, near coastal regions, that the major population centers appeared to be but the place where Selina was leading them was a multi-tiered city built around a large plateau. At its highest levels, buildings with wide flat roofs stretched over the lower tiers like many reaching arms.

Their designated landing platform was on one of these buildings and it was wide enough that they could land the *Lady Hawk* next to Selina's yacht, while leaving enough room for two similar sized ships to land on either side.

As one group, they stepped off the ship to find that Selina waiting for them with her glowing eyed companion Maia.

"Welcome," she said with a warm smile, before she caught sight of Carla and Drackson and turned to them too. "Hello. I don't believe we've met. My name's Selina." She gestured to her companion. "And this is Maia."

Carla and Drackson introduced themselves in turn and once the prerequisite pleasantries had been exchanged, everyone followed Selina into the building via some stairs just beyond the landing platform. Below, they were treated to a splendid view through the floor to ceiling windows that extended the length of the building.

"Nice place," Asten commented. "Is it yours?"

Selina laughed. "What, all this? How rich do you think I am? No, this is an official building of the Phalamkian defense force. But don't ask me what it's for because although I'm certain you're all honest people, I'm not supposed to discuss such matters."

They then noticed military garb on some of the people about the place.

"But," Selina went on cheerfully, "I *can* tell you my father is waiting in a lounge at the end of this wing. And I can also tell you there's a bar there for the patrons of this facility and it is excellent."

"Are drinks on the house?" Asten asked.

"Of course."

When they reached the lounge, they found it empty save for the bartender and one lone occupant. He embodied the typical Phalamkian completely. Tall, broad across the shoulders, and with long plated hair.

"Welcome, all of you," he said. "On behalf of my daughters, I wish to give you a token of our appreciation for saving their lives and the lives of their crew. But firstly, allow me to introduce myself. I am Lord Erama."

Seeing their surprise, he gave Selina a whimsical look before turning back to them. "I see my lovely daughters neglected to mention who I was."

"Selina did tell us you were highly ranked in the Phalamkian forces," Zak told him, glancing at Selina as well. "She just didn't say how high." Then he glanced at Maia. "You said your daughters…"

Lord Erama smiled. "Ah. I understand your confusion. Though she is not of my blood, Maia is also my daughter."

Maia gave Zak a smile. He blushed a little, surprised despite himself. For some reason, it felt as though he were seeing her for the first time. He smiled back before turning to Lord Erama. "I see. Still, your daughters didn't tell us exactly who you were."

"I often travel independently throughout the Federation," Selina explained. "If people found out my father was the Phalamkian equivalent of an admiral, it would make me a rather tempting target for pirates with eyes for large ransoms and other unsavory characters."

Asten thought of young Phalamkians aspiring to careers in the military but decided to keep the witticism to himself. Although Selina seemed to share his sense of humor, he wasn't so certain her father would.

"Which I'm sure you'd agree is most sensible," Lord Erama added. "Anyway, to get down to business, what do you think the leaders of your resistance organization would say to two Phalamkian Battle Titans with full fighter compliments?"

"You'd give us that?" Zak asked.

Erama smiled. "After a fashion. You see, an alliance between the Phalamkians and the Resistance has been on the table for some time. Of course, we are indebted to you for saving Selina and Maia and their crew but there are larger reasons. For a little while now, the Federation has been cordoning off our system, making hit and fade strikes along our borders and subduing our closest allies. A confrontation is at this point inevitable. Even as we speak, we are preparing for war."

Zak swallowed. "Yes, our sources have confirmed a substantial amount of Federation activity in this sector as well. And everyone heard about Kordan of course. Speaking for the Resistance, I'm sorry we weren't able to do anything."

Erama shook his head. "Nobody could have done anything. There was no warning. We had three ships nearby and when we heard what was going on, we sent them straightaway but by the time they arrived, it was too late. There were two other systems as well. The Brae system and the Alandra system, where Selina's mother is from. Understandably, because of this, we cannot spare too many ships at present. We may be able to spare more later but, at the moment, I hope you will place these two fine cruisers in your organization under the command of my daughter Selina. Maia will also be accompanying her."

"But you won't be?" Zak asked.

"My responsibilities lie here," the Phalamkian told him. "However, Selina and Maia would work better with you anyway as they've had more contact with other peoples in the Frontier and the Federation than I have. But though they hold no official rank as yet, they are my protégés and are both fine commanders."

Selina grinned. "And who needs official ranks with all those obligations?"

Asten smiled too, admiring the charismatic woman's free spirit but he resisted joining in with his own support in front of her father. For a moment, he wondered if he was getting a grasp on the whole diplomacy thing.

Then his thoughts turned to all those escort ship jobs he was missing out on. They'd been out of the game so long that the competition may have moved in on some of their clients. They might even have lost some to the damn Shipping Guild.

However, for the moment, he decided these worries could wait. Right now, he was part of something much more exciting than guarding cargo ships and he wouldn't miss it.

Maybe it was leftover euphoria from that heist on the Adari refueling station. Or maybe it was because Selina and her sister were joining up. But right then, he *wanted* to be in the Resistance.

14. The Resistance hits the Shipyards

"TWO PHALAMKIAN BATTLE TITANS?" General Draedon said. "That's no small contribution."

"I've never seen one," Zak said.

"They're serious warships," Draedon said before turning to a man standing on the other side of his desk. "Now, Commander Materson. There's someone I'd like you to meet."

Zak followed the general's gaze and extended a hand to the other man.

"Admiral Garam," Draedon said with a distinctive note of pride in his voice, "this is Commander Materson."

"A pleasure to meet you, Commander," the admiral said, shaking Zak's hand.

"The pleasure's all mine, Admiral," Zak responded in kind, giving the man a quick visual appraisal. He was perhaps a few years older than General Draedon but not more and Zak thought he looked kind. This surprised him for some reason and he wondered why.

Perhaps he'd expected the highest-ranking leader of the Resistance to be an embittered old warrior with a burn scar or two for good measure but whatever his previously imagined concept had been, it was now gone.

He also knew this was a high honor. As the coordinator of the various divisions of the Resistance—each formed around the militia of a different Frontier world—Admiral Garam was a busy man. In his flagship, the Cirtani heavy cruiser *Maiden's Virtue*, he traveled far and wide, making sure all the Resistance's divisions were running as effectively as possible. It was also an honor that Admiral Garam believed Draedon's division, along with General Kalae's, would be the most suitable group to sabotage the new Federation warships nearing completion in the Usile shipyards.

"General Draedon's told me a lot about you," Garam said. "It sounds like you'd give Captain Fera a run for his money these days."

Zak grinned. "I wouldn't dream of it, sir."

"There's no need to be modest," the admiral said. "Your squadron's track record is second to none. In fact, this is the reason I wanted to see you."

"Sir?"

"The general and I have been discussing the matter of our Harskan Corteks, Commander, and who's going to fly them. We fully intend to utilize them at the Usile shipyards when we make our strike there, you understand."

"Of course," Zak agreed. "It'd be crazy not to. I take it that my squadron came up in the list of possible candidates then?"

"It did," the admiral told him. "Would they be willing to make the transfer?"

"I think I speak for all of them when I say we'd be up for the challenge."

"Then it's settled. Report to the hangar at oh-eight hundred hours to begin flight training. We'll need you ready and able when we strike the shipyards."

"We'll be ready, sir."

"Now, where were we?" Admiral Garam asked after Zak had left.

"I believe you were explaining to me why my unit's handling this job alone," Draedon said. "Not that I'm saying we're not up to it but I thought General Kalae was going to be assisting us."

"She still will be," Garam said. "But we've now got a different plan in mind. She'll be hitting the Jaerad supply depot three hours before you hit the shipyards. It'll be another blow against Corinthe but more importantly for you, it'll be a critical distraction. By the time the alert is raised in the shipyards, any loose task force that might have responded will be too far away, having been diverted to deal with Kalae's group."

"Is Kalae's division up to it?"

"It should be. They're not going to stay to deal with all those task forces. We've cracked Corinthe's last few communiqués and we now know where every single sector fleet and task force in the Federation will be positioned at that time. She'll have an hour and a half window before the first of them arrive. Besides, those Narvashae Galleons she's been restoring for the past ten months are all in working order now and General Emerson's supplied her with some of those modified Shokhan Star Keepers he acquired."

General Draedon nodded. "Sounds like she's been busy."

"I think we all have."

"By the way, when are we getting our allotment of those ships?"

"We're working on that," Garam replied. "Emerson needs some time to organize people to transfer them to you. I take it you've got the necessary personnel to crew them then?"

"I've had the necessary personnel for over a month now."

"All right," the admiral nodded, making a mental note of it. "We'll sort it out soon. However, let's work on these shipyards first."

· · ·

A small crowd gathered in the base's main briefing room and General Draedon waited until they were seated before he began.

"Admiral Garam sends his apologies for not being here tonight," he told the assembled group. "He has some work of a different kind to take care of.

"Now before we proceed with this plan, I want to make one thing very clear. This is a hit and fade operation. We're not taking any unnecessary risks. While the defenses seem minimal, they have several wings of fighters in the facility that can be scrambled at a moment's notice so if we outstay our welcome, we could be in for a lot more trouble than we bargained for. I want each and every one of you to understand this. The reason our organization has managed to last as long as it has is that we've always managed risks carefully and I don't want all that hard work wasted now."

He hit a switch by the wall and a large visual display of the shipyards appeared on a screen behind him, rotating to provide a complete view of the facility. The new Federation cruisers clearly stood out, tethered to the perimeter of the shipyards by a number of pylons and passageways that workers used to access them.

"Bloody hell," one of the pilots muttered.

The comment did not go unnoticed.

"Yes," General Draedon agreed, glancing back at the display. And one particular ship in the middle of the yards.

It wasn't large. All Federation cruisers were large. This thing was enormous, more than twice as long as the other cruisers in the yard and probably five times their size. Also, while the standard A and B-Class Cruisers were essentially built around a central pylon, this ship was broad and looked like a giant shield.

"Since you've read Captain Fera's reports, I'm sure you'll have all come across... that. Now, nothing at this stage has been publicly released on any of these ships of course but we assume this is intended to be a new flagship for the Federation navy. And although it appears to be an updated design, it looks like it's modeled off the V-Class Dreadnoughts the Federation used during the Levarc War."

There was a murmur among the assembled. Everyone in the room had seen archival footage of V-Class Dreadnoughts like the *Vigilant* or the *Retribution* and the idea they could see a ship like that once more struck a deep chord throughout the room. Draedon could only imagine the effect that seeing it unveiled would have on Corinthe's supporters in the Federation. With several notable Dreadnoughts destroyed in the war and the last of them decommissioned nine years ago, people thought of the majestic ships with a lot of nostalgia.

"We also believe the Federation has incorporated elements of Levarc dreadnoughts into the design as well," Draedon continued, "as they have a stripped down Levarc warship in the shipyards that they appear to have been studying for some time. They've probably been applying Levarc principles to hull armor design but we don't know for sure. Anyway, all in all, from the size of the thing and our understanding of how Corinthe generally works, this will be as much for show as for its destructive combat capabilities, something to stir the spirit of all who live in the Federation."

There were a few laughs and murmurs of agreement.

"Yes, we're getting well acquainted with how Corinthe romances the Federation," he said with a sardonic smile. "But there you have it. The golden age Dreadnought recreated, bigger and more heavily armed than before."

He resumed the briefing. "If we can hit that one, we could no doubt save ourselves a lot of trouble further down the line. However, as you can see, it's right in the middle of the yards so it might not be easy to get to. It seems that although the Federation isn't expecting an attack, they've taken some precautions." He looked into the ranks of pilots assembled. "How old are these images, Captain Fera?"

From his seat in the middle of the group, Zak turned around and saw the handsome captain of Epsilon squadron a couple of rows back. Although their squadrons were going to hit the shipyards from opposite ends, he was still thrilled by the prospect of more or less fighting alongside him.

"They're the latest ones," Captain Fera said. "I did another fly-by three days ago. The ships were in exactly the same positions as they were last time. They haven't moved in weeks."

The general nodded. "Well then. It doesn't look as though they're going to move them anywhere before we get there." He pointed back at the visuals. "Now, the plan is simple but it's crucial that everyone synchronizes their appearances. The only way this thing is going to fly is if we all strike at the same time. That way, we will confuse the perimeter patrols and the other security forces. Hopefully, it'll take them a minute or two to work out how they'll deploy their defenses. Time we can use to our advantage if we get everything right. Now obviously, the cruisers will concentrate on the demolition work. As for the fighters, you know your job. Protect our ships. Those of you flying the Harskan Corteks will have your chance for one or two strafing runs while the Federation scrambles its defenses but once they're scrambled, you scramble too and get back to defend the cruisers."

He looked around the room. "Any questions?"

"Are we on schedule?"

Captain Merrick turned to his superior officer. "We're making exceptionally good time, sir. Navigation believes we can shave twenty-three hours off our current ETA for the Marno system."

"Then have the *Sentinel* reduce speed by sixty percent," Admiral Roth replied. "And flag to all ships."

Merrick nodded. They were now very close to the Usile system. With several of the Class-A Cruisers at the shipyards barely a week away from completion, it was an ideal time for the Resistance to strike as the admiral had said. And if they did, the *Sentinel* could reach the shipyards in under four hours, and a reduction to forty percent of their current speed would keep them at that proximity for a further two. Captain Merrick felt almost treacherous for thinking it but if the Resistance was planning to attack the shipyards, he hoped they did it soon.

He turned to relay the admiral's instructions. "Yes, sir."

Just as he was turning though, there was a commotion at the communication station.

"Sir!" the officer on duty called out. "Emergency in the Jaerad system. The supply depot is under attack. Four Narvashae Galleons, three apparently modified Shokhan Star Keepers and three squads of fighters, irregular. They're requesting assistance."

"Understood," Admiral Roth replied. "Notify our task forces in the Rinhast and the Dren Vaschal systems and relay the following. Send in all four Class-A cruisers from the Rinhast task force, and one Class-A and six Class-Bs from Dren Vaschal. Captain Heles is to coordinate the defenses."

"Copy."

Merrick frowned as Roth walked away from the station. "What about us, sir? If we leave now, we can reach that depot in three and a half hours."

"Our friends will be long gone by then," Roth told him. "If they're as careful as I believe they are, they will expect the reinforcements we've sent and will leave well before they arrive."

"So why bother sending them then?"

"Because I might be wrong. However, I believe this is a diversionary attack."

"Change course for the shipyards then?"

"Give the order, Captain."

. . .

After a journey of two days, General Draedon's strike force was almost at their destination. Fortunately for all concerned, the fighters had remained in hangars on the cruisers so nobody had had to sleep through the journey cramped up in a small cockpit. Asten had taken advantage of the arrangement as well and the *Lady Hawk* was presently in a hangar too.

He and the others were having a warm beverage in one of the lounge areas on their cruiser when the battle alert was sounded.

"We're approaching the Usile system," a voice came over the loudspeakers. "All pilots to your vessels. All crew members, take your stations." The message was repeated and around them, everyone dropped what they were doing.

"That's us," Carla said, climbing out of her seat.

Asten followed her, with Drackson giving him an encouraging clap on the shoulder. They jogged to the hangars, along with a number of pilots and technicians, and were soon in the familiar cockpit of the *Lady Hawk*. Except for Carla, who was at the other end of the ship manning the rear guns.

"You comfortable, Carla?" Asten asked over the communicator as he powered up the ship.

"It's a little tight but I think I'll manage," she replied. "It's better me being here than Drackson, right?"

Asten grinned at his co-pilot who nodded his own agreement. They'd tried flying the *Lady Hawk* with Drackson on the rear guns once. The seating hadn't exactly accommodated the Harskan's larger frame.

"Right."

"Asten, you there?"

He glanced back at the communicator. "Hello, Zak. I read you."

"Just checking that you're using the right frequency and encryption."

"No problem," Asten replied. "Got to check up on the civilians, right?"

Zak laughed. "Not at all. I just don't want to leave you guys in limbo out there, that's all."

Asten smiled to himself. "Much appreciated."

"All right. You follow my squadron in and I'll get back to you. We'll keep radio silence until we get there."

"Copy that."

"Over and out."

With a click, Zak was gone and Asten resumed the task of getting the *Lady Hawk* out of the hangar without crashing into anything. On the viewscreen, he saw Zak and the rest of Sigma squadron gliding away in their Harskan Corteks.

For a moment, it looked as if they were going in alone. Seeking a little reassurance, Asten glanced at the instrument panel and saw the three Resistance cruisers flanking them, as well as the two Phalamkian Battle Titans. They were frightening looking ships, quite solid with bulky trapezoid shaped prows that made them look like battering rams. But since all their firepower would be directed at the Federation shipyards, there was a certain reassurance in having them along. There were also two squads of Raptor-7s and two Phalamkian squads close behind him; and approaching from the other end of the shipyards, he knew, was Epsilon squadron with their Corteks and another two groups of Raptor-7s.

"Stay sharp, everyone," Zak's voice came over the communicator, ending the brief radio silence. "We're now on their radars."

On the *Lady Hawk*'s viewscreen, the shipyards were coming into focus. As General Draedon had anticipated, there were a few fighters around the perimeter but the bulk of the Wasps and gunboats were still in their hangars. However, they wouldn't be there long.

"All right," Zak said. "This is our window. Let's make it count. On my mark."

He steered his fighter up as if he intended to fly right over the shipyards, drawing the fire of the perimeter guards that way and in the wrong direction. Then as several enemy fighters accelerated towards his squadron from underneath them, he corkscrewed down, diving towards the unfinished Federation cruisers and leaving his pursuers trailing empty space.

With the way clear, he and the others wasted no time demolishing everything they could. Out to starboard, Zak saw his wingman Ja'is flying over the pylons connecting the new ships to the various wings of the shipyards and with precise torpedo shots, he ripped five ships from their anchors, sending them drifting across the yards and tearing into each other.

Zak in the meantime fired at the rear engines of the cruisers. It wasn't always effective but they provided large targets, with critical systems underneath them, and the ships didn't have any active shielding to protect them yet. Other members of the squadron were firing with less discrimination but the overall effect was impressive nonetheless.

"All right, Drackson. Carla," Asten said, watching Sigma squadron's work. "Let's show them how it's done."

He took the *Lady Hawk* underneath the Federation cruisers and Drackson and Carla began probing their underbellies for weak spots such as support joints and exhaust vents.

Then several blasts shot past the ship and a warning light on the control panel told him they'd taken some hits. The Federation had got its remaining fighters into the open.

"Sigma squadron!" General Draedon's voice rang out. "Return to the cruisers."

"Acknowledged," Zak replied before addressing his squadron, which for the time being included the *Lady Hawk*. "All right, you heard the order."

Asten grimaced. Up ahead, eclipsing everything around it, was the new Dreadnought they'd seen in Captain Fera's recordings. With a few more seconds, they'd be right underneath it. But orders were orders and while the Resistance leaders had agreed to the idea of having civilians accompanying them on *this* strike, they wouldn't do so again if they blatantly flouted direct commands. With a sigh, Asten turned the ship around.

"That wasn't much of a window."

Selina glanced at the young ensign who had spoken. "It's more than we had any right to hope for."

"Selina," Maia's voice came over the communicator. She was on the other Battle Titan. "Incoming Wasps."

"They're fast," Selina said. "Whatever else you can say about them, they've got a hell of a lot of pick-up." She turned to the crew of the bridge. "On my mark, fire at will." She watched as the enemy fighters closed in. "Fire!"

There was a heavy concentration of blasts and the first line of Wasps was obliterated, their pilots not having anticipated where the enemy guns were. The next group wouldn't be as foolhardy as the first though and already, their wing commander had them veering off to both sides of the cruisers in an attempt to make themselves harder to track. However, the Phalamkian fighters and the Resistance squadrons had now returned and were maneuvering in to take the Wasps out, leaving the cruisers free to carry out their primary task.

"Hold fire," Selina announced, raising one hand. With her other, she tapped the communicator to open a channel with General Draedon. "General, the preliminary defenses are engaged and we're moving in."

"I read you," Draedon replied. "We'll stay back just far enough to cover you."

In his office overlooking the entire shipyards, Commodore Hallyd was sweating. These Resistance fighters had come out of nowhere. He didn't think he'd been slack in maintaining security, and he'd organized the defenses quickly, but by the looks of things, it had been too little too late. And where the hell had they got all those Harskan Corteks? Was that what the incident at the Adari refueling station had been all about? A ship transfer? How come Corinthe had told Vendon but not him?

"Get the cruisers back from the perimeter," he snapped at the lieutenant behind him.

"They're on their way," the young man replied, trying to keep his voice steady. The kid put up a tremendous effort, Hallyd had to admit. He sounded much calmer than *he* felt right then.

He bit his lip as he watched the scene on the viewscreen. "I count five capital warships out there," he said, pacing back and forth and trying to stay in control, "but those two Phalamkian Battle Titans are our primary concern. Have our cruisers pull up behind them and pummel them before they can turn around."

The lieutenant swallowed. It wasn't good form to talk back to superior officers but...

"Not easy things to pummel, Phalamkian Battle Titans," he said. "They only have shields as an extra measure."

"How do they move if they're so damn heavily armored?" Hallyd demanded.

"No idea, sir," the lieutenant replied. "However, it wouldn't matter much anyway. Two of the cruisers are covering their flanks port and starboard."

Hallyd looked at the viewscreen again and saw them. And a glance at his radar displays gave him a rough idea of how big they were.

"What the hell are they?" he scoffed. "They look like plain old S-7 Cargo Carriers."

"I'd say they've been modified, sir," the lieutenant replied.

One of the things blew a swivel turret clean off the outer wing of the shipyards.

"Considerably," he added.

Feeling more tired than he'd ever felt in his life, Commodore Hallyd returned to his seat with slumped shoulders. How the hell could Corinthe have done this to him? He hadn't seen any action before. Sure, he'd served his time on ships when he joined after the Levarc War but that hardly qualified him for this. Still, he was the man on the scene and it was up to him to salvage the mess. Unfortunately though, there was only one way he could see them getting out of it without a complete catastrophe on their hands.

"Sir?"

Admiral Roth turned to the communications officer. "Yes, Lieutenant?"

"Emergency at the shipyards, sir," the man replied, flicking a switch to divert the call to him.

"— Hallyd, calling all units in range."

Roth glanced at Captain Merrick and switched on his comm. "Commodore Hallyd, this is Admiral Roth."

"Admiral…" The voice on the speaker faltered but only for a moment. "It's good to hear your voice."

Captain Merrick swallowed. The fact that Hallyd sounded genuinely relieved to be talking to Admiral Roth was not a good sign.

"We're under attack," Hallyd said.

"I know," Roth replied. "I'm here with the *Sentinel* and six other cruisers." He nodded at Merrick to give the necessary orders. "We'll be there in eight minutes."

"Understood. Thank you for your assistance."

"It's my duty," the admiral told him. "Now, you've got two cruisers on perimeter duty. I assume they're coming back to defend the yards?"

"They should be here in about two minutes. Do you want me to give them any orders?"

"Yes. Tell them to carry out the contingency plan. Also, if they head out on a vector of point nine, we can cover them as we go in."

"The contingency plan?" Hallyd asked.

"We're not going to turn this around, Commodore," Roth said. "Our job now is to control the damage and minimize our losses. It's not going to get us in the history books but that's what needs to be done."

"I understand."

"Good. Over and out."

Roth switched off the communicator. "Lieutenant Saska, how long before we get the shipyards on radar?"

A woman a few stations down on his left turned around. "Two minutes."

General Draedon smiled. The attack was going well. Surprisingly well when he thought about it. But they weren't in the clear yet.

"Starboard gunnery!" he shouted as something caught his attention. "Cease fire on that ship."

The guns stopped blazing but the men looked a little puzzled. Just a few more blasts would rip the ship the shreds.

"They've got a major turret behind that," Draedon explained, "and right now, that ship's shielding us from it."

For a moment, he wondered why whoever was in charge of the shipyards hadn't seen it. Naturally, they wouldn't want to destroy their own ships but that one was so badly damaged now that it was beyond salvage. If he'd been in their position, he would have finished the job himself, cleared an opening and started firing on them five minutes ago.

He shrugged. If the Federation wasn't throwing everything it had at them, that was fine with him.

"General," a voice came from his side. "There are two Federation cruisers coming in at point eight."

Draedon looked at his scopes. "They're going to fly right by." He looked at the viewscreen. Surely they wouldn't be stupid enough to have a go at the Phalamkians with two of his cruisers sitting right behind them.

However, it seemed they had no intention of engaging them at all since the two great vessels glided past the Phalamkian cruisers as well, right into the center of the shipyards.

"General?"

He flicked on the communicator. "I read you, Selina."

"Shall Maia and I engage those two cruisers?"

"Hold for the moment," he replied. "There are a lot of heavy turrets in the center there. Let's see what they're up to first."

"It's hard to see from here," Selina told him.

"Here too," Draedon agreed. "Just maintain the bombardment for now."

"Copy that."

He switched the frequency. "Commander Materson. Captain Fera. What are those cruisers doing?"

"They're tethering themselves to the Dreadnought, sir," Zak told him. "It looks like they're towing it out of here."

"I see. Commander. Captain. Don't engage. Over."

To his right, a small alarm went off and the radar officer turned around. "Sir, there are seven more Federation cruisers coming in at point three. ETA five minutes."

"All right," Draedon said.

For the life of him, he couldn't work out where *those* ships had come from. Intelligence had cracked Corinthe's most recent communiqués to the navy and checked every last detail and there weren't supposed to be any ships nearby.

However, the situation was still in their favor. They had taken out a sizeable portion of the new ships being constructed and had probably put the shipyards out of commission for at least a month. As for waiting around to engage the Federation's reinforcements, there was nothing to be gained from it that would justify the risk involved. All in all, it was an easy decision.

"All fighters. Return to your cruisers. All cruisers, prepare to withdraw."

By the time Admiral Roth arrived, Draedon's strike force was gone, so for all his precautions he hadn't been able to do much in the end. However, the shipyards, and some of the new cruisers at least, were repairable and the new Dreadnought had been safely escorted out of the fighting as well.

Roth hadn't been happy when construction on that ship had been commissioned. The Dreadnoughts had been formidable ships in their day but their size had often worked against them as they were such obvious targets in engagements. Also, as a Dreadnought was so obviously an instrument of destruction, it seemed wrong to build one in peacetime. But then, he supposed, that was part of Corinthe's reasoning in doing so. He was after all trying to mould the Federation into a warlike state to maintain his prestige and authority.

However, a lot of effort and funding had gone into this new ship's construction and although Roth preferred the Class-A Cruisers, he recognized that the Dreadnought could be a useful ship to have in the future. So while he hadn't approved of its construction, he was still relieved they'd been able to get it out of the shipyards in time.

The same could not be said for most of the other ships in the yard.

"That's incredible," Captain Merrick murmured as he surveyed the damage on the viewscreen.

"Yes," Roth agreed. "I doubt anyone will underestimate these people again."

Merrick let out a long breath. "Well, I suppose I'd better organize the clean-up crews."

"Thank you, Captain."

15. The Time for Action

IN THE OUTER REACHES OF AN UNREMARKABLE system, a small vessel was about to cross paths with a Class-A Federation cruiser, although the four Phalamkians on board had little reason to suspect this. They were traveling far outside their system and although their ship had hidden weapons emplacements to deal with any pirates they might come across, there was nothing they could use when the *Adjudicator* dropped out of lightspeed right in front of them.

"Where did *that* come from?" one of them exclaimed. Although the Phalamkian system was not part of the Federation, they all spoke Corsidan as it had supplanted their traditional language hundreds of years earlier.

"I don't know," another replied. He turned to the pilot. "Come on. Let's get out of here. We've got to get our payload back home."

"What if we get caught?" the first speaker asked. "What if they board us and inspect our holds? We know they're preparing an offensive against our system. If they find out we're working with the security forces, they might kill us to make their job easier. I say we jettison the payload before they get any closer."

"It'll show up on their radars!" the pilot snapped, turning the ship around in a violent motion. "Just keep quiet, will you?"

A sudden impact shook the ship and a moment later, it decelerated.

"What happened?"

"We've taken a direct hit!" the pilot muttered. "Our engines are dead."

"Unidentified vessel," a harsh military voice barked over their communicator. "Your engines have been disabled. Power down and prepare to be boarded."

"What do you want?" the pilot demanded.

"Rear Admiral Kellahav will see you shortly," the voice replied. "You can save your questions for him."

The communicator fell silent, as did the four Phalamkians. Except one.

"Kellahav," he murmured. "The guy who took the Kordan system. Wasn't he a *general*?"

A few minutes later on the *Adjudicator*'s bridge, they waited as the man in question walked towards them.

"Welcome to the *Adjudicator*," he said, favoring them with what he probably thought was a warm smile. "I'm Rear Admiral Kellahav. I must apologize for the manner in which you were brought here. I fear if I'd simply requested an audience with you, you would have refused. *I* would have in your position."

"And as for the damage to your engines," he assured them, "you needn't worry. My men are repairing them as we speak. By the time our business is concluded, your ship will be waiting for you in one of our hangars below."

"Business?" one of the Phalamkians stammered.

"Business," Kellahav repeated. "We have a mutual acquaintance back on Phalamki and he highly recommended you."

"A mutual acquaintance? You've bought someone from the Phalamkian security forces, you mean?" There was contempt in the Phalamkian's voice.

"Bought?" Kellahav asked, raising one eyebrow. "I suppose that's one way of looking at it. The way *I* see it however is that your acquaintance and my people have simply come to an arrangement that's of mutual benefit to both parties."

"And he thought we might also be interested in this arrangement?"

"Indeed," Kellahav said, smiling again. "He highly recommended you, as I said."

"And told you where you might find us as well, I see," one of the other Phalamkians muttered.

"Well," Kellahav replied, "this isn't the kind of arrangement we can discuss on Phalamki. Come. We can talk about it in my quarters. If you gentlemen would follow me?"

At his base of operations in the Therah asteroid belt, General Draedon was reading over inventory reports when he had a welcome visitor.

"Selina," he said, rising from his chair. "It's good to see you again."

"Likewise," Selina replied with a warm smile.

He gestured for her to sit and sat back down himself. "Was there any difficulty in getting those supplies?"

Selina shook her head. "No. The lines seem to be running smoothly, despite all the excitement Corinthe's been stirring up for the past few months."

Since the hit on the shipyards, Corinthe had sent his naval assets scrambling all over the Federation and along the Frontier looking for Resistance hideouts. Although given the futility of the exercise, it appeared to be a publicity stunt more than anything else.

"Well, it looks like all our divisions were wise to lie low," Draedon said. "No one can keep a constant vigil without a visible threat and I imagine Corinthe's not going to be able to keep his 'state of emergency' alive much longer."

"True," Selina agreed. "And more people are asking if he really has any evidence of these so-called 'Minstrahn insurgents' of his."

"A lot of the parading of military strength is being abandoned as well," Draedon said. "It seems most of the navy's warships are being returned to their regular duties."

Selina looked thoughtful. "Or being sent to the Frontier to aid Rear Admiral Kellahav in subduing systems that are allied with the Phalamkians."

"Have more systems been hit?"

"A couple," Selina told him and then she smiled. "Although, it's not all bad news. In fact, it may be that in targeting the Phalamkian system, Corinthe has bitten off more than he can chew. Other systems are starting to take notice. And they're starting to take action."

It was oh-nine hundred hours according to the chronometer. Captain Merrick gave the various stations around the bridge a cursory glance. For the past few days, the crew of the *Sentinel* had been enjoying some planetside leave. Admiral Roth himself had only just returned from the world below.

Close by, Merrick heard the small hiss of a door being released. Satisfied that all was well on the bridge, he went to greet him.

"Captain," Admiral Roth said.

"How was your leave, sir?"

"Most refreshing," the admiral replied. "How is our ship?"

"Running at peak efficiency," Merrick told him, handing him a pad. "However, I have some news. First, you may want to take a look at that."

Admiral Roth did so. "The transcript of Corinthe's address for the unveiling of his new Dreadnought. He's unveiled it ahead of schedule."

"And he's transferred Rear Admiral Kellahav from the *Adjudicator* to take command of the ship," Merrick told him. "I'd say Corinthe's probably granted his request to use it in this campaign of his against the Phalamkian system."

"Well, we knew he was going to do that," Roth said. "General… Sorry. *Rear Admiral* Kellahav doesn't give him any trouble like I do." His intonation rose as he brought the subject back to the transcript on the card. "Now, this is most interesting. Whatever else you can say about our favorite security minister, he's clever.

Why do you think he made this announcement ahead of schedule?"

"Probably so you wouldn't have a chance to review his speech first," Merrick said with a sour note in his voice. "I don't see what's so clever about that. I think there's a more suitable word for that kind of thing."

"What would that be?"

"Sneaky, sir, if I may be so frank."

Roth smiled. "Why, Captain. Listen to you. A year ago, you would have hesitated to even criticize someone like Hallyd in front of me."

"A year ago, I didn't know you as well as I do now," Merrick pointed out.

"Well, I'm glad you feel more at ease now," the admiral replied. "However, the early broadcast was not the act of cleverness I was referring to. Now, ask yourself why Corinthe didn't unveil his Dreadnought a month ago. It was certainly ready then."

"I don't know."

"Well, I assume you read this transcript," Roth said. "But perhaps I can refresh your memory." His features grew solemn as he read from the pad, quoting Corinthe and mimicking the man's manner of speaking. "This was supposed to be a joyous occasion, a proud moment in the history of our fine navy. However, as many of you know, this great ship was nearly destroyed in its infancy during an unprovoked attack on the shipyards where it was being built. A senseless act of violence that claimed the lives of many honest hardworking citizens of the Federation, men and women just like yourselves. After a long and exhausting investigation, we have finally found that the perpetrators who orchestrated this attack were Minstrahn insurgents. In light of this discovery, it is clear we must maintain an even stronger vigil in guarding our borders as we do not know when or where they may strike next. To this end, I am increasing the size of our navy and today, I'd like to unveil the latest addition to our armada. My dear citizens, I give you the greatest ship to have ever graced the navy of the Federation. The *Annihilator*.'"

Merrick frowned. There was something terrifying about the sweeping statements that filled Corinthe's propaganda when one knew that countless millions around the Federation resounded them without question. Some more thoughtful individuals would wonder about them of course but by and large, they would remain silent, choosing to simmer rather than to oppose the growing problem, perhaps some among them fearing that if they spoke out they would do so alone.

"He waited another month to unveil this new ship to give credence to his story about there being an investigation," Merrick said. "And having the announcement ahead of schedule creates the feeling that we're now facing a grave threat."

"So you see?" Roth asked him. "He *is* clever."

Merrick grimaced. "But so are rats."

"True enough. Now, you said that was your first news item. What was the second?"

"Commodore Hallyd's resigned."

Very rarely was the admiral caught by surprise but he was then. "Corinthe threw him out?"

Merrick shrugged. "Maybe. We both know he wasn't happy with him for requesting your help when the Resistance hit the Usile shipyards. But the official story is he chose to leave."

Roth contemplated the news. "Interesting. Is he still on Corsida?"

"Why? Would you like to meet him?"

"Of course. The man was in Corinthe's closest confidence for years. Who knows what information he might have on him?"

"That's a good point," Merrick conceded. "But if he knows as much as you're suggesting, wouldn't Corinthe have him under very close surveillance?"

"Definitely," Roth replied. "But I think the information he could provide would be worth the risk involved in snatching him out from that surveillance."

"If you say so, sir." Merrick sounded doubtful.

"Well, Captain," Roth said, changing the subject, "it seems to me this little lull we've been having is coming to an end. We've got the Phalamkian campaign—"

"That's hardly a campaign," Captain Merrick said. "Corinthe just wants to make a quick example out of them."

Roth shook his head. "No. This is going to be something quite considerable. Rear Admiral Kellahav has been orchestrating a strategy to overrun the Phalamkian system for months now and Corinthe's been supporting him every step of the way. Gamma Five's been keeping me updated on the situation and according to them, it's getting quite volatile."

"Gamma Five?" Merrick commented. "They did that reconnaissance job in the Harskan system, didn't they?"

"That's right. You have a commendable memory for details, Captain."

"It's nice of you to say so, sir. Though—since you've brought it up—if developments in the Phalamkian system are as serious as you say, shouldn't you assign a few more teams to monitor it?"

"Don't worry, Captain," Roth smiled. "They can handle it. Besides, I've assigned most of the other teams to get a reading on how the other systems along the Frontier are responding to these developments."

"And how are they responding?"

"The Phalamkians have a lot of friends in these systems. And the harder Corinthe and Kellahav push this campaign of theirs, the harder the inevitable backlash is going to hit. And they will push harder. For months, Corinthe's had evidence that the Phalamkians assisted the Resistance in that attack on the Usile shipyards. Now that he's officially concluded his investigations and unveiled his new Dreadnought, you can be sure he'll make that evidence available as well."

"But he's already tied the attack to those fictional Minstrahn insurgents of his."

"It doesn't matter," Roth said. "He'll just say the Phalamkians were working with them. He can say just about anything he wants now. And if he can rally the Federation public against the Phalamkians, he and Kellahav won't have to keep their plans under the radar any more. And there'll be no limit to the number of ships they can send in."

"So they could send in an armada if they wanted?"

"Easily. And regardless of how large their strike force ends up being, any overt move against the Phalamkians right now will provoke all their allies along the Frontier. And we could really do without that."

"It would result in a pretty ugly confrontation," Merrick agreed.

"Indeed," Roth said. "And if I can, I'd like to stop it before it happens."

"Sir?"

The admiral was quiet for a moment. "Captain, I'm leaving the *Sentinel* under your command for the next nine days."

"Nine days?"

"That should be enough time."

"For what?"

"To stop a confrontation in the Phalamkian system that could spark a war."

16. The Nearest Escape Yet

"THE RESISTANCE SURE KNOWS HOW TO PICK 'em," Asten remarked as he sized up the tricky landing he was about to attempt. The third moon of Ithera, a lone gas giant in a system he'd never heard of, wasn't the most convenient location to set up an outpost. However, convenience had never been the Resistance's biggest consideration when establishing bases.

Since the attack on the shipyards, Asten, Drackson and Carla had been helping the Resistance in their own area of expertise, escorting ships. Their first job had been protecting big frigates moving essential personnel around. After that, they'd done several jobs escorting supply ships for General Kalae. They'd then worked with her division for a while and were now escorting a frigate full of expensive hardware to one of General Emerson's bases.

To Asten's annoyance, it was at the bottom of a narrow valley, nestled among giant towers of thick ice. Conveniently for the occupants of the base, the ice was just regular water. But it screwed up Asten's depth perception and made the landing more difficult.

He eyed the large frigate descending beside him, wondering how the hell *it* would manage the task. However, once they were below the line of the pinnacles, he realized the valley was much larger than it had first appeared. He relaxed and flicked on the communicator. "Captain Adella. How's it looking?"

"We should be able to manage it from here. Thanks for your help, *Lady Hawk*."

"Don't mention it," Asten replied. "Over and out." He took a moment to admire the beautiful gas giant on the viewscreen looming in the sky above and turned his attention back to the landing. With a little more caution than usual, he brought the ship down and they glided into their designated hangar.

"Nicely done," Carla said, removing her safety straps and getting up.

They disembarked and Asten gave a nod of thanks to the technicians who came to refuel the ship. Leaving them to it, they went to the refreshment station, attracted by the enticing aromas of hot beverages. Once they'd got some, they went to look for the deck officer as they'd been told to meet him once they'd landed.

"Well, there's nothing heading out for the next couple of days," the man told them as he looked at a pad. "So if you'd like to take some ground leave, you're more than welcome." He brought up a new item on his display. "But we've got some light equipment for General Draedon sitting back there in storage if you're interested in another trip. We've been waiting to put it on one of our scheduled cargo transfers but if you're interested…"

"How much equipment are we talking about here?" Asten asked.

"Not much. All told, it's only about five hundred kilos so I'm sure your ship could handle it. And it's packed in sturdy crates. Seriously, it wouldn't take up much more than a cubic meter of space."

Asten smiled. "Actually, we'd like to head back to the Therah base at some stage."

"Yeah, I thought you might," the man replied. "You're all originally *from* Draedon's division, aren't you?"

"Yeah. It'd be nice to catch up with everyone again." Asten smiled, feeling a little embarrassed. "I know. It's not a social club you're running—"

"Hey, I understand," the deck officer said. "I'm the same. When you're cut off from the rest of society, your division's your family. However, before we get your ship loaded, you're not actually heading for the Therah base on this trip."

"Oh?" Carla remarked.

"General Draedon's heading out to the Frontier," the man told her, handing her the pad. "You'll find him at these coordinates. At least for the next five days. But all the information's there."

"I wonder what he's up to," Carla murmured, having a look.

"Is it far?" Asten asked, leaning over her shoulder.

"Yeah, it's a fair way out actually," Carla said. "But we can stop for fuel and still be there with three days to spare. I can chart the course."

"Yeah, we'll be fine," Asten agreed, tapping the screen. "We can stop over at Nemasil."

"No," Carla told him, pointing out an alternative route. "We'll go by the Taeia system. It'll take a bit longer but Taeia's much less of a hassle."

"Shall I have the equipment put on your ship then?" the deck officer asked.

"Yeah, we'll take it," Asten told him. "Thanks again." Once the officer left, he turned back to Carla. "Relax, Carla. Nemasil will be fine."

"I've met a lot of pilots who refuse to land there," Carla said. "Some of them turned down good jobs too."

"Yeah," Asten scoffed. "But they're amateurs." He gave her his custom smile of reassurance. "We'll be fine."

· · ·

Above a dark world of swirling clouds, the *Lady Hawk* dropped out of lightspeed.

"I sure hope we don't get stuck down there," Carla said as she got her first look at the place.

"Relax," Asten told her. "Besides, we're not in a hurry."

Carla sighed. "I suppose. Okay then. Let's run up a fake ID for the traffic control. You're now the proud captain of the *Isabella*."

"Great," Asten said, hitting the communicator. "Control, this is the *Isabella* requesting a landing platform."

"We read you, *Isabella*," came a reply in a distinctive local accent. "Please state your purpose of visit."

"We need to refuel," Asten explained. "And I'd like to get a new fuel converter as well."

"Refuel... Fine. Well, if you're just stopping by, I can give you a grade one landing permit."

"Sounds good."

"Now, are you familiar with our rather unique atmospheric conditions?"

Asten glanced at Carla who gave him her 'I didn't say anything' expression in return. "Yeah, I've heard."

"Right now, you've got a clear window so just follow the guiding beacons down. But if I tell you to abandon your landing, you high-tail it out of the atmosphere straightaway. And I'm not kidding about.

We had a bulk freighter pilot here the other week who thought he knew better than us and a flash storm disintegrated his ship. And his was about ten times the size of yours."

"I understand. Thanks for the warning."

"No problem," the man replied. "It's my job. Besides, we don't want metal debris falling into the vents. The cleaning crews hate it. All right, you're set for platform T-278 and it'll be forty-five credits for the landing permit."

It was a little steep, Asten thought but considering the extra difficulties in having a spaceport in this kind of environment, it was probably fair enough.

"No problem."

"Okay, you should be able to lock onto the landing beacons now."

"Yeah, I've got them," Asten replied.

"Then you're clear to proceed. Keep your communicator on until you land. Over."

"Well," Drackson said as he adjusted his seating straps for what promised to be an interesting landing. "This should be fun."

"Don't worry," Asten replied. "I've been here before."

"You've been shot at before too," Drackson countered.

Asten shook his head. "You're as bad as Carla."

Hot winds buffeted the *Lady Hawk* as it descended through Nemasil's stratosphere and it was a real effort to hold her steady. However, once they broke through into the lower atmosphere, things calmed down somewhat.

Outside, thick black clouds stretched to the horizon on all sides, tinted with a fiery red light that illuminated very little apart from dark rocky formations that tore through the planet's surface and a fine red sand that lay between them and blew overhead in violent dust storms.

It was evening where the *Lady Hawk* was heading but Asten had seen this same area of the planet during the day as well and there was no discernible difference in the amount of light that got through. That thick blanket of black clouds was always there. It covered the entire world and kept it in permanent darkness while trapping all its heat. And the end result was a planet that was more akin to a blast furnace than a place that might lend itself to habitation.

Yet, despite these obvious drawbacks, life thrived here and it was not because of unnatural intervention either. Life had been flourishing on Nemasil for countless millions of years before Federation colonists first arrived. For among the rocks were numerous vents that went far beneath the planet's surface and through these vents, hot steam rose from deep reservoirs, providing basic necessities from which life had sprouted. Apart from things that could only be seen under the microscope, there were no animals but what Nemasil *did* have was plants and it had these in abundance. Dark green tropical plants with beautiful sweeping fronds and colorful flowers adorned the sides of the vents in every conceivable place. On ledges, in caves and even in small cracks. Above the vents, Nemasil was to all intents and purposes a dead world but within them, it was a tropical haven.

It was for these reasons that people had settled here. Botanists came to study the plants. Those with more commercial leanings genetically altered the prettier ones so they could be sold offworld to wealthy enthusiasts and others came to see the tropical underground forests simply for the pleasure of the experience. Some tourists came for the fact that being in the vents was similar to being in the largest and most luxurious sauna one could imagine. Adventurous sorts came to abseil down them in heat proof suits and explore the networks of caves below while some people just came to forget their troubles and be left alone.

All in all, Asten thought as he brought the *Lady Hawk* into his designated vent, it was pretty impressive and he was kind of sorry they were just dropping in and out. Soon, the dark clouds were replaced on all sides by steep walls of rock that dwarfed the ship and all around him, bathed in the red glow that filled the vents, he saw the beauty of the Nemasil forests for himself. Giant fronds hanging over the sides of ledges and precipices and caves filled with great clusters of green leaves and flowers of every color imaginable. Then down below, he saw landing platforms that had been built over some of the rock ledges, leading to structures built in the walls of the vent itself and others built among the forests.

Controlling his descent, he brought the *Lady Hawk* to a gentle landing and powered down the engines.

"Well," he announced, getting out of his seat, "here we are."

"Nice landing," Drackson said.

"Thanks," Asten replied. "Now, just excuse me for a moment. I'm going to find some light clothes before I head out."

"I think I will too," Drackson said, noting that all their clothing was better suited to the regulated temperature of the ship than the sauna outside.

They all got changed and, a few minutes later, assembled by the main hatchway.

"Now, whereabouts do we...?" Asten muttered, looking around. He stopped as he saw what he was looking for. "There. Come on, guys."

He led the group away from the landing platform and towards a cluster of modern looking buildings that appeared in sharp contrast to the great fronds of the trees that loomed over them on all sides. It was a stylish contrast though and the whole place had a very laid-back look, which no doubt contributed to its appeal.

He found the office that handled landing permits and paid for the grade one permit he needed.

"Just come back when you're ready to go," the officer inside explained. "And we'll clear you for take-off, provided you haven't breached your permit conditions."

"Thanks," Asten replied, wondering what kind of technology they had to prevent people from taking off without a clearance. Most places had one permit for all arrangements or had separate landing platforms for pilots wishing to stay for extended periods. The places that didn't however were often quite creative in stopping people from cheating their permit systems, with such tricks as magnetic moorings. Then Asten realized these officials didn't need any tricks. Pilots *had to* check in before leaving because they needed the local spaceport officials to verify it was safe to launch.

"By the way," he asked the man, "where's the nearest place I can pick up fuel converters?"

The officer thought about it. "That depends. How large is your ship?"

"Not large," Asten said. "I generally use A-Standards with the regular fittings."

"Well in that case, it really doesn't matter. There are about six shops in easy walking distance that stock those and the prices are pretty much the same." The man pointed towards the door. "If you turn right and head up the street for a little bit, you'll see one called Kaedran's Tech Supplies. It's the closest."

"Thanks."

Once they went outside, they returned to their landing platform where a technician was waiting to refuel the *Lady Hawk*. Once that was done and Asten had paid him, he went into the ship and fetched a trolley.

"Do we really have to change that fuel converter now?" Carla asked him. "The others are working fine."

Asten shrugged. "I know but since we're here, why not?"

"It would have been cheaper on Taeia," she muttered.

"Yeah but that would have added another day and a half to our trip," Asten replied.

"Didn't you say you weren't in a hurry earlier?"

"Ah, Carla," Drackson intervened, "Asten's just trying to… what's the expression? He's trying to play it cool."

"Ah," Carla smiled.

They walked on wordlessly for a few moments before Asten gave in. "All right. I'm kind of looking forward to seeing Selina again. There."

Carla clapped him on the back. "See? That wasn't so hard."

Asten shook his head with a grin.

Soon they reached Kaedran's Tech Supplies where they were greeted by a Ja'voreal, an interesting looking species with multifaceted eyes like glittering jewels and thin limbs that while spindly, were capable of exerting immense strength, as evidenced by the hard muscles and arteries visible under this one's steely skin.

"How may I be of service?" he asked, his Corsidan heavy with inflections that were unavoidable for a Ja'voreal but easy to understand.

"I need to replace one of my fuel converters," Asten explained. "An A-Standard with regular fittings."

The Ja'voreal lifted a compact but heavy looking tube from behind his bench and put it in front of them. "Is this what you had in mind?"

"That's the one. How much do I owe you?"

"Eighty."

Asten handed the credits over. "There you go."

"Thank you. By the way, would you like to trade in your old fuel converter? Kaedran's Tech Supplies recycles old components and we pay a fair rate for them too."

"I'm sure you do," Asten replied. "But I don't think you'd be interested. Our old converter's fused solid. It might be good for an abstract art piece but that'd be about it."

The Ja'voreal laughed. "Oh well. Who knows? Maybe it'll make you a fortune off some collector."

"Maybe," Asten grinned as he loaded the new fuel converter onto his trolley. "Anyway, thanks for that."

"You're welcome. Have a good day."

"You too."

Outside, Asten turned to Carla. "See? Eighty. That's nothing."

"Yeah, all right."

Asten gave her a sly look. "Also… since we're here, I thought I might stop by one of these other stores and pick up a crate of Kulahri. You know, things are always at their best when you buy them straight from the source, right?"

Carla shrugged. "You're the captain. Go for it. Drackson and I can change the fuel converter while we're waiting, can't we Drackson?"

"Yeah," he replied. "No problem."

"See you back at the ship," Carla said as they took the trolley off Asten's hands.

With a wave, Asten saw them off. Then he wandered around and a modest store caught his eye. As he entered, he noticed that it joined onto an outdoor café where several small groups of people were enjoying their beverages under the dark green canopy of the cavern forest above.

There was something rather odd about what he saw though and it took him a few moments to realize what it was. Sitting around one of the tables were three men who probably imagined they were nondescript in their appearance but had military written all over them. And at the same table were four Phalamkians. He hoped for a moment this was a meeting between Resistance members but then he saw the insignia of the Federation fleet on some of the men's gear. So while they weren't in uniform, they weren't trying to be nondescript after all.

Something was very wrong. Phalamkians were not famed travelers. Sure, Selina traveled. But she was special. And for the life of him, Asten couldn't imagine what four Phalamkians were doing talking to Federation special operatives.

Then he realized he'd been staring and worse still, the occupants of the table had noticed. Trying to act nonchalant, he glanced about the café as if he were looking for someone else. Then having not found this imaginary friend, he turned to leave. But before he'd reached the door, he knew it had been a pointless ploy. His unconcealed curiosity had landed him in trouble. One of the Federation agents had risen to his feet and another had pulled out a communicator. Now the only thing remaining to be seen was exactly how *much* trouble he was in.

One thing was certain. He was not going to be able to check back with the spaceport authorities before they left so they'd have take their chances with Nemasil's famous storms on their own. But maybe with a little hide and seek, he could at least get to the *Lady Hawk* without the Federation operatives knowing which ship he'd boarded. As the door slid shut behind him, he ran as fast as he could, weaving his way between the buildings and changing direction several times to throw off the man who was no doubt following him.

When he was sure he was out of sight, he ran into the trees and hid behind some large fern-like plants to catch his breath. Within moments, his pursuer appeared around the corner and glanced to his left and his right. Asten glared at him. He hadn't had half the time he needed to get his breath back. He reached for his blaster, ready to rip it out of its holster if needed. Then another man from the café appeared. The first man nodded for him to go left, while he went right. After hesitating for a moment, Asten followed the first man. Given how good this guy was at following him, it was probably better to be behind him than in front. And just to be on the safe side, he drew his blaster as well.

The man led him behind the main cluster of buildings. The forest threw shadows everywhere and the red glow of the vents, mixed with the green light from that same glow and filtered through translucent leaves, provided good cover. But better still, there was no one else nearby.

Then the man heard him and spun around, tracking his weapon on him. Asten though was one step ahead and shot the gun from his hand before he could fire. The man clutched his weapon hand with a cry that was made more in anger than pain, although the shot had seared half his hand to the bone. He recovered quickly, grabbing his communicator from his belt with his good hand. But before he could flick it on, Asten knocked him to the ground and kicked it away.

"What were you talking about with those Phalamkians?" he demanded.

"Get lost," the man muttered.

From amongst the buildings, Asten heard raised voices. He looked back at his would-be-assailant.

"Yeah, they're all looking for you," the man told him. "But if you want to sit here asking questions that I ain't going to answer, then don't let me stop you."

It was unlikely the man was acting tougher than he really was. The fact that he hadn't even given his injured hand a second glance was enough to tell Asten that he wouldn't be intimidated by anything he might threaten him with. Besides, he didn't have what it took to do this kind of thing anyway.

The best thing to do, he realized, was to just get back to the ship as fast as he could. With a small flick, he set his weapon to stun and shot the man in the chest. He then took a moment to check his vital signs and satisfied that he hadn't killed him, he picked up the man's communicator and headed on. He wouldn't have been averse to killing the guy under other circumstances but not in cold blood.

Flicking the communicator on, he tried to listen in on the conversations of the men who were after him.

"Corban's down," someone said. "He's not responding."

"All units head that way then."

Asten turned the thing off, took a breath and headed for the landing platforms. Carla and Drackson weren't going to be too thrilled with him, that was for sure.

As he reached the ship, another one of the men from the café appeared and fired a couple of shots at him. Asten ducked behind a slight protrusion on the hull and shot back several times to scare him off. Then he leapt through the hatch and sealed it shut.

"Carla! Drackson! Get in the cockpit! We're in trouble!"

"What's going on?" Carla asked, running out from the engine room with Drackson in tow.

"We've got to go," Asten told her, jumping into his seat and powering up the ship. "We've got to go now."

"Why?"

"We're in trouble."

"Did you check in with the—?"

"No time," Asten cut her off as the *Lady Hawk* rose from the platform. "How did you go with the fuel converter?"

"We changed it," Drackson told him. "We were just cleaning up. Asten, there's some kind of modified Wasp up there."

Asten looked up and saw the ship in question. It was larger than an ordinary Wasp and more armored. It also had additional stabilizers and the modifications made for a strange looking ship. However, it made sense. This thing was designed for stability, not speed, because in the vents, speed was a good way to get yourself killed. Also, several more had just glided over the rim of the vent to join it.

Asten weighed up his options and gave Drackson a tight smile. "Hang on, guys."

Drackson tried to say something and a look of horror fell across Carla's face. Then they experienced the nauseating sensation of free fall. They were heading deep into the vent, with the Nemasil security forces on their tail. A blast hit the wall of the vent in front of them, throwing burning debris into the red and green mists surrounding them.

"Where are we going?" Carla asked.

"You're going to have to trust me on this," Asten told her, not that he was giving her much of a choice.

Then he saw what he was looking for. An enormous cavern that glowed with a faint light seemingly of its own. The real source of the light though was an adjoining vent and that was his next destination.

With a surge of power to steady its descent, the *Lady Hawk* leveled out and in a deft maneuver, Asten brought it roaring into the cavern on a tight line between the forests covering its floor and the ceiling of rock above.

The pilots of the modified Wasps came straight after them and despite the dangerous speed the *Lady Hawk* was traveling at, several of them were keeping up.

Asten nudged the ship's acceleration a little more, although he was already pushing his luck as it was.

One of the pursuing fighters dipped too low and was torn apart in the trees, causing a brief but deadly inferno that clipped one of the others, sending it spiraling into the rock above. The other Wasp pilots were able to avoid the debris that came hurtling at them from ahead but in doing so, they fell behind.

Moments later, Asten reached the far end of the cavern and drove his ship towards the surface with everything it had.

He let out a cheer but his elation was short-lived. They emerged from the vent to the sight of turbulent black clouds and electrical surges so bright they were almost blinding. One of Nemasil's violent storms had moved in, sealing off their escape route.

"Carla," Asten said without turning around, "get on the rear guns."

"Okay." With a single motion, she was out of her chair and out of the cockpit.

"So," Drackson remarked, "what's the plan?"

"We'll hug the surface until we're clear of the storm," Asten replied. "And then we're going to get the hell out of here."

However, hugging the surface wasn't as easy as he thought, which became apparent a moment later when a pocket of heated air exploded out of one of the untamed vents beneath the ship, throwing it several hundred meters overhead.

"What the hell was that?" Carla complained on the communicator.

"Rising air from the vents," Asten explained. "Are you okay?"

"Yeah, but if you could avoid flying through any more of that, it'd be really appreciated."

Asten smiled tightly. "I'll do my best."

There was a burst of fire from the rear of the ship.

"Did you get one?"

"Dusted him," Carla said. "Although you might want to speed up a little. We've got another six on our tail."

"Copy that." With steady control he'd honed over several years, Asten brought the ship under a natural rock arch then drove hard for higher altitude before sending it into a downward spiraling corkscrew maneuver through a small canyon. The fancy tricks had the desired effect, throwing the pursuing Wasps off and taking out two of them that tried too hard to match him.

"Nice work," Carla told him before another explosive burst of fire sounded out.

"You got another one?" Asten asked her.

"Yep."

"How many are left?"

"Three and if you're waiting for your window, we're just ahead of the storm now. I'm not exactly keen on this but if you gun it now, it's the best chance we'll get."

"Now?"

"Now."

Asten braced himself and pulled the ship up, putting it on a straight trajectory out of the atmosphere and hopefully ahead of the storm. With a jolt, they shot into the permanently dark sky. As they drove into the stratosphere, the ship shook and the rattling of more parts than he knew the thing had put him in a cold sweat. But when it seemed they were about to be ripped apart, the violent movements came to a stop and they were in the safety of space. Still, lifeless and without so much as a light breeze to buffer them.

Asten let out a breath and wiped his brow. They'd made it. "All right, Carla. We're good."

"Yeah. I'll be right up," she told him.

"So," Drackson said, eyeing him critically, "I suppose you're going to tell us what that was all about now?"

"Yeah," Asten replied. "As soon as Carla gets here, I'll fill you both in."

"All right," Drackson eased off. Then he laughed.

"What's so funny?"

"I was just wondering," Drackson told him, "whether you wanted to go back for your Kulahri."

17. Meetings of Very Different Kinds

SITTING ON THE LOUNGE IN HIS APARTMENT

on Corsida, former Commodore Hallyd stared at Admiral Roth half in horror, half in shock. "Did you kill those men?"

"Don't be naive," the admiral replied, taking a seat across the room from him. "It's wearing thin. I just had the local authorities pick them up. Corinthe's surveillance team were all dressed in civs so my men took their identification tags and made an anonymous call. You see, without proper identification, nondescript government agents on surveillance detail look a lot like loitering hoodlums."

"The local authorities will contact Corinthe to verify their story though," Hallyd pointed out.

"Eventually," Roth agreed. "But we'll be out of here by then."

"We?" Hallyd asked. "What exactly have you dragged me into?"

The admiral smiled. "Well, you may not believe it but by finally standing up to Corinthe, you've become a person of some use to me."

"Well, I don't want to be used," Hallyd told him. "I think I've been used enough."

"That nonsense won't work with me," Roth said, his voice cold. "All right, you've been used. You were Corinthe's buffer between him and the senior ranks of the navy. You lent him credibility through your support. Well, when you're playing the victim, Hallyd, remember that you went along with it. You sat there, telling us to carry out Corinthe's directives, wasting my time and the time of everyone else who walked into that office of yours and you were handsomely rewarded for it. Your phony commission. Your obscene salary. This place. So don't you dare sit there sulking and telling me how hard you've been done by."

"I left," Hallyd told him, hanging onto the precious little dignity he had left. "When Corinthe lied through his teeth about that incident at the shipyards, fabricating the number of casualties and planting the whole thing on Minstrahn insurgents, I made a stand."

"Yes, you did," Roth told him. "But if you think that pardons all your past sins, then you've got another thing coming."

"What are you going to do? Throw me in the brig?"

"It's tempting," Roth replied, "but no. You've got a lot of inside information on Corinthe, Hallyd. That's why he's got you under twenty-four hour surveillance and that's why I'm moving you to a secure location where he can't watch you. We're leaving straightaway."

"Why?"

"These men who've been following you will kill you if they think you're a threat to Corinthe and believe me, you are now."

"Because of you?" Hallyd demanded.

"Yes, because of me," Roth conceded but without apology. He stood up and several men Hallyd didn't recognize entered the room behind him. "However, given the amount of rubbish you've thrown my way, I think I'm entitled to return the favor. Get used to it, Hallyd. You backed the wrong man. Didn't you think that was going to catch up with you?"

"Where will you take me then?" Hallyd asked, giving in as he climbed to his feet.

"I'm not taking you anywhere," Roth replied. "I have pressing business to attend to and I'm on a rather tight deadline. My men however will take you off Corsida to a secure location for about a week or so, by which time—one way or another—your troubles will be over. You will of course cooperate with them in all their inquiries and provide them as much information as you can about Corinthe's activities."

"Or what?" Hallyd asked him.

"Or they'll bring you back here and we'll let Corinthe form his own conclusions about your absence."

For the crew of the *Lady Hawk,* the remainder of the trip to where Draedon's ships were waiting was uneventful. It was an overnight trip as far as their body clocks were concerned and when they woke the next day, they felt well rested.

Soon the ship was nestled in a hangar, the equipment they'd brought was unloaded, and Asten and the others went to find the general.

To his pleasant surprise, Selina was with him.

"Well," Draedon said after Asten had recounted what had happened on Nemasil. "What do you make of it, Selina?"

"No doubt what everyone else has," she told him, drumming her fingers on the desk beside her. "Whoever these men are, they're clearly up to no good and I can only assume it's connected with the upcoming attack."

Asten furrowed his brow. "What attack?"

Draedon grimaced. "Bad news travels so fast now, it's impossible to keep up. Corinthe's about to carry out his attack on the Phalamkian system."

"How do you know that?"

"It's hardly a secret," the general replied. "The entire *Federation* knows about it."

Asten was quiet for a moment. "It's because Selina's Battle Titans were involved in the attack on the shipyards, isn't it?"

"Not exactly," Draedon said. "As I'm sure Lord Erama mentioned to you, Federation forces have been making moves against the Phalamkian system for some time. However, Corinthe's now released his evidence that the Phalamkians are assisting us so he can push his schedule forward. And with the public support he's gathered, he can send a much larger task force now."

"How large?" Asten asked, not sure he wanted to know.

"Several sector fleet divisions at least."

He glanced across the room at his half-Phalamkian friend.

Selina shook her head and smiled. "It's all right, Asten. I've told General Draedon and I'll tell you. We knew this might happen when we involved ourselves in the Resistance and we accepted the risk. We want to stop Corinthe's suppression of the independent worlds along the Frontier just as much as you do so believe me when I tell you, we have no regrets."

"However," she said, addressing everyone, "now that we're facing the consequences of the risk we took, we have to work out how we're going to deal with them. And I think the four traitors Asten found are important."

She turned back to him. "Do you think you would recognize them if you saw them again?"

"Well, I don't know if I could pick them from a line-up of the entire Phalamkian race," Asten replied, "but I think I'd know."

"Good," Selina nodded. She clasped her hands as she thought everything over, then addressed the room. "When the Ipaatid system was taken, we saw it was necessary to upgrade our planetary shield to withstand an attack from Federation cruisers." She smiled. "Now, I'm not afraid to boast when it comes to Phalamkian technological know-how and when I say our shield can now repel any attack, I mean it. It's been tested. Seriously tested, with dozens of Battle Titans firing at it with everything they had."

"You fired on your own planet?" Asten asked.

Selina shook her head. "We fired on our own *shield*. Of course, it was carefully monitored from the ground and the firing was controlled but we made sure it worked. Now, I'm not saying this to brag or go jingoistic on you all but I think this is related to Asten's little run-in on Nemasil."

"I see," Draedon said.

Selina nodded. "I think the Federation must know about our shield and if any attack on the Phalamkian homeworld is to have even a *chance* of success, they'll have to take it down. Preferably beforehand. Because once it's up, no one's going to be able to go planetside to make a strike on the generator."

"So the only chance the Federation has is to put saboteurs in place before their warships even arrive," Asten told her. "And you think these four characters I saw on Nemasil could be the saboteurs they have in mind."

"Exactly," Selina said. "I mean, they're hardly going to send a contingent of shock troopers. Good saboteurs should blend right in so no one realizes they're there until it's too late. Which is why I was hoping you could remember what these particular individuals looked like."

Asten felt as though a huge weight of responsibility had been laid on his shoulders. Yet... he cared about Selina. And her homeworld was about to be attacked by the largest task force the Federation had used so far in its campaign of annexation.

"Well," he said, "it looks like I'm going to be liaising with the Phalamkian ground security then. Did Corinthe broadcast the attack date?"

"It's in a week."

"That doesn't give us much time then. I'm going to need to familiarize myself with the complex where the shield generator is housed and meet the people who operate it. Maybe with some luck, I can find your saboteurs before the attack. Assuming of course the ones I saw on Nemasil aren't middlemen and the real saboteurs are a different group entirely."

Selina frowned. "The thought had occurred to me. But we'll see."

"When are we going?"

Selina looked at Asten with a touch of pity. She knew how attached he was to the *Lady Hawk* and how close he was with Drackson and Carla. "Today."

Asten nodded and glanced at his crew, such as it was. "Well…"

"Do you want us to come with you?" Carla asked.

"Up to you," Asten said. "I don't know what you could do to help though."

At this point, Drackson spoke up. "I don't know either but I do know that the *Lady Hawk* is a damn good ship to have in a fight. So if the Federation's intending to bring a task force to surround the

Phalamkian homeworld, then we should be there too, holding the line."

"I don't know…" Asten replied, glancing Draedon's way. "Who else will be holding the line?"

"The whole resistance," Draedon told him. "Eight or nine months ago, we wouldn't have had the strength to hold back an attack of this nature. I had my poor pilots sitting by helplessly, recording footage of forced occupations to counter Corinthe's propaganda machine, all the while telling them not to get involved. However, times have changed. Actually, you've played a large part in that because through your efforts, we've gained some very strong allies. But anyway, I spoke with Admiral Garam this morning and he said the attack on the Phalamkian system could mark the most critical point in our campaign. He's already alerted all our divisions and soon, every fighting unit in the Resistance will be making its way to the Phalamkian system, including our own.

"And it seems the other independent worlds along the Frontier are taking an interest in this too. It looks like they finally understand what we've been telling them all along. That if they don't help each other then sooner or later, they'll find their own worlds under threat and they'll be very much alone. So when I say the whole resistance will be there, it's more likely an understatement than an exaggeration. Phalamki will be unlike anything we've been involved with before."

"Talk about things moving fast," Asten said.

"Well, they say the whole universe can change in the blink of an eye," Draedon told him with a smile.

"True," Asten replied. "But I've never seen it demonstrated so literally before."

"Neither have I, to tell you the truth."

"Still though, that changes things a little." He turned to Drackson. "Are you sure you want to be caught up in the middle of that?"

"We've seen action before," Carla reminded him before Drackson could reply. "Quite a *lot* of it recently."

Asten sighed. "You're right. And I guess you and Drackson can take care of each other."

Drackson smiled. "That's right."

"But," Asten asked, "can you really handle the *Lady Hawk* with just the two of you?"

"May I make a suggestion?"

Everyone turned to Draedon.

"I've always been interested in ships and I think I know a bit about your precious *Lady Hawk*. Now, if I'm not mistaken, it's from the A.N. Ynarvon line of gunboats that were manufactured on Tanem several years back. An LM-505 made to specifications set by

Novatech Systems and Aurora Prime during one of their brief joint ventures. Is that right?"

"Yeah," Asten said, impressed.

"It wasn't much of a line," Draedon continued. "The decision to have external contractors build them seriously backfired in terms of quality control. Construction standards were highly inconsistent and most of the gunboats were subsequently melted for scrap metal. However, for a little while, a number of them were made really well and I'm guessing that's when you picked up the *Lady Hawk*. Then it was hit and miss until Novatech Systems and Aurora Prime abandoned the line. Honestly, I don't know why they ever have joint lines. They always end in tears and lawsuits. But anyway, how am I going so far?"

"Pretty good."

Draedon smiled. "It's like I said. I'm interested in ships. It's useful obviously to know a bit about them in my position but it's also something of a hobby. Anyway, your *Lady Hawk* was actually designed to be crewed by five people. Four in the cockpit and one rear gunner. So I'd suggest you talk to our pilots and see if some of them might join your crew for the duration of this thing. The way I see it, it'd be a win-win situation for everyone involved. Zak, for instance, could command Sigma squadron from a more heavily shielded ship while one of our trained pilots who doesn't have their own ship yet can fly his Harskan Cortek, and another pilot in the same situation can man your rear guns. Then instead of two people trying to fly the *Lady Hawk,* or even the usual three, it would have a full crew. And just imagine how good it would be in a fight then."

"And perhaps my sister Maia can join the crew as well," Selina added. "Then you'll have two experienced commanders on board. Plus, she's been training with Sigma squadron for the past couple of months to keep up her skills as a fighter pilot. She and Zak work well together."

"Sounds good," Asten said, turning to Drackson. "Well, you're the captain now. What do you think?"

"I think that should work nicely."

"Well then," Draedon said, "I'll leave you to make your arrangements then."

"Sure." Asten turned to Selina. "Ready when you are."

"Well, you'd better say goodbye to your friends," she told him, "because we're going right now."

"Sure." He turned around. "Well, you heard the lady."

"Yeah," Carla said, hugging him. "Be careful, Asten."

"You too."

As she released him, she brushed away a few sudden tears. Leaning toward her, Asten brushed some she missed and she gave him a little smile.

Asten then clapped a hand on Drackson's shoulders. "See you later, big guy."

"Look after yourself," Drackson told him.

"I will," Asten replied. "Take care of the ship."

Drackson smiled. "I will."

"And take care of yourself too." Asten turned back to Selina. "All right. I'm ready."

Tejav was a very important planet within its region of the Federation. Though neither a tourist draw-card nor a major center of industry, it supplied several worlds with basic agricultural produce they could not grow themselves. But it was still a sparsely populated planet of large uninhabited spaces that, apart from the cargo carriers that came to transport its produce, was ignored by the rest of the Federation. So it was ideal for the meeting Admiral Roth had arranged with his agents.

There was a groan from the engine compartment as he eased back on the thrusters of the nondescript transport he was flying. It wasn't much of a ship but that was the point. Nobody would take much of an interest in it. To all observers, he was a farmer returning home after a short trip offworld. It hadn't cost him much and it had felt good to get his hands dirty, making the thing flyable again.

Below him, fields stretched to the horizon, punctuated by occasional lakes, forests and the odd mountain range here and there. He eased his ship down to one of the latter and landed near the edge of the foothills beneath it. As he disembarked, he took in a deep breath of the clean air and admired the view. Sunlight glistened off patches of snow on the ridgeline above while around him, a few scattered trees marked the dividing line between a small forest further back in the hills and the rolling green country below.

After a cursory look at his surroundings, he made his way down the hill to a small unremarkable house resting on the edge of the plains. The farmer who built it had abandoned it years ago when it became obvious he couldn't grow his specialist crops there. The nutrient mix in the soil kept the grass flourishing but little else, and trying to change it had been more trouble than it was worth. However, his efforts hadn't been wasted. When Roth's agents discovered it, they had recognized its potential as a useful meeting ground and Roth had made a point to keep it well maintained.

Aside from deep space, if there were anywhere in the Federation where he could have a face to face meeting with one of his intelligence units without a chance of a third party listening in, this was it.

Turning the wooden handle, he opened the door and stepped inside. Natural light pouring through large windows filled the various rooms, although there were electronic controls that served to lower insulation panels over those same windows to keep the house warm during the winter months. It was an interesting contrast of the traditional and modern. The plastered brick walls were more in keeping with the overall aesthetic of the place though.

He walked down a short hallway and stepped into a circular room in the center of the building. There was a small lounge that curved around one half of the room, affording anyone who sat there a lovely view of the mountains stretching away outside.

He smiled at the woman seated there. "Khalin."

His operative, however, didn't smile back.

So much for best laid plans. "What's wrong?"

She nodded to the room's other entrance. "I'm sorry, Commander."

"It's not your fault," Roth told her, turning to the entrance. There had always been the possibility this might happen sooner or later.

"Why don't you come in, Corinthe?" he suggested. "There's plenty of room for the both of us."

With a solemn expression, Khalin's partner Epcar entered the room and stood behind him. Following him, two armored soldiers stepped through the door and flanked the entrance. Then Corinthe appeared.

Here was a man whose face was known to everyone in the Federation. He was tall with thinly cut gray hair and a lined face with cunning gray eyes. Surprisingly, given the enormous popularity he enjoyed, it was not a charismatic face. But he had an authoritative quality about him and had practically built his career on it.

"I hope we can put aside any pretensions, Admiral," he said. "Your people told me everything."

"I know," Roth replied, staring him straight in the eye. "I instructed them to cooperate if they were ever put in a situation such as this. They're good people and I would not have them bring undue risk to themselves. And you might as well let them go. They aren't going to tell you anything else. They can't. They have no knowledge of the whereabouts of the other units I have working for me and no way of contacting them unless it is provided to them by me."

Corinthe smiled. "Commendable. I see though that you have no compunction about bringing undue risk to yourself, Admiral."

"If that's a threat, you're wasting your time." It wasn't false bravado. Admiral Roth had fought in the Levarc War as both a pilot and a member of elite commando units. As well as being placed in the heaviest fighting in the entire conflict, he'd escaped from a Levarc prison camp. After all that, there wasn't much that could rattle him.

"Come now, Admiral," Corinthe replied. "There's no need to be uncivil. I was complimenting you on your leadership." He took a few steps forward, putting himself in front of his men. "You see your problem, Admiral, is that you play everything close to the chest. You guard your various agendas closely and you think everyone else does too. For the entire time I've been in office, you've been playing espionage games behind my back, looking for my concealed hand." He raised his hands in front of him with open palms. "But you see, Admiral, both my hands are in plain sight. They always have been. I want to bring the Frontier nations under Federation control and that's what I'm doing."

"Maybe so," Roth replied. "But it's not as open as you claim. If we're not playing charades any more, then we both know there are no Minstrahn insurgents threatening the Federation and that you've been maintaining this lie for several years now as a pretence for your campaign. Also, you must have had your own side operations to infiltrate mine."

"Actually," Corinthe said, "I infiltrated your side operation with the official intelligence network. You were always rather unfair on them, you know. They're far better than you give them credit for."

"That's not the reason I didn't use them."

"I see."

At the other end of the room, several more armored troops appeared in the doorway. Roth gave them a glance before turning back to the security minister. "So, I'm to appear missing in action under unknown circumstances then?"

"Pretty much," Corinthe told him with a shrug. "You will be presumed dead but your body will never be found. However, there are plenty of unsolved mysteries in the Federation. Your disappearance will simply be one more in a growing pile, along with the circumstances related to it."

Roth nodded. "And I suppose my people here won't be allowed to leave either?"

"No. I'm afraid not."

"Hm." Roth looked at the floor for a moment. "If I'm a dead man anyway, would you at least have the graciousness to satisfy me on a point of curiosity?"

Corinthe smiled. "Now why would I do that?"

"Why indeed?" Roth murmured. It had been worth a shot but he hadn't really expected Corinthe to talk more. Besides, it was clear the time for words was over and already, beneath the facade of his calm exterior, he was priming himself for action. While his ground combat in the Levarc War was a long way behind him, his reflexes still remained.

Throwing his full weight into a powerful cut, he struck Corinthe below the jaw. With a horrible sound, the security minister reeled back, blood gushing from his chin. Behind him, Epcar leapt at the guards there, grabbing one of their weapons while Khalin hit the floor. The guards at the other side of the room seemed unsure of where to train their weapons as the fighting was so close. If they fired at Epcar, they'd hit their own men and if they fired at Roth, they'd most likely hit Corinthe. And the admiral was taking care of that already.

With one hand, he pulled Corinthe's head down and with the other, he landed him another blow. This time, it was a hard fist to the stomach that caused him to utter a muffled cry of agony that ended in a spluttering cough.

Behind him, the nearest guards were down and Epcar had fired on the guards across the room before they had a chance to shoot back.

Now that the coast was temporarily clear, Roth shoved Corinthe across the room where he crashed headfirst into a wall. The security minister stumbled about in pain and dizziness for a moment and collapsed, rolling across the floor to lie staring at the ceiling with his arms sprawled to either side.

Khalin grabbed a gun from one of the fallen guards and aimed her newly acquired weapon at Corinthe but Roth placed his hand over the barrel, lowering it.

"Not like that," he told her. "He'll die a martyr and then one man's madness will become the Federation's obsession."

He ushered Khalin and Epcar through the door they'd come through. Close by, he heard more troops running towards the room, mingled with breaking windows and doors being blasted from their hinges.

"I'll deal with him later," he said as he took one last glance at the room and its sole occupant, who was trying to focus his furious gaze on him. "Where everyone can see."

"So why did you really want to meet us?" Khalin asked as they strode away from the building.

"I was hoping you could do an information raid on Corinthe's office," Roth told her. "Acquire whatever evidence we could use to convict him. However, that'll no longer be necessary."

"But we'll never be able to prove what happened here today."

"I have something rather different in mind," Roth replied. "Come on."

. . .

Inside the homestead, Corinthe's reinforcements poured into the room where the drama had unfolded but they didn't give pursuit. Not yet. The first ones to appear set up a small protective perimeter around the room to shield their leader while the next rushed over to attend him. With an agonized groan, Corinthe sat up with their assistance, wincing at the onslaught of a vicious headache.

"Are you all right, sir?" the trooper closest to him asked.

Corinthe glared at him. "What do you think?"

"I'm sorry, sir. I didn't mean—"

"Admiral Roth has gone AWOL, Commander," he cut him off. "And it looks like he's killed four of my men. Or at least incapacitated them. I want you to get back to the ship and inform Corsida. Tell them he is a highly dangerous and wanted fugitive."

The trooper started to his feet but Corinthe grabbed him and pulled him back down again. "However," he muttered, drawing the other in close, "just off the record, let's make one thing clear. I do *not* want to find him alive."

18. The Armadas Gather

Sнiрs ALL OF KINDS AND SIZES FILLED THE VOID above the Phalamkian homeworld, drifting in controlled orbits and occasionally adjusting their courses to avoid collisions. Asten stared at them in awe. Among them were Resistance cruisers with their markings bold and clear, as well as numerous warships from the various worlds of the Frontier, including some he recognized and many he didn't.

He turned to Selina. "Do you really think the Federation would risk a confrontation with this armada?"

Selina shrugged. "Your guess is as good as mine. I must admit, though, I had no idea there'd be this many ships here. I mean, I heard all the reports but seeing them like this is something else."

"If Corinthe presses ahead with this mad scheme of his, a hell of a lot of people will get killed," Asten pointed out. "On his side too."

"And if he doesn't, then what?" Selina countered. "Corinthe places great store in keeping face. In fact, I'd go as far as to say it's his defining characteristic. If he backed down now, his reputation as the Federation's ironclad leader would fall to pieces. However, since whether he presses ahead or not is outside our control, there's not a whole lot of point in worrying about it, is there?"

"I guess not. Well, we'd better head down. You're still coming with me?"

"I am," Selina told him. "I'll be staying with you the whole time."

"What about this ship?"

"It'll rejoin the rest of the defense fleet, along with the other one."

"Under your father's command?"

"They'll *all* be under his command."

"But you don't need to tie yourself up with me down at the shield generator."

Selina gave him a wry smile. "I don't intend to 'tie myself up' with you anywhere but I think you're going to need someone you know down there because you'll feel pretty lonely otherwise. Also, just in case anything goes wrong, I think it's better that you have at least one person you can trust."

"You don't trust the people down there?"

"Personally, yes, but officially, everyone's a potential saboteur until the danger passes."

Asten shook his head. "You're one cool-headed woman."

"I try to be," Selina replied. "Anyway, ready when you are."

They took a small shuttle to the surface with five armed Phalamkian soldiers. The shield generator itself was built on a large rocky bluff and a small city lay on the plains below. A cable car ran between the two, transporting people and equipment between them, while there was a small landing platform next to the generator for those coming in by air.

"Here we are," Selina announced as they touched down. "Let's go and meet the gang."

Asten followed her with their armed escort taking up a flanking position behind them. As they descended the shuttle ramp, he saw several Phalamkians waiting for him but by the looks of things, they hadn't been assembled for long. And some of them seemed flustered. Adopting the suspicious mindset he'd decided his task required, he filed this observation away for later.

"Young Selina," one of them said, stepping forward. "It is of course a pleasure to welcome you to this facility but I must tell you we were not informed of this visit."

"That was intentional," Selina replied. "This is a random inspection, Supervisor Tallec. We are here to make sure everything is in order and will remain here until we've repelled the Federation's attack."

"I understand," Tallec replied. "We shall extend you and your men every possible courtesy during your stay." As he said this, he seemed to take in Asten for the first time but his gaze didn't linger. While not common, there were humans living on the Phalamkian homeworld, including Selina's mother, the Lady Erama. So as a general rule, Phalamkians didn't see anything out of the ordinary with them apart from the fact that, like so many humanoid species, they somehow got by with only two arms.

"Our needs are very simple," Selina said. "We know there are basic quarters here for visiting technicians and maintenance crews. These will suit us fine. And as for catering, whatever you normally have will be fine with us too. The only other courtesy we require is access to all the areas of this facility and at all times."

"Of course," Tallec agreed.

"Oh, and there's one more thing," Selina told him. "Would it be possible to have someone show us around the place? The more we know about the facility, the better we can do our job."

"I'm sure we can accommodate you," Tallec said. "In fact, I'd be happy to give you the tour myself at your earliest convenience. We could go right away if you'd like."

Selina smiled. "That would be wonderful."

"Very well. Follow me."

First of all, Tallec showed them where their quarters were, nestled behind the rest of facility and accessible by both lifts as well as stairs cut into the rock for those who felt like a bit of fresh air. After that, they saw the main control deck, which was directly accessible from the landing platform by a short tunnel and a security checkpoint. It was an impressive space with various workstations on raised platforms that formed a rectangle around the room. All the workstations faced the middle where there was a large holographic projection of Phalamki, along with a visual representation of the planetary shield. There were also holographic projections of all the ships in orbit of accurate scale and appearance. At a glance, one could distinguish between Phalamkian Battle Titans, the cruisers of the Resistance or Federation warships. And not only that but the projection displayed their real-time movements.

"This is nothing new," Tallec pointed out for the benefit of his guests, although Selina used similar technology on the Battle Titans albeit on a smaller scale. "We're just using the standard planetary display adopted by most of our command centers. It enables us to use the shield more effectively."

"You see," he said, walking over to one of the workstations, "there is a finite amount of energy we can project into our shield. It is a lot of course but it cannot absorb impacts from collisions or sustained bombardment indefinitely. However, if we perceive that one part of the shield is under particular stress, we can re-route energy from other parts of the shield."

He gave a nod to the technician at that particular workstation. While continuing with his previous task with his upper set of arms, he started tweaking a different set of controls with the second set. Asten was awestruck before he'd even seen what was being demonstrated. He found it difficult enough to coordinate unrelated actions with just two hands, let alone four. He wondered if Selina felt as though she'd missed out on something by not inheriting this unique gift.

His attention was brought back to the demonstration at hand as the transparent blue sphere representing the shield warped, becoming thicker in one part.

"Here, we've simply drawn energy from other areas of the shield's surface to reinforce one particular point," Tallec explained. "To be honest though, our shield's capacity is large enough that I doubt we'd ever need to do this. However, it is best to be prepared for all eventualities, is it not?"

"It is indeed," Selina agreed.

"Now, shall we move on?" Tallec asked, waving one hand to the exit on the other side of the room.

"All right," Selina said.

They followed him through the doorway and down a ramp of grilled mesh, under which machinery hummed and lights glowed.

"What's the deal with the mesh?" Asten asked. "Is that so you can keep an eye on all the electronic equipment down there?"

Tallec laughed. "It's cheaper." His tone changed when he caught the puzzlement on Asten's face. "That was a joke. No, it gets very hot down there. The mesh walkways are just another way we keep it ventilated."

"Another way?"

"There are ventilation grills on the outside walls of the facility. I don't know if you saw them or not. And behind each one, large fans extract the hot air. Also, the machinery goes under the main control deck too, as you saw."

"Where are the maintenance access tunnels?" Asten asked.

"We're heading down one right now," Tallec told him. "Also, there are ladders built into the railings near several of the workstations back on the control deck. You just pull a lever and they slide down. Then there are passageways down the bottom that allow you to walk around and get close to all the machinery. However, don't ask me about the workings of it all. I leave that to our engineers and maintenance crews."

"Fair enough."

"However," Tallec said as they reached the end of the ramp and stepped into the next area, "I do know about this particular piece because it's the reactor that's powering the whole shield."

Remembering the job he had to do, Asten took it all in. He guessed this particular room was on the front face of the rock bluff, which meant there was nothing below them for several hundred meters. In fact, he'd seen it from the outside on the way in when they'd come down in the shuttle.

A few meters from the ramp they'd come down were two more grilled mesh walkways that extended back to the area under the control room, meeting each other to form a 'U' shape. He also noticed some closed trapdoor hatches on each side of the reactor and a conventional hatchway on the side furthest from him.

Casually, he walked over to it and found the release switch. "Do you mind if I look outside, Tallec?"

"Not at all," his guide replied.

If he was one of the saboteurs, Asten thought, then he was good. He'd seen a brief flash of annoyance in Tallec's eyes before he answered but it had disappeared without a trace.

The hatchway opened onto a small platform and when he stepped out onto it, Asten felt a rush of wind that almost forced him back inside. Regaining his balance, he stepped out for another look. It was nerve-racking standing on the platform, seeing how far down the ground was. Above and below, strong cables and support struts held the platform tightly against the main structure, providing resistance against the wind and there were more struts and structural cables below the whole thing, anchoring it to the bluff. Above him, rungs were built into the side of the structure, leading to the top.

He stepped back into the comfort of the reactor room and closed the hatch. "Nice view out there."

"True," Tallec agreed. "It's a bit too hair-raising for me, I'm afraid, but you can certainly see a long way. However, there is a better viewing platform above the main control deck where we monitor incoming traffic. I sometimes stretch out there to relax. Actually, if we've seen everything we want to see down here, I might take you there now. That's also where the kitchens and other recreational facilities are."

"Yeah, let's check that out," Selina said. "Before we go though, can this reactor be manually shut down?"

"It can," Tallec told her, showing her around its outer surface. "Although as you can see, there are no switches or other such interfaces. A qualified technician would have to do it."

"Are any qualified technicians on staff here?"

"We don't have any, no. However, if we put in a call to the command station down in the city, they can send us one in under two minutes."

"That's fast," Asten remarked.

"It's necessary," Tallec explained. "If the reactor was overheating, you'd want it shut down as soon as possible."

"Would shutting down the shield help in that situation?"

Tallec shrugged. "Maybe. Maybe not. It's something we might try in that type of scenario but hopefully, we'll never have to."

"And where would you shut down the shield from?" Selina asked him, taking over from Asten.

"Back at the control deck," their guide explained, "at the same workstation where we raise and lower the shield from."

"I see," Selina said. She was quiet for a moment. "Can we see that on the way up to the traffic control room?"

"Of course," Tallec said. He motioned them back towards the ramp they'd come down. "Shall we?"

Zak Materson, leader of Sigma squadron, ran his hand over the controls of the *Lady Hawk* as he settled himself into the pilot's seat. "I've got to tell you," he said to Drackson, "I've wanted to fly this ship ever since I laid eyes on her."

"Well, now you've got your chance," the Harskan replied. "Welcome to the crew."

"Thanks. It's good to be part of it." Zak turned around to see how Carla and Maia were doing. "Is everyone good back there?"

"Yep," Carla replied as Maia gave her own okay.

Zak's gaze lingered on Maia a moment. After she'd started training with Sigma squadron, offering her skills as a pilot, Zak had been amazed by how natural she was in the cockpit. And this was in addition to experience as a commander in the Phalamkian defense forces. There was a lot more to Maia than she'd first let on.

Catching his gaze, Maia gave him a private smile.

Zak smiled back before checking on their rear gunner. "And how are *you* going, Hellesis?"

"I'm good."

"All right then," Zak said. "Now, we've got about thirty minutes before we need to get back. Let's take this thing for a test run."

A few light-years outside the Phalamkian system, half the Federation's armada lay in wait with the *Annihilator* at the spear-point of the formation. On the bridge of the gigantic vessel, Rear Admiral Kellahav was growing anxious and the nervousness he detected in the face of the young officer approaching him did nothing to alleviate the feeling.

"What's the latest word from the forward scouts?"

The officer saluted him then read from a pad. "The size of the force defending the Phalamkian homeworld is far larger than we anticipated." He flicked the display screen to bring up another item. "Also, the scouts have had a flood of intelligence reports from various systems along the Frontier. They've been communicating with ambassadors from the Resistance and other independent systems and many of them have sent their own task forces to aid the Phalamkians. The scouts say this largely accounts for the number of ships that are presently there."

Kellahav raised his eyebrows. "Largely accounts?"

"Yes, sir," the young man replied, hesitating. "The rest of the ships are clearly marked as belonging to various divisions of the Resistance. It seems intelligence has underestimated how large the organization is. They believed the attack on the shipyards was carried out by a single division and they estimated there were three or four such divisions at the most. But going by the number of their ships in the Phalamkian system, it's more likely that there are seven or eight of them now."

The officer handed the pad over. "There's a full count of all the ships there as well as a breakdown of the different types and the number of each type."

"Thank you, Lieutenant," Kellahav said, looking over the information. "That'll be all for now."

"Yes, sir," the young man replied with another salute before turning about with parade ground flair.

Kellahav's feelings of anxiety morphed into dread. He wished now that he'd never gone along with Corinthe's schemes, even if it meant being a general again. Corinthe had pushed his luck too long and too hard, along with the worlds of the Frontier, and the mess they were now in was the inevitable result.

He walked up to the communications officer. "Is our strike force assembled?"

The man shook his head. "Not yet, sir. Just about every ship you requested is here but there are still eight warships we've been unable to raise."

Kellahav grimaced. "Is the *Sentinel* one of them?"

The officer swallowed. "Yes, sir."

Admiral Roth's disappearance was common knowledge now and it was a touchy subject for most of the fleet. A lot of the men were fiercely loyal to him and it was a safe assumption that the crew of his own flagship would side with him against Corinthe. In fact, both Kellahav and Corinthe had had mixed feelings about requesting the aid of the *Sentinel* in the first place. In the end, they'd decided that most of the men would feel that something was out of place if they didn't. Now though, it looked as if it had been an academic dilemma.

"Well then," Kellahav said, "we'll have to make do without them. Signal to all ships that we're ready and instruct them to await my commands."

As he turned away, he simmered with fresh frustration at Corinthe. Of all the people in the Federation, what had possessed him to make an enemy with Admiral Roth? Kellahav didn't exactly like the man—Roth had brought him up on rather heavy disciplinary charges once and he had always felt sore about that—but he didn't go out of his way to get on his bad side either.

It was time to have a word with the security minister.

Presently, he was standing on the other side of the bridge with his back to him, looking at the main viewscreen. Bracing himself, Kellahav made his way over to him and cleared his throat just loudly enough to be heard.

"Sir?" he asked.

A smile creased Corinthe's lips as he turned around. "Admiral Kellahav."

"Rear Admiral, sir."

Corinthe's smile didn't falter. "That was your rank, Admiral, but in light of recent events we won't dwell on for the present, not any longer."

"Does this come from Rear Admiral Calaom or yourself?"

"Rear Admiral Calaom," Corinthe told him, "but as usual, at my request."

"It's just that I find it very hard to imagine that the Rear Admiral would feel happy promoting me above himself, sir. He was quite vocal in his disappointment when Admiral Sharnost and Admiral Keigen promoted Roth to supreme command over him. It seems strange he would willingly pass himself over."

"You have a suspicious mind, Admiral."

"Thank you, sir."

Corinthe sighed. "Both the Rear Admiral and I believe you are the man for the job, Admiral Kellahav. Calaom knows he is old and he understands that the future of the Federation lies in the hands of the next generation of commanders."

"Very well, sir," Kellahav replied. "If I may however, I wish to speak to you about another matter."

Corinthe raised his eyebrows. "And what is that, Admiral?"

"I believe it may not be wise to press ahead with our attack. The size of the force defending the Phalamkian homeworld rivals that of our own task force and we could take quite heavy casualties if we proceed." He offered Corinthe the pad. "I have the numbers right here if you'd like to see them for yourself."

"No thank you. I do not doubt the authenticity of your word, Admiral. However, I believe that the size of the armada that stands against us only makes it that much more important that we bring the fleet in. Admiral Kellahav, these people are in open defiance of the Federation. If we back down, more will join them and they will all start acting more boldly, perhaps even aggressively. I think you follow me, Admiral."

"I do, sir. But while you're advocating that we should advance on the Phalamkian system and crush this force as swiftly as we can, we don't actually have a significant leverage over the enemy. If we move in, there'll be disastrous losses on both sides."

Corinthe motioned for him to follow him. "I think we should talk in my quarters."

It wasn't a long walk as his quarters were positioned right next to the bridge and a few seconds later, they were speaking in private.

"You forget several things, Admiral," Corinthe told him, his voice stern. "First of all, you doubt the ability and the fighting spirit of the men under your command. Secondly, you doubt this very ship. There is not a single vessel that can rival the *Annihilator* in size or firepower and you shall have the honor of witnessing this yourself as you command it during its first action."

"I wasn't worried about this ship."

"And you seem to have also forgotten about our plan to bring down the Phalamkian planetary shield," Corinthe reminded him, ignoring the remark. "A plan *you* orchestrated. In fact, this whole campaign against the Phalamkians was your idea."

"This isn't what I had in mind," Kellahav told him.

But it was clear that Corinthe was no longer listening.

"So the campaign has become something larger," he said. "The objective remains the same. The only difference is that now, instead of simply crushing the Phalamkians, we might squash this whole resistance organization as well. And I can tell you that once that shield is down and we've commenced the planetary bombardment, most of those fools supporting the Phalamkians will give up and cut their losses."

"Maybe. Or bringing down the shield might just harden their resolve against us."

Corinthe lowered his voice. "Have a care, Admiral Kellahav. You are only here because I put you here. You can forget about what I just told you about Rear Admiral Calaom. That was for the benefit of any eavesdroppers on the bridge. Calaom is an officer well past his use-by date but in return for continued privileges, he carries out my directives so I keep him on staff. *I* run the Federation now, Admiral Kellahav. Not the government, not the former supreme commander of our naval forces or Rear Admiral Calaom, and certainly not you. And before you try to claim the moral high ground over me, remember that your own record isn't exactly spotless either. Or have you forgotten what happened at Ipaatid?"

Kellahav swallowed. He wondered how Corinthe had known.

"That isn't the issue right now, sir."

"Nevertheless," Corinthe told him, "you ordered the men on the *Adjudicator* and the other warships under your command to fire on the ships of fleeing refugees and even to maintain pursuit out of the system for the simple reason that they'd wounded your pride. Roth would have had a field day with you if he'd found out. As I recall, he nearly had you thrown in the brig once, didn't he?"

Kellahav glowered. "Yes, sir."

"Let's see. That was for firing on a neutral vessel with only a negligible warning, correct?"

"That's correct but I've never hidden that fact and I received a formal discommendation over the incident. Which you were well aware of the time."

"Nevertheless, it could have been a lot more public, Admiral, and it *would* have been if it had not been for my interventions. Now, I don't know what happened in your past to make you so quick to anger and aggression, although I suspect you may have had a rough time in the war."

Kellahav glared at him, seething at the manner in which Corinthe dismissed the atrocities he'd faced as a young man. The security minister knew full well that he had witnessed the destruction of his homeworld.

"However," Corinthe continued, "it seems clear from your colorful record that your temperament tends to get you into trouble. Ipaatid's the most recent example that comes to mind and there was of course your discommendation, but there have been other... indiscretions, shall we say. Now, as Minister of Security, it is my responsibility to keep records on such matters but given how instrumental you've been in our campaigns on the Frontier, I'd prefer to keep those records confidential. After all, there may have been mitigating circumstances in these incidents that the records neglect to mention—"

Kellahav cut him off. "So now it's blackmail?"

"That's a rather vulgar thing to suggest," the security minister replied. "I have no interest in tarnishing your career. That would serve neither of us. Think. If I denounced you after I made you the effective commander of the entire navy, that wouldn't exactly do my career any favors now, would it?"

Kellahav said nothing. Corinthe had him there.

"However," Corinthe added, "since I more or less had Calaom give you your new position, a lot of people in the navy no doubt see you as one of my men."

"What exactly are you driving at?"

"I'll tell you frankly, Admiral," Corinthe replied. "If we don't go ahead with this attack, I'm finished. The entire Federation will demand that I relinquish my powers and step down. And when everyone's after my head, they'll be after yours too. Make no mistake about that."

In horror, Kellahav stared into the man's eyes. It was only now that he understood him. Kellahav had never wanted this. All he'd wanted was the challenge of command. Now, he realized he had irrevocably thrown in his lot with a madman.

"You see, Admiral," Corinthe told him, "there is only one way either of us will emerge unscathed from this."

19. The Battle of Phalamki

ON THE BRIDGE OF HIS WARSHIP, LORD ERAMA checked his chronometer. It would not be long before they knew if Corinthe's invasion force would come.

He leaned over his communicator. "Admiral Garam, are all your fighting divisions in place?"

"They are. What about your own?"

Erama smiled. "All accounted for. I am assuming that while we'll keep communication open between us, you will still be commanding your own forces and I'll be commanding mine?"

"That's what we agreed was best."

"Just checking, my friend. And all independent task forces will be operating under localized command. Now, I make it eight minutes until the enemy's fleet arrives. How about you?"

"Eight minutes," Garam replied.

"Good. With luck, Corinthe may even stand down this time. But if he doesn't, I wish you happy hunting."

"Likewise. Over and out."

Lord Erama looked at the bridge's holographic display and at the void around it that, if Corinthe carried through with his threat, would soon be filled with enemy ships.

For a moment, it looked as though nothing would happen. Then the Federation's armada arrived with a massive warship at its head. The bridge fell silent and everyone listened as a transmission was broadcast.

"This is Vilastrian Corinthe, Minister of Security for the Federation Department of Security and Defense, and I am addressing you from aboard the Dreadnought *Annihilator*. Who is in command of this force?"

When Lord Erama replied, his tone was calm and courteous but his manner was firm. "Minister Corinthe, this is Lord Erama of the Phalamkian Defense Forces. I speak for everyone in this fleet you see before you and I must inform you that your task force is in violation of our sovereignty. Members of the Federation and vessels originating from within it are welcome at any time. However, we cannot allow your armed force within our system."

"And what of the other armed forces I see here?" Corinthe countered. "You have in your midst Narvashae Galleons, Koratav gunboats, Hie'shi Tridents and countless others. As well as that, you have eight divisions of warships that bear the markings of a terrorist organization that is responsible for the deaths of numerous innocent citizens of the Federation."

"Regarding the armed forces you mention, these ships are operating under Phalamkian command and as such are considered to be part of our own defense forces. As for your accusation that we are harboring known terrorists, we refute it outright. The organization that you refer to has only *ever* attacked military targets. However, if you would like to discuss these matters further, you are welcome to come aboard my flagship. You may bring your own people with you if you'd like, provided that they come unarmed, and you will not be harmed in any way or detained against your will."

"I thank you for the offer, Lord Erama, but I cannot accept. I can offer you the same terms aboard my own ship though."

"I'm sorry, Minister, but as this is our system, it is our right and duty to host any face to face discussions."

"Then let us have our discussion as we are," Corinthe told him and there was a distinguishable harsh note to his voice. "We have come to exact payment for damage done to Federation interests by Phalamkian parties involved with the terrorist network that calls itself the Resistance. If you surrender, there will be no loss of life. We will send Federation crews to take command of all your warships and soldiers to collect your weapons. You will then be transported to the surface of Phalamki and that will be the end of the matter. If you refuse though, then you will leave me with no choice but to declare war on this system. I would prefer not to do this as I'm sure you can imagine the loss of life would be extremely high. However, our fleet is prepared for this if necessary. It is your choice."

Erama sighed. "We cannot allow the Federation to continue attacking independent worlds along the Frontier unprovoked. If you choose to carry out your threat, then we must defend our system."

"Then war it is."

"So be it." Erama flicked the communicator off.

On the viewscreen, he saw the Federation cruisers moving into an attack formation, a sweeping arrow head with the *Annihilator* at the point. Today, the people of the Federation and the Frontier systems would find out if that ship was everything it was said to be.

"All ships," he announced, "you heard what Corinthe said so there's no need to be chivalrous. Mark your target once it's in range and open fire. Divert all power from your rear deflection shields to the front and fire at will."

Within moments, there was a barrage of exchanges between the two armadas.

"Damage report?" Erama asked.

"A lot of scorching down the port side but nothing critical," the chief of engineering told him. "And one of the starboard weapons emplacements has been dislodged."

"Copy that." Erama set the communicator to address the other ships. "Are any vessels critically damaged?"

"Sir, the *Hydra* took a heavy barrage from the *Annihilator* and we've had to seal off several hull compartments."

"Fall back and see to your crew. The *Pegasus* and the *Gorgon* will bridge the gap."

"Sir," the radar officer called out. "Enemy fighters coming in. Eighteen wings from different cruisers. Looks like the first wave."

"Hold tight everyone," Erama instructed. "Revert your shields to their default energy distribution levels. We won't have to worry about our fronts as much now. Those cruisers won't fire on their own fighters."

Filling the space between the two lines of warships, the Federation Wasps came in, firing at full power and making strafing runs over the cruisers. Meanwhile, from amongst the Phalamkian Battle Titans, squadrons of Phalamkian Kites emerged and while they were not as formidable in deep space combat as the Raptor-7s of the Resistance or their new Harskan Corteks, they could maneuver more closely between the capital warships and their rear gunners took a number of Wasp pilots by surprise.

Elsewhere, a small group of Resistance fighters with Sigma squadron at its head cut their way through the sea of enemy fighters between the Federation ships and the Phalamkian Defense Forces.

"Asten would have a fit if he knew what we were doing," Carla remarked.

"And he'd be jealous he missed out," Drackson added.

It *was* absurd though. Even if they avoided taking a direct hit from a blast, the chances of a fatal collision alone should have ruled out such foolhardiness.

"We're breaking up their formations," Zak pointed out. "And it's working." He veered the ship out of the way of an exploding Wasp. "And while they're trying to avoid crashing into *us*, half of them are crashing into each other. Look."

Carla had to admit that Zak's reckless stunt was paying off. Flying across the enemy fighters instead of taking them head on had thrown them into disarray.

However, while they were having some luck, the *Annihilator* was on the move. Edging forward, it opened fire on one Phalamkian Battle Titan, concentrating its attack on this single ship while the surrounding Federation cruisers lay down a barrage of cover fire, and in under fifteen seconds, the massive Dreadnought had ripped the smaller ship to shreds.

Then when everyone was still trying to come to terms with that particular shock, it singled out a Resistance cruiser and systematically pummeled *that*. It was clear this time that some of the *Annihilator*'s batteries were overheating but this second assault ended as the first had, with a cruiser that had been running at full capacity with its shields intact disintegrating in a fireball.

The guns on the *Annihilator* fell silent but it brought little relief to the assembled forces defending Phalamki. It was clear they were simply recharging and it was only a matter of time before they opened fire again.

As the rest of the *Lady Hawk*'s crew stared in shock, Carla looked at her radar screens. "Some of our ships are leaving."

Maia leaned over to have a look. "You're joking." However, the dots on the radar moving behind the main group and away towards the edge of the system didn't lie.

Carla didn't say anything. They had probably had no idea what they were heading into when they came to hold back the Federation's attack and the *Annihilator*'s onslaught had taken everyone by surprise. But she understood how Maia felt. Abandoning comrades in their time of need was a pretty low thing to do.

"Forget them," Drackson said.

"Sigma leader," a voice cut in on the communicator. "Bank portside. I'm coming through."

"Ah," Zak replied. "I read you, Hurricane." He adjusted the communicator frequency. "You heard him, Sigma squadron. Bank now!"

Following the *Lady Hawk*, the fighters of Sigma squadron corkscrewed back towards the Phalamkian defense line, while a lone Harskan Cortek shot through from the opposite direction. At its controls, Lieutenant Rillei "Hurricane" Brais from Epsilon squadron guided his ship towards the *Annihilator* and the center of the Federation fleet. He fired a torpedo that shot over the enemy cruisers and exploded into tiny fragments. Then, without decelerating, he pulled his ship around and gunned it back to the relative safety of the defense blockade.

In the void above the *Annihilator*, several of the torpedo's fragments moved of their own accord. Lights activated on them and small lens surfaces swiveled down towards the Federation cruisers.

"Are the surveillance pods transmitting?" Hurricane asked.

"All good, Hurricane," a man replied. "We should have a count of the *Annihilator*'s guns shortly. Good job."

"Happy to be of service," Hurricane said, heading back to join Captain Fera and the rest of Epsilon squadron.

Moments later, the count was done. The engineering officer who had just spoken to Hurricane swiveled around in his chair to face General Draedon. "The *Annihilator*'s stats have come through, General. Sixty heavy cannons, one hundred repeating cannons and ten torpedo tubes. The probes are still scanning for structural weak points."

The figures had a sobering effect on the bridge crew.

"Well, that checks," Draedon murmured.

"What was that?" the engineering officer asked.

"We'll have to send the fighters in to do a strafing run," Draedon said, brushing off the question. "There's no way any of our cruisers can go up against it, broadside or head-on, unless we take out some of those guns."

"Shall we send them in now?"

"Not yet," Draedon told him, looking over his radar display. "We need to draw these fighters away first." He switched on the communicator. "General Kalae. Do you read me?"

"Loud and clear, General Draedon. Go ahead."

"I want your division to move towards those Federation cruisers at the far end of the assault formation. With luck, we might draw off some of the enemy fighters down here and clear the way for our own fighters to head into the Federation lines."

"Lucky them," Kalae replied. "If we go ahead with this though, I might hold the assault from that end and press on towards the center of the group."

"That would work," Draedon agreed. "However, I suggest you liaise with the Phalamkians over there and get them to cover you."

"Will do. Good luck, General."

"Thanks. You too."

To the portside, he saw Kalae's cruisers moving towards the end of the Federation armada and they crippled the first cruiser they encountered. Kalae pressed on as she'd said she would, moving head-on and attacking them on their broadsides, inflicting maximum damage on their ships while risking only minimal damage to her own.

The Wasp pilots in the meantime, or their commanders, realized that until a few more assault shuttles arrived, they were the only ones in any position to pose a substantial threat against Kalae's ships. The Federation cruisers there could not move fast enough to get into better firing positions and the remaining cruisers were held down by enemy fire as well. Unanimously, the Wasp pilots abandoned their attacks on the center of the Phalamkian barricade and flew towards the end of their own lines to assist their cruisers. As they neared their destination though, groups of Phalamkian cruisers at the far side of the formation pummeled them.

Draedon smiled. All in all, the plan had gone well. However, there wasn't any time to enjoy the show. He had work to do. "Epsilon leader. Sigma leader. Come in."

"Sigma copies."

"Epsilon leader. Go ahead."

"We need to take out some of the enemy's guns," he told them. "You'll be strafing the *Annihilator*. Don't slow down for extra shots or you'll be blown to pieces. Sigma squadron, take the starboard side on your way in and the port side on your way out. Epsilon group, port side in and starboard out. Don't crash into each other on the turn."

"We read you, General."

Bracing himself, Zak drove the *Lady Hawk* towards the enemy lines with his fighters trailing behind him. The view outside was not daunting; it was terrifying. Enormous cruisers filled the black void and bright flashes of deadly fire shot towards them from all directions. Any one of them could rip the entire ship to shreds in an instant and for the most part, it seemed to be sheer luck that none of them hit.

Then before they had time to register it, they were flying over the vast hull of the *Annihilator* itself. The dark gray mass below was covered in protrusions of various sizes, including the distinctive shapes of weapons turrets and right now, all of them were firing madly at the *Lady Hawk* and the fighters behind it.

Not wasting a second on hesitation, Zak and the others fired back with a barrage of their own with a number of torpedoes for good measure. As a general rule, Zak never felt comfortable firing on enemy targets. There was a world of difference between destroying an abandoned hulk for target practice and attacking a crewed vessel. But in light of the destruction he'd just seen the *Annihilator* unleash, he couldn't help feeling a sense of vindictive satisfaction as turrets and protrusions exploded across its hull.

He and the others then passed Epsilon squadron as they swooped around behind the *Annihilator*'s enormous rear engines and they lined themselves up for their exit runs. As they soared over the Federation's flagship, their weapons blazed ceaselessly, while their torpedoes exploded into its hull, ripping armored plating apart and tearing turrets from their bases. Then they shot over the end of the ship and headed back to the Phalamkian blockade.

"That oughta slow them down a little," Carla said.

"I hope so," Zak replied. He wiped a layer of sweat off his forehead. He'd done a lot of crazy stunts since he joined the Resistance but that one left them all behind.

Meanwhile, Asten was growing restless. Perhaps they'd all been wrong about those Phalamkians he'd seen on Nemasil. Maybe they had nothing to do with whatever was going on today. He met Selina's gaze and she shrugged. With little else to do, they turned their attention back to the holographic display in the middle of the room. Stray shots from the Federation armada were hitting parts of the shield but overall, it didn't appear to be under much strain.

Which was strange because right then, an alarm blared from some hidden speakers.

"What's going on?" Asten asked Tallec.

The supervisor looked flustered as he leaned over one of the work stations. "I don't believe it. We've got a malfunction. One of the main circuit breakers has melted down."

"That can't be right," Asten murmured to Selina. "Otherwise, something down there would be overheating."

"It could be a malfunction," the Phalamkian seated at the console suggested, overhearing the remark.

"Possibly," Tallec conceded, "but all the same, we have to bring in an emergency crew to have a look at it. Assuming the rest of our equipment's in good order, that alarm would have been relayed to the base so a crew should be on its way right now."

He moved for the exterior entrance and motioned some of the other staff to follow him. "Come on."

Asten and Selina also went after him with their armed guard.

As they came outside, a cable car was coming up. In a few seconds, it stopped at a platform just below them and four figures leapt out, wearing gas masks and carrying bags of miscellaneous equipment.

"Tallec," Selina said. "Check these guys for IDs."

Tallec nodded and took several steps towards the newcomers but before he could say a thing, they barged right past him, mumbling apologies and running inside.

"What—?" Tallec cried out.

"I think these men might be saboteurs!" Asten said, chasing after them with Selina and the armed guards hot on his tail.

As they reached the main control deck, the four men disappeared down the ramp that led to the reactor room.

"Stop right there!" one of the Phalamkian guards called out, drawing his weapon. "No one enters this facility without an ID clearance."

"Sorry, sir," the last of them replied, turning around just long enough to answer. "It's an emergency!"

"No one enters this facility without an ID clearance," the guard repeated. "Regardless—"

A shot through his chest cut him short, leaving a smoking wound. With a gasp of escaping air, he collapsed to the deck dead.

Asten swiveled on his heels to see where the shot had come from and saw the Phalamkian who'd been in charge of the work station where the alarm had sounded. Tallec looked at him with an expression of disbelief and anger. "What do you think you're—?"

The Phalamkian fired again and Tallec fell with an anguished cry, badly injured but alive. One of the remaining four guards rushed to his side while the other three opened fire on the traitor. However, he was too fast for them, crouching under the cover of his work station and retreating down the ramp.

"Get everyone out!" Selina shouted.

"But the shield—" one of the technicians exclaimed.

"It'll hold for now!" she snapped. "Come on, Asten."

As they rushed over, a cloud of thick black smoke poured out of the doorway to the ramp, forcing them back coughing.

"Smoke grenade!" one of the guards called out. "Get away, quickly." He hit the release for one of the ladders that extended from the platform and it slid down to the walkway below. "Hurry, before they get to the bottom of the ramp."

He scurried down and Asten and Selina followed with two more guards behind them. The last remaining guard assisted Tallec out from the control room with the rest of the staff who worked there.

On the deck below the main control room, everyone drew their weapons and ran to the reactor room but several shots made them take a few steps back. One of the guards leaned out to see where their assailants were and saw that one of them was about to lob another smoke grenade. Before he released it from his grip though, the guard shot him and as he fell, he dropped it on the ground—its contents enveloping the group.

"Stay back," the guard warned the others. "They've got gas masks so they'll still be standing. And now they're hidden in the smoke."

"That traitor from the control deck didn't have a mask though," Selina pointed out. "So he'll be down at least."

"Good," the guard replied. "I'd like to have a few words with him later."

"I'd like to throw him over the side of the landing platform," Selina said.

"Yeah. Me too." The guard leaned forward while he waited for the smoke to clear. "Don't make this harder on yourselves!" he called down the space between the various pieces of machinery. "Surrender now and you might receive some clemency."

"Save your clemency," one of them called back, his voice filtered through his gas mask. "Everyone in the Phalamkian Defense Forces is a dead man, including you! Besides, while you're offering clemency, Corinthe's giving us money. Tons of it."

"Only good if you're alive to spend it," the guard replied. "And you won't be if you keep this up."

The smoke cleared enough for him to get another shot in. One of the saboteurs was down, although he wasn't sure if it was the same one he'd injured earlier or not.

"Just to show you we're not screwing around," he told the others.

Then something clattered across the mesh walkway and landed at his feet.

"Neither are we," another saboteur called back. The guard had only a moment to react. He leapt away without looking at the object and crashed into the others behind him. A moment later, the walkway exploded where he'd been standing and a blast of hot shrapnel tore into his back. Then he slid into the gaping hole in the mesh the blast had left, pinned down by debris.

"Stay with him!" Selina told the other two guards. "Watch ahead!"

She gave Asten a gentle push but he knew what she wanted. He headed around the U-bend and ran up the other side of the walkway back towards the reactor room.

As he emerged, a saboteur fired at him and he ducked back. Then he heard a short hiss followed by the sound of some kind of electrical discharge, a blaster pack overheating. It was known to happen with some of the cheaper blasters around.

Taking a chance, he stepped out and fired. He caught one of the saboteurs in the shoulder but the remaining two were ready for him. One of them had opened one of the hatches he'd seen earlier when Tallec had shown him the room and as he looked around, the other grabbed him and threw him into the room beneath it. As he climbed back to his feet, he heard a scream and the sounds of someone struggling and a moment later, Selina crashed into him as well. Then the hatch was closed overhead and they heard something heavy sliding across it. They were trapped.

Selina tried to force the hatch but it was useless. With a scream, she hit it. Asten pulled her back and in embarrassment, she tried to turn away from him.

"We can't get out that way," he told her. "But there might be another way those creeps haven't thought of."

She nodded.

"Don't worry," Asten said with an easy smile. "We're not alone down here. And there are only three of them left and at least one of them is injured."

Selina sighed. "Yeah, you're right. Now, let's have a look around."

In orbit, Lord Erama knew nothing of his daughter's predicament as he had his own problems to deal with. A number of the Federation's cruisers had broken through the lines. Some were attacking the allied ships where they were vulnerable and had few guns to fire back with, while others were moving on to pummel the planetary shield. Making it worse was the number of deserters. He didn't know what these people thought battles were *supposed* to be like but clearly, they hadn't expected the ferocious assault the Federation had unleashed. However, most of their allies were still holding fast and in the end it was more than he could have asked of any of them.

Still though, something had to change. The Federation was getting too confident and his own officers needed something to lift their spirits fast. Otherwise, it would be a toss-up as to whether they surrendered or were blown apart. It was time for an advance.

"All cruisers," he announced. "Move in formation. We're heading in between the enemy ships. Engage them broadside and hit them with everything you've got but steer clear of their flagship."

"What about the shield?" one of his captains asked. "If we move out, we'll give the enemy the chance of a direct bombardment."

"We will," Erama agreed. "However, we'll have to risk it."

"Here," Asten called out, throwing aside some boxes of cables to clear some space.

Selina rushed over and crouched beside him.

"I think we can move this paneling." Asten looked around. "Here, hand me that rod over there."

Selina got it for him and he pried it into a groove around the outside of the panel. He pulled down, groaning with the exertion. He tried to lever it a little more and finally, it came free. He tossed the rod aside and slid the panel across the flooring. Underneath the deck was about a foot of space and another panel bolted onto some metal support beams. He pulled out his blaster and tried to shoot the bolts out. It wasn't entirely successful but they had melted slightly. Then, gripping the edge of the hole he'd made so he didn't fall through, he kicked at the bottom of it several times until the piece of metal came free and fell away into empty space.

Asten recoiled in fright. It was a hell of a long way down to the ground. Outside, it was getting darker as the sun was setting and there was a howling wind.

Selina grabbed him to keep him steady.

"Thanks," he said.

"Now what?" she asked him.

"Look." Asten pointed down. "There are some external support beams down there. We can climb down and make our way back up on one of them. I saw them on the first day we got here."

This time, it was Selina's turn to recoil. She felt a wave of nausea as she leaned over the hole. "That's insane. We'll fall for sure."

"No, we won't," Asten told her. "Also, it's not going to be 'we'. You wait here. I'll come back for you."

"No!" Selina protested, clutching his arm. "We're going together. What if something happens to you?"

"It won't," Asten replied.

"All the same, I'm coming with you."

"All right. But I'll go first. Follow my lead and whatever happens, don't let go."

Selina nodded. For a moment though, neither of them moved. Selina pulled Asten towards her and kissed him. Then embarrassed, she pulled away and gave him a smile. "Good luck."

Asten smiled back. He wanted to say something but no words came. He kept smiling a little longer and as he did, he realized he was in complete awe of this woman and the idea that she might feel something for him in return was more than he could have ever hoped for. Then, worried that he was just sitting there grinning like an idiot, he forced himself to move.

"All right," he muttered. "Let's see."

He gripped the edge of the hole and lowered himself down. An easy step brought him onto the first support strut then he ducked his head so he could see better. The surface of the beam was rough, which made it easier to hold onto than it would have been otherwise. Also, it was large enough to provide a comforting sense of having something under him, without being so large that it was hard to grip.

"It looks good," he told Selina. "Just crouch down and you'll be on a good solid beam. Follow me."

He crawled up the beam and waited for Selina to emerge.

She came out and steadied herself. Then she lay down on the strut, hugging it tight. She tried not to look down and at the same time, tried to ignore the sound of the wind. It felt as though a sudden gust would blow her off into the dusk sky at any moment. Hanging on, she made her way towards the end of the strut where Asten was waiting.

Once he was sure she was okay, he reached out and grabbed a thick cable. Taking a firm grip with both hands, he held onto it as he stepped out onto another support strut which branched off at a right angle to the one he was on. He was now standing underneath the platform outside the reactor room he'd seen when Tallec had given them the tour of the place and the strut he was standing on was one of several holding it in place. He stepped onto the next beam to make some room for Selina and gave her a hand up. "How are you going?"

"Terrified," she said. "Aren't you?"

"Absolutely. I'm not crazy." Asten gave her a reassuring smile and looked at the platform above them. "Well, we're almost there." Taking a deep breath, he pulled himself up his support strut, grabbed hold of the platform and turned around. "All right. Your turn. You ready?"

"Well, the sooner it's over, the better, right?"

"That's the spirit."

Swallowing her anxieties, Selina made the climb and Asten kept her steady as she turned around to hold the railing. Then he helped her over before climbing over himself, and he gave her a moment to catch her breath. "There. That wasn't so bad, was it?"

Selina let out a nervous laugh. "I don't know *what* your basis of comparison is."

Asten laughed a little too. The worst part of the climb was over. However, they still had a little further to go. He looked at the rungs he'd seen when he had first set foot on this platform, rungs that led back up to the control deck. He smiled at Selina, gauging whether she was ready for the last leg of the climb. "Shall we?"

She nodded and he saw some of her fiery determination coming back.

"Let's go then."

Hand over hand, Asten climbed up the side of the facility until he was standing on the landing platform outside the control deck. The others were there as well but the guard who'd been assisting Tallec earlier had gone. Asten hoped he was okay. He turned around to help Selina up.

"Come on," he said and ignoring the questioning glances and queries from the staff of the facility, they headed back inside. As soon as they reached the all too familiar control deck, they were greeted by the sound of blaster fire from below. They leaned over the railing and saw that all the guards were all right. Two of them were covering the one who was wounded, while the one who'd been helping Tallec was now down there as well, covering the other side of the U-bend.

Asten tapped the railing just loud enough to get the attention of their comrades. One of them glanced up and the look of relief on his face was visible even from the distance Asten was above him. Asten mouthed a question and the guard held up three fingers.

He nodded. So the one he'd injured earlier was still fighting. He motioned Selina to keep quiet and led the way down the ramp. Thankfully, all the smoke from the saboteurs' grenade had now cleared. As they reached the bottom, he looked around the corner.

There was one saboteur blocking each end of the U-bend walkway. Standing back behind the nearest one was the saboteur he'd injured earlier, making the best of his remaining limbs. He had two arms clutching his injured shoulder and supporting the arm that hung limp from it, while he held onto his blaster with his last remaining free hand.

Asten was thankful for the fact that with their attention entirely focused on the guards, all three saboteurs had their backs turned to him. But he had to be careful. He and Selina would only get one shot at this. He stepped out and motioned for her to join him. In silence, they raised their blasters. Asten nodded for

Selina to take the saboteur who was nearest to the ramp and he indicated that he'd take out the injured one behind him.

He raised three fingers and Selina nodded her understanding. He nodded once, then a second time and with a third nod, he fired on his man, blowing a burning hole in the back of his head. Selina took her man out at the same time. Instantly, the remaining saboteur whirled around to open fire on them both but the guard who was covering him at the other end of the walkway got him first and, with a thud, the traitor hit the deck. When the gun he dropped stopped rattling and came to a halt, a heavy silence hung over the reactor room.

Finally, one of the guards emerged and Asten and Selina walked over to him.

"I think we've got them all," the guard said, looking over the bodies sprawled across the deck. He paced around the room a little more, giving them each a prod with his boot to make sure they weren't going to leap up and start shooting again.

"So," Selina said to Asten. "are these saboteurs the same individuals you saw on Nemasil?"

"I'd be curious to find that out myself," he told her, crouching down next to one of them.

He turned the dead saboteur's head around and pulled the gas mask off. "Yeah," he said, standing up while still keeping his eyes fixed on the lifeless face. "They're the same guys."

The guard who was with them looked at the control deck technician who had let the saboteurs in and checked his pulse and vital signs.

"I wouldn't want to be him when he wakes up," Asten remarked.

"Yeah," the guard agreed, rolling the traitor over and cuffing his hands behind his back. "He's going to be in more trouble than his little mind could even begin to comprehend."

"So is anything down here actually damaged?" Asten wondered, pacing around and eyeing the thing up and down. "Everything looks fine to me."

"I'd say there was nothing wrong with any of the circuit breakers," Selina said. "The technician didn't have to actually damage anything to get the saboteurs up here and I don't see any way he could have. We pretty much knew where everyone was the whole time. But we couldn't see what everyone was *doing* at those work stations all the time. And I imagine it wouldn't be very difficult for someone with a bit of technical know-how to hack into the computer systems and program an alarm to go off."

"I agree," the guard said, standing up. "However, we can investigate that later. Right now, we've got injured people to look after and a shield generator to operate."

"Right," Selina said. "By the way, is your other man okay?"

"He's still stuck back there," the guard replied. "But he's not hurt. And now that we don't have to worry about being shot at, we should be able to pry him out without injuring him."

Selina smiled. "Well, that's a relief. Right then. I'll go and tell the staff up there that the area's secure. I'll come back soon and give you a hand. And if he *is* hurt, I can put him on the cable car with Tallec and send them down to the medics at the base."

20. The Frontier United

As HE SURVEYED THE FIGHTING FROM HIS command chair on the bridge, Admiral Kellahav was worried. The warships that had broken through the Phalamkian barricade should have been pummeling the surface of the planet by now. Something was wrong.

He turned to the communications officer. "Lieutenant Cardal. Contact our Phalamkian surface team. Ask them what's causing the delay."

"Yes, sir," the man replied and set up the necessary encryption to mask the communication. However, after a good twenty seconds or so, all he'd received for his troubles was static. "Sir, they're not responding."

"What's going on?" Corinthe demanded, appearing beside Kellahav's chair.

"It looks like our Phalamkian friends on the surface have been incapacitated," his newly appointed admiral told him. "I'm going to call off the planetary bombardment and recall those warships. As long as that shield's up, they're wasted there. They can re-engage the Phalamkian defense forces."

"Keep them there," Corinthe countered. "So our friends below failed in their simple task. All that means is that it's going to take a bit longer. That shield can't withstand that kind of bombardment indefinitely."

"And as long as they're firing on the planetary shield, we'll have to tie up precious ships to cover their flanks," Kellahav snapped. "I'm sorry, sir, but you're not a military strategist. I don't presume to tell you how to do your job. Don't tell me how to do mine."

His outburst startled Corinthe so much, he took a step back in surprise. Then he looked about the bridge and saw that everyone's attention was fixed on their confrontation. Even though it was not his style to back down, Corinthe knew it would be dangerous to press his position under the circumstances.

He allowed a few seconds to pass in order diffuse the tension and smiled. "My apologies, Admiral. Carry on."

With a nod he backed away, leaving Kellahav to ponder how long he would remain Admiral after this was over.

For the forces defending the Phalamkian homeworld, the battle had turned in their favor. The word had quickly spread that the Federation's plot to sabotage the planetary shield had failed and the Federation forces that had been pummeling it moments before were now taking a heavy bombardment themselves as they tried to turn their ships around. Meanwhile, Lord Erama's advance into the midst of the enemy was paying good dividends as his Phalamkian Battle Titans separated the Federation's ships and threw them in disarray.

General Draedon smiled as he watched it all. Then a familiar voice broke in over the bridge loudspeaker. "Attention all Resistance forces. This is Admiral Garam. We're making an attack on the *Annihilator*. All ships hold back."

After the click at the end of the transmission, several of the officers on the bridge looked at Draedon in bewilderment. "What's going on?" one asked.

Draedon shrugged. "I guess we'll see. He did say he had something special planned but he's been playing it close to the chest."

From the midst of the Resistance ships holding back the Federation's advance on Phalamki, one warship broke away and steered towards the Federation's command ship.

"Sir," the chief radar officer called out to Kellahav. "Incoming cruiser on our portside at eleven."

"They don't appear to be firing, sir," another officer added from his post.

Kellahav looked at the viewscreen. There was something strange about the way the ship was moving. The trajectory was too straight, it was taking no measures to avoid the occasional blasts that came its way and it was moving too fast. At the rate it was speeding towards them, it would collide with them for sure.

"Sensors, scan that ship!" he called. "How many on board?"

In the space of a few heartbeats, several lieutenants carried out his request and did it again to make sure.

"No one, sir," one of them called back.

"It's rigged with explosives," Kellahav concluded. "We have a remote controlled bomb on our hands."

Because of its size, he knew they couldn't turn the *Annihilator* out of its path in time, which meant the only option was to blast the incoming ship to pieces before it hit them.

"Portside gunnery," he ordered. "Concentrate all fire on that ship!"

Unfortunately, while sound, the plan had little chance of success as the several gun emplacements that were in the best position to fire on the enemy cruiser had been badly damaged when Sigma and Epsilon squadron had made their strafing runs. Where Kellahav had hoped to see the most fire, there was nothing.

Around him, the gunnery officers complained that the batteries weren't responding but he didn't reply. There was no point. Some officers were getting hits in—good hits too—but it was not enough to slow the projectile hurtling towards them. In fact, there was only one thing they could do.

"All hands brace for collision!" Kellahav shouted, gripping his command chair.

Even though he was holding onto it with all his strength, the impact threw him and sent him sliding across the deck. And the sound of the explosion that followed was deafening, even when muffled through all the decks, paneling and structural framework that separated the bridge from the point of the collision. On the viewscreen, he saw huge pieces of debris tumbling into the darkness and it was obvious the damage was serious.

It took several seconds after the impact for the deck to stop vibrating from the shock and as he climbed to his feet, his head was ringing. He touched his forehead and saw blood on his hand.

Around the bridge, most of the men weren't in much better shape and all around, he heard pained groans as everyone tried to resume their positions. For a number of them, it was too much effort and they collapsed on the deck. He nodded to some officers who were still more or less all right. "Check on these men and take anyone who needs further attention down to the sick bay."

"Damage report?" he inquired as he lowered himself back into his seat.

"We've lost all power to the port side engines," someone called out. "Life support systems are down all over that side of the ship and we've lost steering control. The automatic safeguards are sealing off the damaged sections..." He trailed off and Kellahav didn't press him for the rest of the details. The *Annihilator* was crippled.

"Alert the *Charioteer*, the *Titan* and the *Adjudicator*," he instructed the communications officer. "They're closest. Tell them to take position in front of the ship."

"Yes, sir," the man replied and got to it.

Kellahav then heard the sound of slow deliberate steps behind him. There was only one person he knew who walked like that and he had genuinely hoped he'd been knocked unconscious when that flying bomb had plowed into them.

"The Resistance forces are still clearly in our sights, Admiral," Corinthe said, bruised and disheveled but still carrying the unmistakable arrogance that characterized his every action. "And even with all the damage we've taken, we still have a number of operable guns on our starboard side. As you so rightly said, I am not a military man but surely we must take advantage of any opportunity we are given to inflict whatever damage we can on the enemy. Wouldn't you agree?"

"Yes, sir," Kellahav muttered. He raised his voice to address the bridge. "Fire at will on the enemy cruisers. Use any and all remaining batteries."

There was an uncomfortable silence.

"Well?" Corinthe demanded. "You heard the admiral. What are you waiting for?"

"Sir," the radar officer said. "A number of our own ships have just moved between us and the Phalamkian defense forces."

"Those three ships we just contacted?" Corinthe scowled, giving Kellahav a sideways glare.

"Um... no, sir," the young man replied. "These ships have only just dropped out of lightspeed."

Corinthe's expression hardened. "How many?"

"Eight, sir."

"And is the *Sentinel* among them?"

The young man swallowed. "Yes, sir."

"What do they think they're doing?" Corinthe said. "Putting themselves in the line of our fire."

"Raise the *Sentinel*," he told the communications officer. "And put it on the loudspeaker."

"This is the *Annihilator* calling the *Sentinel*," the man said. "Do you read?"

They didn't have to wait long.

"This is Captain Merrick," came the reply. "I read you."

Corinthe smiled but only to suppress his anger. "Captain Merrick, this is Corinthe. Put Admiral Roth on."

"Certainly."

There was a sound of people shuffling positions on the other ship. While he waited, Corinthe plotted imaginary acts of revenge to punish the captain for the insolent tone in his voice

"Hello, Corinthe," a familiar voice greeted him. "How nice to see you again."

"Admiral Roth," Corinthe told him. "You're wanted for treason and resisting arrest. Tell your men that unless they wish to join you in a labor camp somewhere, they are to move their ships out of the way. I will speak to the captain now."

"Very well." There was another click. Corinthe wondered about the ease in which Roth had acquiesced. No doubt he was up to something.

"Captain Merrick," Corinthe said, putting heavy emphasis on every word he spoke. "Do you know you are acting under the orders of a traitor?"

"Oh, we're not following your orders any more, Minister," Merrick replied.

"Think carefully, Captain," Corinthe warned him. "Our ship may be crippled but we still have half our starboard batteries operating. And if that doesn't persuade you to move your ships back, then I suggest you take a better look at the armada behind us. Because as far as I can see, you just have eight warships."

"Is that a threat, sir? Because I think you'll find that Federation naval officers don't fire on their own ships."

"I'm warning you, Captain," Corinthe told him. "Move your ships out of our way. And I order you to place Admiral Roth under arrest."

"We're not moving, sir. And I have orders that *you* are to be placed under arrest. For the authorization of this unprovoked attack on the Phalamkian system and a number of similar offences against other independent systems."

"I am securing this system," Corinthe replied. "And whether the Phalamkians agree with me or not, I am acting in their best interests. We are acting out of necessity, Captain. Now, stand down."

"The admiral has also instructed me," Merrick continued, "to tell you that you've failed to supply sufficient evidence to support your claim that Minstrahn insurgents are threatening the Federation. He suggests if you have any such evidence in your possession, it may help you during your court martial."

"This is mutiny, Captain. And high treason. I trust I don't have to explain the implications of those charges."

"We're sending a shuttle over to escort you back to Corsida," Merrick finished, ignoring him. "It will arrive in four minutes."

With a click, the communicator fell silent and all eyes on the bridge turned to Corinthe. He gritted his teeth. Everything he had worked to achieve hinged on this moment.

"Admiral Kellahav," he said, standing straight, "prepare to open fire."

Kellahav rose from his chair. "No."

For several drawn out moments, Corinthe stared at him in silent fury. "Then I am relieving you of command," he told him. He turned to the rest of the bridge. "Those men out there are traitors and if we allow them to stand between us and the Phalamkian defense forces, they will increase our losses tenfold. Starboard gunnery, fire on my mark."

No one responded.

"They won't fire on their own men, sir," Kellahav told him. "And countermanding the orders of the senior officer aboard a ship is against regulations."

Corinthe turned to him with a cold gaze. "Do you want to be under arrest as well, Admiral?"

Kellahav shook his head. "It's no good, sir." He straightened his stance and spoke in a loud clear voice so everyone on the bridge could hear. "Corinthe, I hereby place you under arrest for the willful misuse of military resources, for the authorization of attacks on independent systems without provocation and for the reckless endangerment of the lives of the officers, pilots and soldiers of the Federation naval forces."

Around the bridge, Corinthe heard the murmurs of assent and he knew he wouldn't be able to talk his way out of this.

Kellahav turned to the guards standing by the entrance to the bridge. "Men, take the minister of security into custody."

Corinthe wanted to protest but the words caught in his throat. The guards hesitated for a few moments but they overcame their anxieties soon enough and carried out the order. As they placed handcuffs around his wrists, Corinthe found himself unable to muster the slightest strength to resist and all the fight that had been burning inside had left him. Hanging his head in defeat, he went without a word as he was led off the bridge.

"Raise the *Sentinel* again," Kellahav instructed the communications officer. The man nodded and within moments, they were in direct communication once more.

"Captain Merrick, this is General Kellahav. I have placed Corinthe under arrest and I am deferring command of this entire task force to Admiral Roth."

"I will inform the admiral," Merrick replied.

A moment later, Roth came back on. "General Kellahav, I accept command of this task force. I would also like to commend you on having the courage to do what needed to be done."

"Thank you, sir. Your orders?"

"Alert the rest of the fleet and inform them of the situation. Then order them to hold back. I am going to contact the Phalamkian defense forces to negotiate a cease-fire."

"Yes sir."

Twenty minutes later, the Federation ships had all retreated to the outer system with the exception of four that were evacuating personnel from the stricken *Annihilator*. Meanwhile, a small meeting was taking place in an antechamber just off the bridge of Lord Erama's flagship.

"Admiral Roth," the Phalamkian said with warmth in his voice as he shook the Federation commander's hand. "Welcome back. It is good to have the pleasure of your company once more."

"Indeed," Admiral Garam joined in. "Although you cut it rather fine. We were beginning to wonder if you were going to show."

"I must apologize," Admiral Roth replied. "It took me a little longer to assemble my small task force than I expected."

"Well, you got here," Lord Erama said, "and we are very grateful that you did."

Across the room, Draedon, Kalae and the other commanders of the various resistance divisions looked at Garam and Erama in surprise.

"So how long have all of you been working together?" Draedon asked.

Garam smiled. "Actually, Admiral Roth only very recently established contact with us. Just several days ago in fact."

"It was crucial that we did meet however," Roth explained, "because if we hadn't, your commanders might have fired on me when I placed my ships between the Federation's armada and your own."

"And we thought it best to keep the meeting quiet," Garam added, "even from all of you. It may have undermined the admiral's case against Corinthe if it were known that he'd been working with us before the battle had even started."

"Ah," Draedon said, turning to Admiral Roth as something clicked. "You were the one who supplied Admiral Garam with the information on the *Annihilator*'s guns."

"Yes," Roth smiled. "Although I hear you did your own count anyway."

"Well, discretion is the better part of valor, as they say."

"True."

"I should also mention to you all," Garam put in, "that it was the admiral who proposed the plan we used to disable the *Annihilator*."

"I'm just glad it worked," Roth said. "Although, it was unfortunate that it had to be done. We killed a lot of people with that act of subterfuge."

"On balance though," Garam pointed out, "I think we saved many more."

"Perhaps," Roth conceded. "Although, one way or another, a lot of lives have been lost because of Corinthe's activities."

"Yes," Erama agreed. "However, it's over now and we can begin to repair the damage. But before we get started, satisfy the curiosity of an old Phalamkian war horse. What will happen to Corinthe?"

"He has grossly abused the privilege of his position," Roth told him. "He will be tried and most likely, he will be sentenced to life imprisonment. Also, despite his role in helping me put an end to the matter, General Kellahav may unfortunately be facing a lengthy prison term for his complicit involvement in Corinthe's operations and serious crimes committed during the invasion of Ipaatid."

"General Kellahav?" Draedon asked with a pang of sympathy. "Could he perhaps be pardoned? After all, he was the one who arrested Corinthe."

"Perhaps," Roth said. "However, I suspect he may not want to be as he turned himself in of his own volition after handing over his command. Corinthe could have said something as I think he knew about the incident but he didn't. And given the fact that Kellahav had ordered his arrest, that's a little surprising. Although I think he was in such a state of shock at the time that the thought didn't even occur to him. And yes, there were other guilty parties that would have known about Ipaatid as well but they could hardly report Kellahav without incriminating themselves. So you see, he really could have stayed silent about the matter and no one save a handful of people need ever have known."

"It sounds as though he's had some kind of epiphany," Draedon remarked.

"Yes," Roth said. "It certainly makes you think. A couple of days ago, I would have said the man was irredeemable but there you go. He proved his worth tonight. Perhaps, I may be able to argue for clemency on his behalf."

The room was quiet for a few moments.

"What will happen with regard to the planets that were unlawfully annexed?" Erama asked, changing the topic.

"They will of course be compensated. Prisoners taken during the attacks will be released and the proper governing bodies will be restored."

"You know," Kalae said, "a number of our worlds would not have been averse to joining the Federation if there had just been an open offer from Corsida to all interested parties. It was the false pretence under which we were approached. The aggressive manner. As well as planets being turned into supply depots for Corinthe's war machine. That made a lot of people very angry."

"And understandably so," Roth agreed.

"What about Corinthe's other associates on Corsida?" Garam asked. "Rear Admiral Calaom and Commodore Hallyd?"

"They're interesting cases," Roth replied. "They could both be charged for aiding and abetting, although I think it won't be necessary to deal with them in the same manner as Corinthe. Calaom's so old, there'd be little point in an extended trial. He'll probably just retire in disgrace, while Hallyd has agreed to testify against Corinthe in exchange for clemency. And I'm sure you'd agree it is far more important to put away Corinthe than to put away his tools."

"That makes sense," Garam agreed. "Although it sounds like there's a lot of work to be done to clean this all up."

"Indeed," Roth said with the faintest trace of a sigh. "And I imagine there'll be a fall-out in the Federation over this as well. Corinthe has a lot of supporters and while most of them will see sense when the situation is explained to them, I expect a few will cry foul. And I'm not looking forward to dealing with that."

"I'm worried about what will become of our Resistance organization too," Draedon admitted, more tired than he'd ever been during his long campaign. "It's not as if we can all pretend that everything's normal and go back to regular jobs. Sure, a large group of us can go back to the defense forces of our home planets. But for a lot of the people who joined us along the way, the Resistance has been like an extended family. For me too. We need to decide what to do with all the resources we've acquired but also, we have a lot of fine officers, pilots and specialists in numerous fields and I'd hate to see that all go to waste."

Roth considered this. "During the Levarc War, the worlds of the Frontier became the United Frontier, working closely with each other to defend their systems. I'm sure most of you are old enough to remember it. And Admiral Garam, I believe you were quite personally involved in it."

"I was actually," Garam said, looking a little surprised. "But how did you know?"

"I remember hearing your name when I was involved in a joint operation between the Federation and the United Frontier, back when I was with the Battle Meteoroids. I believe we met actually. But it was quite a while ago."

"Ah. I think I remember, now that you mention it."

"Anyway, my point is that there's no reason why you can't have something like that again. The Phalamkians already have a similar system in place, coordinating a defense network between a number of systems, with allies in the Narvashae, Hie'shi and Kordan systems, among many others." He turned to Lord Erama. "Given the Lady Erama's background, presumably you have ties with the Alandra system as well?"

"We did," Lord Erama said. "And after the annexed systems of the Frontier are returned to their people, we will again.

"It's a good idea," Garam agreed. There were a few murmurs of assent from the others around the room.

Draedon stirred. "Now, there's something else that concerns me that we haven't addressed yet and that is that we have no idea how far Corinthe's corruption has spread. There's no telling how many regional governments might be in his pocket or his schemes, or how many other 'associates' he had in the fleet." He turned to Admiral Roth. "Can you be sure that all your systems will step in line now or that Corinthe doesn't have any more die-hard loyalists in the navy?"

"No," Roth said. "We're going to need an overhaul of the entire Federation. However, I'll certainly keep the systems of the Frontier informed on anything that comes up that could be a potential problem. Like aggressive governors or rogue task forces."

"Actually, while we're on the topic of stability in the Federation, let's not forget all the other Resistance groups out there," Kalae pointed out. "There are a number that we're not aligned with, including groups formed within the Federation. We'd have to convince them to halt their activities as well. Also, I think some of them might keep on fighting regardless of whether Corinthe's in charge or not. I've had reports that while a lot of these groups are made up of genuinely concerned individuals, many of them are just pirates using the resistance movement as a thin pretext for raiding systems. And if we can't convince everybody that the situation is in hand, these groups will keep drawing support."

"Yes," Lord Erama said, getting everyone's attention. "There are a lot of issues that we need to discuss." He motioned people to the table in the middle of the room. "So why don't we make ourselves comfortable?"

It was a beautiful morning where Asten and Selina were and while the diplomats lay in bed exhausted from all the discussions the night before, they were up and enjoying the sunshine. Once their job was done, they hadn't waited around the shield generator and now, they were standing on one of the balconies of that same defense building that Asten had visited on his first trip to Phalamki. The *Lady Hawk* was once again on the landing platform on the roof, while Drackson, Carla, Zak, Maia and their one-off rear gunner Hellesis were inside the main lounge area.

Zak and the others had all had a late night celebrating with Sigma and Epsilon squadron. Asten and Selina had missed it, being down on the planet, but that had been all right. They had wanted to check on Tallec and the injured guard, and to spend some time alone.

"Funny, isn't it?" Selina remarked. "How suddenly, we can all come out in the open and act like nothing's happened."

"I know what you mean," Asten agreed. "But not everything's the same." He gave her the most charming smile he could devise. "So what are we going to do about us?"

Selina sighed. "I don't know. We definitely felt something back there—still do—and I think it's more than just that moment under the reactor room. But..."

"But what?"

"What now? Somehow, I can't see you going off on diplomatic errands and negotiating reparations between the Federation and the worlds that it unlawfully occupied."

Asten shrugged. "Not really. Although I can't see you doing that either. You're not really your father, are you?"

Selina laughed. "No. He and I have certainly established *that*. Still... I get the feeling that you just want to go back to flying about in the *Lady Hawk* with Drackson and Carla."

Asten shrugged. "Maybe. But you could always come with us."

"There's a thought."

"There's a whole galaxy out there to see," Asten said with a playful grin, holding her around her waist. "I'm planning another trip to the vents of Nemasil, you know. I wanted to pick up some Kulahri when I was there before but the planetary security forces chased me out before I had a chance. We could just hang around the vents if you wanted. It's like the biggest sauna you've seen. Also, I promised Drackson that we'd go back to the Harskan sector again sometime so he could spend a little more time there. We saw some incredible places when we were flying over El'aesi too. You'd love it."

"That sounds nice," Selina said. "But the *Lady Hawk's* a pretty small ship."

"It's a fine ship," Asten told her.

"Absolutely," Selina said, placing a placating arm around him. "But I just can't help thinking that it might get a bit crowded. I'm hearing things, you know?"

"Yes?"

"Well, it seems your friend Zak is keen on my sister—"

"Zak's a good guy," Asten told her with a reassuring smile, pretending to misunderstand.

Selina nudged him with her elbow. "And Maia says she's keen on him."

"So if you come with us, Maia comes because you two are inseparable and therefore, Zak might come as well?"

"Possibly. Possibly not. But I think I'd like a bit of space. That's all."

Asten frowned. "You know, I thought Zak was from the Ellast Defense Forces like most of the other guys in Draedon's division. He's not going back there?"

"No." Selina laughed. "You don't know where your friend comes from?"

Asten shrugged. "He doesn't know where *I* come from."

Selina shook her head. "Well, I suppose that makes it all right then. Where *are* you from, by the way?"

"Halea."

"See? That's how you find things out. Anyway, Zak, Ja'is and a few of the others in Sigma squadron trained at the Koratav academy."

"That's a tough place to get into," Asten said.

"Yeah," Selina agreed. "So he's not from Ellast. He's a free agent."

"Well, I guess we'll just have to see what he and Maia want to do," Asten said. "However, as for us, I think I've got an idea that might work."

"Oh yes. What's that?"

"Well, I was rather hoping that in return for helping your guards stop those saboteurs that you might be able to put in a good word for me with your father."

Selina shook her head. "You've lost me completely."

"Well," Asten said, "now that the Resistance isn't giving us free meals every day, we're going to have to find something else to keep food on the table and to tell you the truth, I'm a little worried that since we've been out of the game so long, our old clients might have taken up contracts with our competitors. But I thought perhaps the Phalamkian defense forces might appreciate having another ship around to look after smaller transports."

Selina considered the idea and smiled. "I suppose we could set something up. Let's see. A ship large enough to carry passengers or supplies. A hangar with room for the *Lady Hawk* and maybe a few fighters. I can more or less do the same thing *I* was doing before and you can do the same thing *you* were doing. We can handle the Phalamkian government jobs and then we don't have to worry about funds. And we can do a few private jobs too if they pay well. Then we can take some trips on the side to wherever we'd like to go. Yeah, I think that would work."

Asten placed his arm around her waist again. "Come on then. Let's go and tell the others about our new business venture."

As the transparent doors slid open, Carla and Drackson beamed at them and raised small glasses. Grinning back, they raised their hands to show them they were empty.

"Here," Zak said as they came inside, handing them drinks. "We'd hate to have you missing all the fun."

"Thanks," they replied more or less at the same time.

"So," Carla smiled, taking a sip from her own glass, "you two were out there for quite a while. What were you talking about?"

With all his friends grinning at him, Asten felt himself blushing. Putting on an air of nonchalance, he waved a dismissive hand but their expectant stares remained. Finally, he gave in and gave Selina a glance. She smiled and shrugged.

"I was just talking to Selina about expanding the business," he said, "and well, now she's my new partner."

"In our 'business'?" Carla asked.

"Well, our business... and maybe something else on the side."

A short appendix: Harskan dialogue and translations

Kallajai'es, saherai jaehl'adaesol. Gael jea Drackson fei Araujion eliman. Cha jea est jeraes est tae'is alaesu.

"Greetings, honorable warriors. This is Drackson of the Araujion family. I am on an errand of great importance.

Drackson? Saes jea kerimach est chara. Araujion eliman haelim jea-dra esj'aerae-tach omajen. Benisa, jor-esch dechae jea-tach leseia-tach saes-esch amon'gaetol, saes-dra. Harim'fae, saes e'lisas laie'fron.

"Drackson? You are known to us. The Araujion family name is not held highly. However, its shame was brought about by your brothers, not you. Therefore, you may proceed."

Elas'maie-ensa ch'aj, gael jea Lamas'ca fae'ra haledaes. Amaeris memans saes-tal, haelim est saes-esch ch'aj del saes-esch je'sari.

"Incoming ship, this is Lamas'ca control. Please identify yourself, the name of your ship and your destination."

Lamas'ca fae'ra haledaes, gael jea Drackson fei Araujion eliman est
Lady Hawk. *Cha jea talist-ensa est neraji est Ha'jaest in'fael'jion*
Cha he'laemi si da'frae afra'jae aleia.

"Lamas'ca control, this is Drackson of the Araujion family on
the *Lady Hawk*. I am heading for the city of Ha'jaest as I wish
to see a friend there."

Edae'saritach, Drackson. Amaeris ja'haiel esen'fae chara de'trahal
kalam-ensa tra'ja.

"Acknowledged, Drackson. Please wait while we assign a
landing platform."

Edae'saritach.

"Acknowledged."

Habrast ularcach si kalam est tra'ja heil-daes jeic.

"Permission granted to land on platform 63."

Helaeshi.

"Thank you."

Kallajai'es, Braesk fei Helas'jar eliman.

"Greetings, Braesk of the Helas'jar family."

Kallajai'es, cha-esch nemo'liatol Caeras del Arasil. Kallajai'es, cha-esch nemo'lowae Ramani.

"Greetings, my lords Caeras and Arasil. Greetings, my lady Ramani."

Kallajai'es, Drackson fei Araujion eliman.

"Greetings, Drackson of the Araujion family."

Del mia jea saes-esch nes'paratol?

"And who are your companions?"

Hae'jia jea Carla Casdan del gae'jia jea Kalai Asten Korr fei Lady Hawk.

"The woman is Carla Casdan and the man is Asten Korr, the captain of the *Lady Hawk*."

Cha bes'iam Lady Hawk *jea ch'aj gael jea onai heia chara*?

"I assume the *Lady Hawk* is the ship that is here before us?"

Gael jea vasara.

"That is correct."

Cha karai'es. Draes, aji Cha besiam gael Carla del Asten hes'para Corsidan?

"I see. Now, can I assume that Carla and Asten speak Corsidan?"

Gael jea heli vasara.

"That is also correct."

Ka'hai. Esen'fae jera jea elesa'ia, galia chara jea chara-esch milash est Corsidan.

"All right. While they in our presence, let us conduct all our business in Corsidan."

Laie'fron est melaji.

"Go in peace."

...dreish'na kaer'dai-dres ch'ajol del Harskan Cortekol...

"... light assault ships and Harskan Corteks..."

Elas'maie-ensa ch'aj, hesj'on.

"Incoming ship. Respond."

Cha laej'ast saes.

"I hear you."

Laie'fron elstae tralaesta. Sevaerai haledaesol est basaec neravast-ach laherst. Jera hesta aleia jea chaj braecol anestalensa est mei del a'estra jea ilae taleshem si jea tae'laes.

"Proceed with caution. Federation authorities aboard the station have called a lock-down. They say there are ship thieves operating in the area and the timing is too convenient to be a coincidence."

Karai'esach.

"Understood."

Sevaerai jaehl-ch'aj laie'fron est chara.

"Federation warship coming towards us."

Nemo'lowae Braec

"Lady Thief"